MW00449728

Sunset Dead

A Murder on Maui Mystery

Robert W. Stephens

Copyright 2017 Robert W. Stephens

All rights reserved.

For
Felicia Dames

Chapter 1
Paper

This question is just for the female readers. If your husband gave you a gift of paper for your first wedding anniversary, how would you react? I don't mean to imply that I think you might be a materialistic person who would toss that gift right back in his face. Instead, I'm just curious as to whether or not that item is acceptable. I know that's not the right word, but I can't think of another.

My anniversary was fast approaching, so I Googled anniversary gifts. I came across a website that listed items you're supposed to get for each year. Paper was for year one. I'm assuming the list referred to some nice stationary one might use to write letters or cards to loved ones versus a ream of printer paper from Staples. Nevertheless, my wife doesn't really write letters anymore. She rarely even sends an email. It's almost always text messages now. Of course, I could be completely missing the point, and paper really refers to the title on a new car or beach house, maybe even tickets to a two-week European vacation.

I decided to ignore this list and made the short drive to a jewelry store. After all, you can never go wrong with diamonds. The owner and I are now on a first-name basis since I've spent a considerable amount of money in his establishment. I browsed for almost half an hour and ultimately decided on a pair of diamond earrings. I'd already bought Alana a pair, but I assumed she could always use an upgrade. Diamonds, by the way, are what you're supposed to purchase on your sixtieth wedding anniversary, so I was getting way ahead of myself.

"What do you think, Ava? Will Alana like these?" I asked my niece.

At the tender age of one, she just sort of looked at me with this blank expression. Then a wide smile appeared on her face as if I'd just done something incredibly funny. I took that as a sign that she agreed with my purchase.

I thanked Mr. Banks for his recommendation, paid him what was probably an over-inflated price for the earrings, and placed the small jewel box in the front pocket of my cargo shorts. I carried Ava out to my vehicle and strapped her into the car seat. I handed her her stuffed elephant. She can't go anywhere without that thing.

If you've read any of these tales before, you know I usually drive a tiny BMW. Well, I'd bought the Lexus SUV several months ago when I started watching Ava on a regular basis. I know that might sound ridiculous to make such an expensive purchase when the main reason was to chauffeur around a kid who wasn't even with me every day, but I'd been planning on getting something bigger anyway since I often needed to haul stuff around.

My two-seater BMW roadster was certainly not a safe choice for an infant, nor did it have any room in the trunk for other items like all the plants, bushes, and small trees I'd been buying recently since landscaping the new yard had become somewhat of a hobby for me. Anything larger than a shoebox simply won't fit in the BMW. Don't worry, I still have the car. I would never dream of giving it up.

I climbed behind the wheel and plugged my phone into the radio so I could play music for Ava. She likes this album called Zen Spa, which is basically eastern-sounding flute music with the sounds of gentle waves or rainfall mixed into the melodies. It soothes her little mind, or maybe it's more for me. Who knows, but it's usually what I play when we drive around the island.

I started the car and made the short drive back to Kaanapali where Alana and I live in a house on the ocean.

Please forgive me for not immediately introducing myself. My name is

Edgar Allan Rutherford. As I'm sure is quite evident, my late parents were huge fans of the mystery writer. I disliked the name immensely for most of my life for obvious reasons. Children can be cruel, teenagers especially, and the name Edgar was not the easiest name to have. My best friend, Doug Foxx, started calling me Poe in high school, and the nickname stuck. Most people call me Poe these days. However, you may call me Edgar if you wish. The name has grown on me, and I'm no longer embarrassed by it.

As you read just a few sentences ago, Alana is the name of my wife. She's a detective with the Maui Police Department, and we met a few years ago on my first trip to Maui. Foxx had been after me for years to visit him. I don't know why I kept pushing the trip off. It was probably just my busy work schedule. I tend to easily get obsessed with work, and the firm had a habit of overloading us. I worked as an architect for several years until I lost the job in the great recession. After they informed me that I was no longer needed, I realized I didn't have anything to show for all those hours in the cubicle except for the knowledge that I'd spent several years doing something I really didn't like doing with people I didn't care to be around. It was a depressing thought, and it left me in a major funk.

After I lost my job, I spent about six months lying on the sofa and not doing much of anything. It was kind of ironic since I really didn't need the job. My late parents had left me with a considerable amount of money. I'd been investing that money and having fairly good luck with it. Still, I'd been determined to live off the income I earned as an architect, and I saw it as lazy and entitled to dip into my inheritance. Maybe you think I was crazy for feeling that way, and I probably was, but that was my mindset at the time.

There was also my girlfriend. Our relationship had turned toxic, but I was having trouble removing myself from it. I think I was just apprehensive about being alone. I'm sure that doesn't put me in a good light with you, but I believe many of us have had trouble removing ourselves from bad situations. The best we can do is to try to learn from it and hopefully not repeat those same mistakes.

It was my girlfriend who made the move to end things when I caught her on a dinner date with another man. It was awkward to say the least, but it did provide me with the momentum I needed to get away. It was also the deciding factor in finally accepting Foxx's invitation to Maui. Unfortunately, the vacation didn't go as planned.

Foxx got arrested on my first night on the island. He was accused of murdering his girlfriend, a successful artist worth millions. Alana was the detective who got the case, as well as the person who showed up at Foxx's house to make the arrest and read him his rights. I spent the entire trip conducting my own murder investigation since I was the only one who thought Foxx was innocent.

It was during this investigation that Alana and I crossed paths multiple times. I knew I was pressing my luck with her, and I had the real potential to get arrested myself for obstruction of justice or interfering with an investigation or something of that nature. Fortunately, that didn't happen. We did end up at a dinner date that went way farther than either of us expected it to go. I wish I could say it was smooth sailing after that, but there was that pesky murder to solve. Eventually, I helped prove Foxx innocent, and I decided to relocate to the island since Virginia really didn't have anything interesting to offer me, namely Alana's presence.

So, what have I been doing for the past few years? I ended up getting involved in a second murder investigation, which brought me to the attention of a local attorney named Mara Winters. She hired me to investigate a few more murder cases despite my lack of official credentials. I proved myself to have a knack for solving crimes since I'm pretty decent at reading people and figuring out their hidden motivations. I was really beginning to think that it could be a new career for me until Alana was almost murdered in our home.

She and I were working a case that involved a close childhood friend of hers. I don't want to spoil the details of the investigation in case you decide to read that story next, but the attack on Alana left me gutted. We were just a few months from our wedding, and I was completely convinced I was going to lose her. Fortunately, she pulled through, despite her spleen being removed from the vicious beating she took at the hands of a sociopath.

There was also an incident that occurred at the end of the case. I don't want to say what it was, at least not yet, but it left me with the realization that

I had changed, and I wasn't sure I liked this new version of me. Being around the dredges of society has a way of altering you, as well as your outlook on life. I hated the fact that I had become so pessimistic and had begun to question everything and anything people said and did around me.

I reluctantly gave up those private investigations and spent the last year exploring the island and watching over Ava. I also tried to find the version of Poe that had first come to Maui, even if he was a more naïve version of my current self. I haven't been very successful in that endeavor. Once you've changed, it's almost impossible to go back.

Ava has played a large role in my self-guided therapy. It's hard to be in a bad mood when you have a cute kid looking at you. It's also hard to be too self-aware when most of your energy is tied up caring for someone else. Her parents, by the way, are Foxx and Alana's sister, Hani. Their short relationship could best be described as "friends with benefits." They've tended to avoid each other at all costs since Ava's arrival, and I've unofficially become a sort of go-between. It's an unfortunate situation, but I haven't been able to come up with a solution to change it, nor has Alana. Foxx often comes to my house to pick up Ava, or I'll drive to Hani's to get the baby or return her when Hani gets off work. I don't mind, though. It's a fun way to spend my time, and Ava and I have had the chance to bond.

Back to my morning trip to the jeweler. I got home and took Ava to the backyard after putting the earrings away in my upstairs office and changing into my swimsuit. I have an in-ground pool that overlooks the ocean. Ava likes it when I let her splash around. My tiny dog, Maui, is obsessed with being in the middle of everything. He's scared of the water, so he jumps on our raft so he can still be close to her without having to get wet.

I wasn't the only one who suffered a personality change due to these murder cases. The dog's personality changed after the attack on Alana. He no longer lets anyone get close to the house or one of us without going into a crazed fit of barking. I realize most dogs bark when strangers approach, but Maui has taken it to a new level. I was worried when I first introduced him to Ava. I had no idea how he'd react to her, but he had some sort of instinctual recognition that she was a welcome addition to our family. He took an instant liking to her, and they've become attached at the hip. He tends to get depressed for a few hours whenever she leaves the house.

Shortly after getting out of the pool, I received a text from Hani saying that she would swing by the house to pick up Ava after work. She'd gone to a meeting at a hotel in Kihei for an upcoming wedding. Hani had planned my wedding to Alana, much to my initial dismay. However, she'd done a pretty good job of it and had used that experience to start a new business. Our wedding got a fair amount of media attention since the bride was a decorated cop who'd almost gotten killed in the island's biggest crime in years. I assume they saw the wedding as a major come-back tale for Alana. A popular local magazine gave it a huge story, and Hani managed to get herself quoted several times. She was flooded with calls after that and has been consistently busy for the past year planning weddings of all sizes.

Ava was still napping in one of the upstairs bedrooms when there was a knock on the door. It was actually more of a pounding. I looked at my watch and saw it was a good two hours before Hani was due to arrive.

Then I heard another round of pounding on the door and a man's voice yell, "Mr. Rutherford, open up. This is the police."

Maui the dog barked and ran for the front door.

My first instinct was that something bad had happened to Alana. I hadn't heard from her all day, and I had no idea what she was working on. There was a third round of banging on the door before I could make my way through the foyer. I looked through the peep hole and saw two uniformed officers, a man and a woman, standing beside a man in civilian clothes. There were also a few police cars in the background as well as a blue cargo van with the words "Maui Police Department" on the side.

I picked up the dog so he wouldn't bite anyone and opened the door. It was the man in plain clothes who addressed me.

"Mr. Rutherford, my name's Detective Austin Shaw. I'm arresting you on the suspicion of murdering Brooklyn Van Kirk."

The female officer grabbed my free arm and twisted it behind my back.

"What the hell is going on?" I said.

"We also have a warrant to search the premises," Shaw said.

He briefly held up a piece of paper but then almost immediately shoved it into his coat pocket.

"You have the right to remain silent," the female officer said. "Anything you say can and will be used against you in a court of law. You have the right to speak to an attorney, and to have an attorney present during any questioning. Do you understand these rights as I have read them to you?"

The male cop grabbed Maui from me and put him on the ground. The dog then proceeded to attack the cop. I saw him put his hand on the butt of his service weapon.

"You hurt that dog and you'll have me to deal with."

"Are you threatening my officer, Mr. Rutherford?" Shaw asked.

I felt my second arm get yanked behind my back, and the handcuffs were snapped hard around my wrists.

"Do you understand the rights as I have read them to you?" the female officer repeated.

"This is absurd. I haven't killed anyone. Where's Alana? Does she know you're here?"

"Detective Hu will be made aware of this in short notice," Shaw said.

"I'm not going anywhere. There's a baby upstairs."

"One of the officers will care for it until the child's parents can be contacted."

"You're making a huge mistake."

"Do you have any idea how often I've heard that?"

Shaw got within a few inches of my face.

"And I've never gotten it wrong," he continued.

They yanked me out of my house and dragged me toward the police cars in the driveway. Shaw motioned for the other officers who'd stayed by their vehicles to advance toward the house. I saw two plain clothes employees, people I assumed might be forensics investigators, climb out of the cargo van.

I was going to jail, and I had no idea why.

Chapter 2
Unthinkable

Perspective: Alana

My name is Alana Hu. If you've read any of Poe's previous books, you'll know exactly who I am. If you haven't, then the first thing I usually say about myself is that I've been a detective for the Maui Police Department for several years. It's a job I love, and it's something I always dreamed of doing. I guess many people don't know what they want to be when they're growing up, or they pick a career or a goal they don't come close to achieving. I was lucky in that I got exactly what I wanted.

I certainly don't consider myself a writer, so please forgive me if I fumble through this. I've never contributed to his stories, mainly because I view myself as a supporting player, but he can't exactly write about something he didn't experience. Poe's only request is that I be as honest with you as possible.

I don't have an issue with that, but sometimes I feel he's too honest with his readers, especially when it comes to our love life. For example, I didn't think it was necessary for him to go into such detail about our first date in Aloha Means Goodbye. It didn't exactly cast me in a good light, although I know it wasn't his intention to make me look bad. I'm well aware, though, that there are still double standards when it comes to the behavior of men and women. He swears people find our initial encounters endearing. I'm not so sure.

I guess I'm getting a bit distracted, so let me get back to the main story. So, where was I when I found out about Poe's arrest? I was at the tail end of an interview with a shop owner who'd been robbed. It was the second time that week that a store had been hit on that part of the island. The owner of the first store had a security system, but it hadn't worked in years. You'd probably be surprised how often that's the case. The second owner hadn't even bothered purchasing a security system.

He hadn't witnessed anything suspicious the day of the robbery or the days leading up to it. He'd locked up the store the previous night, at least he said he thought he'd locked it up, and he went home, only to find his cash register and office safe empty the following morning. Why hadn't he removed the cash from his register at closing time the day before and why hadn't he bothered to lock the safe? Your guess is as good as mine because he didn't really have an explanation for either of those questions, and I knew there was little chance of me ever figuring out who'd hit his place. It was probably an inside job, though. It almost always is.

I was moments from wrapping up my conversation with the store owner when my phone rang. It was my supervisor, Captain Price. I see and talk to him most days in the office, but he rarely calls me.

I turned to the shop owner.

"I'll be in touch soon. If you think of anything else, you have my card."

He nodded in return, and I exited his store as I hit the talk button on my phone.

"This is Detective Hu."

"Alana, where are you right now?"

"In Wailea. I'm about to head back to the station now."

"I need you to go your house first."

"Why? What's going on?"

He hesitated, and I knew this couldn't be good.

"Is Poe all right? Has something happened?"

"Your husband was just taken into custody. He had a child with him."

"Is he hurt? Is my niece hurt?"

"They're both physically fine. Is there someone you can call who can come get the child?"

"What are the charges?"

"I don't want to go into that right now."

"I'll take care of the child, but I'd ask that you to tell me what's going on."

"I will when you get back here."

Price ended the call before I could protest again.

I knew my sister, Hani, was probably not that far from where I was now, but Foxx was probably at work in Lahaina, which meant he was much closer to the house than I was. I dialed his cell phone as I walked back to my car. All I got was his voicemail. I left a short message for him to call me. Then I phoned the number for Harry's, which is the bar he and Poe own.

"This is Harry's. How can I help you?"

I recognized the voice instantly as belonging to Kiana, who has worked at the bar since it opened under the original owner.

"Hey, this is Alana. Can I speak with Foxx?"

"He just stepped out. You should try his cell."

"I just did, and he didn't pick up. I'll try calling him again. If you see him soon, please tell him to call me immediately."

"Is everything fine?" she asked.

"Yeah, it's fine. I just need to talk to him."

I ended the call and phoned Foxx a second time. The phone rang several times, but all I got was the voicemail again. I didn't leave a message this time, but I did send him a text and told him it was an emergency. I then dialed Hani's number. Maybe she was already on her way back and could swing by to collect Ava. Unfortunately, I got her voicemail, too.

I got into my car and started the drive back to Kaanapali. I hit the sirens and pushed the car as fast as I could without potentially causing a traffic accident.

By the time I got to my house, there were several vehicles parked in my driveway as well as along the street. I also saw neighbors from the surrounding houses standing at the edge of their driveways. There's nothing like flashing police lights to draw out the gawkers.

I parked behind one of the police cars and climbed out of my vehicle.

"Is everything okay, Alana?"

I heard a woman call out to me, but I wasn't sure exactly who'd asked the question. I turned and saw our next-door neighbor.

"It's fine," I said, but I'm sure she didn't believe me.

I walked up the driveway and made my way to the front door. An officer named Allison Jenkins stepped outside and approached me. She had Ava in her arms.

"What's going on?" I asked.

"Detective Shaw is inside."

I took Ava from her.

"Can you let him know I'm here?"

"He already does. I heard someone tell him when you arrived. That's why I came out."

"Why did he arrest my husband?"

"I'm sorry, ma'am, but Detective Shaw specifically told us not to say anything to you."

"Allison, how long have you and I known each other? Put yourself in my shoes. Wouldn't you want to know what happened?"

"I'm sorry, ma'am."

"Allison, please. I need to know."

She looked back toward my house. We were the only ones outside. She turned back to me.

"The charge was murder. The victim's name was Brooklyn Van Kirk," she whispered.

"And why do they think Poe did it?"

"I don't know, ma'am. I heard something about an affair but not much more than that."

I hadn't expected to hear either of those things, and I felt like I'd been kicked in the stomach.

"All right. Thank you for letting me know. Where's my dog by the way?"

"I took him out back. He was going after everyone in the house."

"Can you get him for me? I don't want anyone thinking I'm trying to sneak in through the back. I'll wait right here."

She looked toward the front door again, but there was still no one there. Then she turned and headed toward the backyard.

My phone rang a second later. It was Foxx.

"Foxx, where are you?"

"I just got back to the office. What's going on? Is everything all right?"

"No, it's not all right. How soon can you get to my house? I need to give you Ava."

"What's happened to her?"

"She's fine, but Poe has been arrested."

"Arrested? For what?"

"Please, Foxx. Just get here as fast as you can."

"I'll be right there."

I ended the call just as Allison brought Maui back to me. She'd put him on a leash, and he started wagging his tail as soon as he saw me.

"Thank you, Allison. You better get back inside before Shaw accuses you of colluding with me."

She made no move to go back to the house.

"Did he tell you to stay outside and keep me from entering?"

"Yes, ma'am."

"I understand. I'm going to be here until Ava's father arrives. Then I'll leave."

"I'm sorry, ma'am. I really am."

I walked with Ava and Maui down to the edge of the driveway. Foxx got to the house about ten minutes later. He parked his SUV in front of us and climbed out.

"What the hell is going on?"

I handed him Ava.

"I don't know, but I'm going to the station now."

"Call me as soon as you hear something."

"Can you take the dog, too?"

"Sure."

"There's something I need to ask you."

"What is it?"

"In the car. I don't want anyone listening to us."

I put Maui the dog into the backseat of his SUV. Foxx placed Ava in her car seat, and we both climbed into the front of the vehicle.

I looked back to the house and saw Shaw standing on the front porch. He was looking directly at Foxx and me.

"Who's that?"

"He's the lead detective on this case, at least I assume he is."

"He looks like an asshole."

I didn't respond to his insult. I'd never really had an opinion on Shaw's personality, but now I tended to agree with Foxx.

"I know Poe is your best friend, but I need you to be completely honest with me."

"Of course."

"Was Poe having an affair?"

"Are you serious?"

"I'm not joking. Don't cover for him. It's better if I know the truth."

"Alana, there's no way he would cheat on you. It's a zero percent possibility. Why would you even ask that?"

I told Foxx about the murder charge and the allegation of an affair between Poe and who I assumed was the victim.

"That's crazy. He would never do that. He sure as hell wouldn't kill someone."

"Has he been acting strange recently? Has anything been bothering him?"

"No. He's been acting fine, and I've seen him just about every day this week. Have you noticed something odd?"

"No. He's been the same around me."

"What evidence do they have?"

"I don't know. Has he taken up another investigation that he might not have wanted me to know about?"

"No. I thought he gave that up. As far as I know, he hasn't had one since before you guys got married."

"Okay. I better get going and see why they're trying to pin this on him."

I opened the door, and Foxx placed his hand on my arm.

"Alana, there's no chance he's done this, the affair included. You're the most important person in his life. He wouldn't risk messing that up."

"I'll call as soon as I can."

I climbed out of his SUV and walked over to my car. I turned on the ignition and made a U-turn to head out of the neighborhood. I couldn't stop thinking about Allison's statements. Murder and an affair. Those two things sometimes went hand in hand. Did that mean I thought Poe was guilty? No, I didn't think that, but I've seen too many strange and unpredictable actions to ever discount anything. I hate to admit my reservations to you, but it's how I felt, and Poe wanted me to be honest.

Chapter 3
The Evidence

Perspective: Poe

I was brought to an interrogation room once I got to the police station. Ironically enough, it was the same room I'd been in the last time I was here, only that time I was the one asking the questions of a guy who'd been locked up.

The officer opened the door and pushed me through it. He led me over to one of three chairs that were placed around a small table. He told me to sit on one of the chairs. He undid the handcuff off one of my wrists. He took the free handcuff and connected it to a metal ring on the table. He said Detective Shaw would be in soon to question me.

There were no clocks in the room, and I didn't have my phone or watch, so I had no idea how much time had passed before Shaw arrived. My best guess was that it was around three or four hours later. That made sense since I assumed they'd take a while to search my house.

I didn't know if Alana had been told about my arrest. Maybe she had but they weren't going to let her see me for the obvious conflict of interest. I'd made it a point to tell the police that I wanted my lawyer, Mara Winters, to be contacted. I hadn't gotten a reply, even after I'd repeated that request several times to multiple officers.

There I sat, completely alone and completely confused as to what in the hell was happening to me. I kept trying to listen for possible voices outside the room, but I never heard anything.

Eventually, the door opened, and Detective Shaw walked inside with Mara Winters a few paces behind him. Another police officer was behind her.

"Are the handcuffs really necessary, Detective?" Mara asked.

"Yes, they are," Shaw said.

Shaw and Mara walked over to me. He placed a white plastic container on the table. I couldn't see what was inside of it. I did see there was a manila folder on top.

Shaw and Mara sat on the other two chairs around the table. The police officer shut the door behind him, but he made no move toward the table. Instead, he leaned against the door and kept his eyes on me. It was clearly an intimidation tactic since it was obvious I wasn't going anywhere.

I looked to Mara. She had a neutral expression on her face. I didn't find that comforting.

"Mr. Rutherford, can you please tell me your whereabouts this past Monday morning."

I had to think about it a second. I didn't know if it was because I was getting older, but the days had started to all blur into each other.

"I'm pretty sure I was watching my niece that morning."

"You're pretty sure or you're positive?" Shaw asked.

"I'm sure. My sister-in-law had some appointments that morning, and she asked if I could watch her daughter."

"Do you routinely babysit your niece?"

"Yes. At least three days a week."

"At what point did you meet up with your sister-in-law?"

"I think it was around 10 or 10:30. Hani asked me to meet her in Kahului."

"Why there when your house is in Kaanapali?"

"I told her I'd intended to go swimming at Baby Beach that morning. I offered to cancel my swim, but then she suggested we could just meet in Kahului since it was on my way back, and it was close to her first appointment."

"What time did you go to Baby Beach?"

"Maybe 8:30 or so. I swam for a little while and then I hung out on the beach."

"Was there anyone you knew on the beach with you, someone who could verify your story?"

"No. The beach wasn't very crowded that morning. There were a handful of people but none that I recognized."

"Mr. Rutherford, please describe the nature of your relationship with Brooklyn Van Kirk," Shaw said.

"Where is Alana?" I asked.

"Detective Hu isn't allowed in here. It would be inappropriate."

"Does she even know that I've been arrested?"

"I'm not going to comment on what she does or doesn't know."

"Have you spoken with Alana?" I asked Mara.

"No. I haven't had a chance yet."

"Let's get back to my question. What kind of relationship did you have with Ms. Van Kirk?" Shaw asked.

"I'm not even sure who Ms. Van Kirk is," I said.

"You're going to deny knowing Brooklyn Van Kirk?"

"I met someone last year named Brooklyn, but I don't know what her last name is."

Shaw reached into the folder he'd brought with him and removed a photograph which he slide across the table to me. It was a crime scene photo showing a young woman who'd been killed. There was substantial bruising around her neck, and her eyes were wide open. I recognized her at once.

"That's Brooklyn Van Kirk. Know her now?" Shaw asked.

"I didn't have a relationship with her."

"So you're still going to claim you didn't know her?"

"I didn't say that. I knew Brooklyn, but there was no relationship."

"How did you know her?"

"I met her during my last investigation."

"An investigation? So you're a licensed private investigator?"

"No. I'm not licensed."

"What do you do then?"

"I've been asked to help on various cases from time to time."

"You like to play cops and robbers?" Shaw asked.

17

"There's no reason to insult my client," Mara said.

"How am I insulting him? He just said he likes to run around the island and chase criminals."

"You know that's not what he said."

Shaw turned back to me.

"When was the last time you saw Ms. Van Kirk?"

"It's been more than a year. I haven't seen or spoken to her since that investigation concluded."

"How many times did you see her during this case?"

"Maybe three or four times. We always met at an art gallery where she used to work."

"How soon after your investigation did you start seeing her?"

"I didn't see her. I just told you that. It's been more than a year since I last spoke to her."

"You're denying you had an affair with her?"

"An affair?"

"I think my client has already said multiple times that he didn't have a relationship with Ms. Van Kirk," Mara said.

"There was no affair?" Shaw asked again.

"No. There was no affair. I don't know how else I can say that. This is absolutely preposterous. Why have you arrested me?"

Shaw reached into the container and removed a clear plastic evidence bag. He placed the bag in front of me.

"Do you know what that is?" Shaw asked.

I looked at the bag and saw an empty bottle of Purple Haze beer inside.

"It's a beer bottle."

"Are you familiar with this brand?"

"We sell it at my bar."

"What bar is that?"

"I co-own a bar in Lahaina called Harry's."

"Is this a type of beer you like to drink?"

"My business partner just started ordering it for the bar. He liked it and asked me to try it."

"We found this bottle and two more like it at the bottom of the recycling container in Ms. Van Kirk's apartment. All three bottles have your fingerprints on it. How do you suppose those bottles got in her place?"

"I have no idea. I certainly didn't bring them there. I don't know where she lived."

"You never went to her place during your previous investigation?"

"No. Like I said before, we always met at the photography gallery where she worked."

Shaw opened the folder again and slid another color photograph across the table to me.

"Is that your car?"

I looked at the photo and saw a silver BMW Z3 convertible parked outside some building.

"I can't say."

"You can't say or you won't say?"

"It's difficult for me to read the license plate on this photo."

"How many silver convertibles like that are on Maui?"

"I don't know."

"Have you seen another since you've lived here?"

"No. I can't say I have."

"Fortunately, I had the photo blown up," Shaw said, and he reached back into the folder.

He grabbed a third photo and tossed it across the table toward me.

"Is that your license plate number?"

I looked at the photo.

"Yes. It is."

"That photo was taken outside Ms. Van Kirk's apartment complex. You still going to deny you didn't know where she lived?"

"Who took that photograph?" Mara asked.

"A neighbor of Van Kirk's."

"Some neighbor just decided to take a photograph of a random car in the parking lot?"

"We spoke with her about that. She took a photo of the storm clouds.

When she was later going through the photos on her phone, she realized it had the convertible in it that she'd seen outside Ms. Van Kirk's apartment. She'd heard about the murder of her neighbor. She put two and two together."

"She decided to take a photo of storm clouds? That's awfully convenient," Mara said.

Shaw shrugged his shoulders.

"Sometimes we catch a lucky break."

"I'm sure," she said, and there was no denying the sarcasm in her voice. "This neighbor, is she claiming to have seen my client the day Ms. Van Kirk was killed?"

"No."

"Did she say whether she saw his car outside Ms. Van Kirk's apartment on the day she was killed?"

"No."

"There are dozens of cars in that parking lot. Are you suggesting they're all suspects? Did you interview the owners of each and every car?"

"It goes to your client's claims that he hadn't seen Ms. Van Kirk in some time. It clearly shows he's lying."

"It says nothing of the sort. It just says a car like his happened to be in her apartment complex. We haven't even had a chance to have an expert examine that photograph. It could have been manipulated."

"You don't really expect me to believe that, do you?" Shaw asked.

"Photographs get manipulated every day. I'm surprised you don't know that," Mara said.

Shaw ignored her dig and turned back to me.

"I'm guessing a car like that is hard to miss, especially in a place like the complex where Ms. Van Kirk lived. Let's be honest here. It isn't exactly the nicest place on the island."

"If you say so. I've never been. I don't even know what part of the island it's on."

"How do you suppose your car got there then?" Shaw asked.

"I don't know. I certainly didn't drive it there."

"What about the photo? Photos don't lie."

"Like Mara said, photographs lie all the time. There are dozens of editing programs that can make a photograph say anything you want it to say."

"Who else has access to your car?"

"My wife."

"How often does she drive your car?"

"She never drives it."

"So why bring her up?"

"You asked who had access to it, not who drove it."

"Don't be a smart ass."

"Let's cut to the chase, Detective. None of this paints my client as a murderer. Beer bottles and a car. You'll get laughed out of court," Mara said.

"I saved the best for last."

Shaw reached into the container a third time and removed another plastic bag. He placed it on the table in front of Mara. It had a cell phone inside.

"Is that your phone, Mr. Rutherford?"

"No."

"Then how did it end up in your desk drawer in your home office?"

"I don't know. That's not my phone. I have an iPhone. I don't know what kind of phone that is."

"We found multiple text messages on Ms. Van Kirk's phone that show she was in a relationship with you. The text messages match what's on this phone."

"I was not in a relationship with her."

"Van Kirk was pregnant. Was that what pushed you over the edge?"

I said nothing.

"Here's what I think happened. Your affair probably started shortly after your investigation last year. She was a good looking girl. I can see how you'd be tempted. I'm guessing you told her you'd leave your wife. Guys always say that, but Ms. Van Kirk got tired of the broken promises. Then she gets knocked up. She figured she needed to get something out of the relationship since it was obvious it wasn't going anywhere. She threatened to tell your wife if you didn't pay her money, big money. You're a smart guy, and you knew this wasn't going to end with one payment to get her to shut up, especially with a child to support. You were terrified of losing Alana. The problem was you didn't know how to make Van Kirk go away. You were desperate, and there was only one thing you could think of. She had to die. You'd worked with the police enough to know what we look for at a murder scene, and you convinced yourself you could get away with it. You strangled Ms. Van Kirk. You wiped your prints clean in the apartment, only you didn't think to look at the bottom of the recycling container for those beer bottles."

"That's absurd."

"Were his prints only on the bottles?" Mara asked.

Shaw didn't answer her.

"You're suggesting my client had a months-long affair, and he managed to wipe all his prints expect the ones on those bottles?"

"Maybe he met her at local hotels. Maybe he only went to her apartment that one time when he killed her."

"He went to her apartment to kill her, and he had three Purple Haze beers first?"

"You can't make those text messages go away, Rutherford."

"Why did I hang on to the phone? I'm a smart guy, according to you. Why didn't I destroy the phone and dump it in the trash? Why didn't I just pull over to the side of the road and toss it into the ocean?"

"It's best if you admit what you did. Maybe the judge doesn't give you life in prison. Maybe you're out in twenty. Tell me what happened. Was it an accident? Did you two get in an argument and you got carried away?"

"I didn't kill her."

"You said you found corresponding messages on her phone. Where was that phone?" Mara asked.

"In her apartment."

"Where in her apartment?"

"On the coffee table, not far from where her body was found."

"If my client was so smart as to cover most of his tracks, why didn't he take her phone as well? He was bound to know you'd look at it."

"What would be the point? He knew we'd be able to get a warrant for her phone records."

"Okay, speaking of phone records, I'm sure you determined where my client's phone was the day Ms. Van Kirk was killed."

"We did."

"And where was that phone? I'm guessing it showed him in Kaanapali, which is a good one hour from Ms. Van Kirk's apartment complex."

"He wouldn't have brought that phone with him. He knew he needed to leave it at his house. Plus, he had the burner phone."

"Okay, which car did he drive to her house? Did he take the BMW?" Mara asked.

Shaw didn't answer her.

"There are bound to be traffic cameras he would have had to drive past to get to her home. Do any of them show the BMW?"

"I'm sure he wouldn't have driven that car over there to murder her."

"Which car did he take then? A rental? Do you have a copy of his credit card bills showing he rented a car? You can't rent a car with cash."

Shaw said nothing.

"He didn't take a rental car, either? What about an Uber? Oh, that requires a credit card payment, too. So he didn't drive his BMW over. He didn't rent a car. He didn't take an Uber. How did he get there? On a skateboard? Did he walk? Did he ask a friend to give him a ride? Did he hitchhike? You can't place him at the scene of the crime. Beer bottles don't do it."

"He had motive. He had the means, and he had the opportunity."

"This interview is over, Detective Shaw. I'd like to talk to my client alone," Mara said.

"This is your last chance, Rutherford."

"We're done talking," Mara said.

Shaw stood.

"Take your time, counselor. He's not going anywhere."

Shaw walked across the room and exited the door, along with the other police officer.

I turned to Mara.

"When can I speak with Alana?"

"I'll try to arrange it was soon as I can. I promise," she said.

"How bad is it?"

"It's all circumstantial. Unfortunately, the phone was probably enough to get you charged. He's right when he said it's speaks to motive."

"It wasn't my phone."

I expected Mara to say that she believed me. She didn't.

"Have you seen the messages yet? What do they say?" I asked.

"I haven't, but I will. If this is a setup, though, I have a pretty good idea of what's on it."

I'm sure you caught her use of the word "if." I certainly did.

Chapter 4
He's My Husband

Perspective: Alana

I was only a mile from my house when it occurred to me that Poe needed an attorney. I grabbed my phone off the passenger seat and dialed Mara Winters. Her assistant told me Mara had already left for the police station, so I ended the call and immediately dialed her cell. All I got was her voicemail.

I left a quick message and ended the call. I drove the rest of the way to work. I parked the car and walked into the station. Everyone seemed to go out of their way to avoid talking to me or even making eye contact. I had no doubt that word had already spread of Poe's arrest. We have a small department, and we're certainly not immune to gossip. Plus, Poe isn't exactly the most welcome person. His investigations have garnered a lot of press. It's not something he's ever gone after. In fact, I know he dislikes the media attention, but it's had the unfortunate side effect of making my department look foolish when we've arrested the wrong person or failed to solve the case ourselves. I'm sure there are a few people here who would appreciate him getting put in his place, even on something as serious as a murder charge.

I didn't bother going to see Captain Price. That conversation would have to come later, and I already knew what he was going to say. What I didn't know, and one of the things I'd been stressing about, was what I was going to say. I knew he wouldn't give me many options, and I might have to do something extreme.

I made my way to the interview rooms since there was a better than average chance Poe was still there. I was intercepted by a fellow detective named Abigail Ford. She and I had come on the force around the same time. She was a solid person and someone I considered a friend, but friendships have a way of falling apart when your job is on the line. I thought she would try to prevent me from seeing Poe, but she leaned in close to me and whispered in my ear.

"I just heard they found a few hairs on one of your husband's shirts. They're too long to be his and too light to be yours. They've sent the hairs to the lab to be tested."

"Where was the shirt?"

"I heard it was in the hamper."

She gave me this look of pity.

"I'm sorry," she continued.

"Is there anything else you can tell me?"

"I'm sorry," she repeated.

She turned from me and headed off.

I walked the rest of the way to the interview rooms. Poe was in the last one. I stood outside the door and looked through the window. He was seated at the table. His head was down and his shoulders were slumped. They'd handcuffed him to the table. I had no way of knowing if that was Shaw's decision or the officer who'd brought Poe into the room. I opened the door. He looked like he was about to stand, but then he looked at his handcuffed wrist and stayed seated.

"Are you all right?" I asked.

I knew it was a ridiculous question as soon as I asked it.

"How is Ava?"

It was typical Poe, always more concerned about his family than himself.

"She's fine. Foxx came and got her."

I walked over to the table and sat on the chair beside him.

"Do you need to hear me say it?" he asked.

I didn't mean to do it, but I hesitated. I saw the look of hurt in his eyes.

"I didn't have an affair with Brooklyn. I certainly didn't kill her."

"I know."

"Have you seen the evidence?"

"Be careful what you say in here. They're recording everything."

"I assumed as much. Have you had a chance to talk to Mara?"

"Not yet. I tried calling her on the way over."

Poe filled me in on his interrogation by Detective Shaw, as well as his and Mara's defense of the evidence presented.

"When was the last time you saw Brooklyn?" I asked.

"It was at the end of the investigation last year. She's the one who told me about the person who attacked you."

"She was involved? Why didn't you tell me?"

"Because there was no proof."

"Then how did you get her to talk?"

"I came up with what I thought was the only way the killer could have gotten into the building," Poe said, referring to a photographer who'd been murdered in his own art gallery. "I knew she had to be involved. I made up a story about a non-existent security camera that supposedly captured her helping the guy get inside the gallery through the back door. Fortunately, she fell for it, so I must have guessed right."

"That's when she told you my attacker's name?" I asked.

"It was either that, or I told her I'd contact the police, namely you. She talked after that."

"She never contacted you later?"

"No. There was no reason to. I haven't even seen her from a distance. I kind of thought she might have left the island."

"Why would you assume that?"

"Wouldn't you flee Maui, especially if I'd just told you that I knew you played a part in the murder of your boss?"

"Good point. Let's go over this evidence. You said you'd never been to Brooklyn's apartment complex. Is there any way you might have been there to see someone else?"

"There's a chance, but I don't think so. I'm pretty good at remembering those places. I didn't recognize anything in that photo, but the picture didn't show the entire building."

"The beer bottles. Have you had that brand before?"

"Yeah. I tried it at Harry's and liked it."

"Have you just had the beer at Harry's?"

"Yes, but I got a six pack and brought it back to our house. I haven't even had any there, though. They should all still be in the refrigerator."

"So you've just had them at the bar?"

"Yeah."

"Any place else?"

"No. I don't think so."

"How good of a look did you get at that photo of your car in Brooklyn's parking lot?"

"Pretty good," Poe said. "They had my license plate number."

"Any chance that it might have been altered?"

"Could be, but they did a good job if they did. The shadows usually give it away. Everything looked legit, but I didn't spend a long time examining it. I'd want another look."

"The only time when you didn't have the car was when it was in that auto shop. Is that correct?"

"Yeah. They had it for eight weeks. Someone might have taken it from the shop. Maybe one of the employees took it for a joy ride."

"And he happened to drive it to her apartment complex?" I asked.

"Who knows? Maybe he lives there, too. Maybe my car was stolen."

"But why would they have returned it? You would have thought the owner of the shop would have told you."

"Maybe not. It makes them look bad, and they did get the car back, if it was stolen, that is."

"I can't think of any other way someone might have gotten it without you knowing, especially since you park it in the garage every night."

"I really haven't driven the car that much since Ava's arrival. Now I mainly drive the SUV."

"Did they bring up the SUV? Did they claim to have photos of it at her apartment?"

"I got the impression they don't even know I have the SUV, but they must have seen it in the driveway today. Mara asked them specifically about traffic cameras showing me driving to and from Brooklyn's place. They don't have anything. Do you think you can get a wider shot of that apartment complex? Maybe I'm wrong. Maybe I did go there."

"I'll ask where the place is. I'm sure they're not going to let me see any of the files, but I should be able to find out. Now the phone. How often do you look in your desk drawer?"

"I don't think I've opened it in weeks. Most of the stuff I frequently use is on top of the desk. Did you hear whether or not the phone had my prints? Shaw didn't say anything about that."

"I didn't hear, but if they did have your prints, he would have said so."

"I don't see how my prints could be on it. That might be the way we shoot this thing down. There would be no reason for me to wipe my prints if I'd been keeping the phone in my home office."

"You wouldn't have even had the phone if you'd killed Brooklyn. You'd have tossed it into the ocean."

"I already made that point to Shaw."

"How did he respond to that?"

"He didn't seem to have a problem overlooking it. Is he considered a good detective?"

"I haven't worked a case with him, but his reputation is solid."

"I was hoping you were going to tell me he was like the other guy."

I knew exactly who Poe was referring to. We had a detective who had a habit of getting things wrong. He'd even arrested Poe on erroneous charges, but I'll have to tell that story another day.

"When do you think I'll go before a judge?"

"Probably tomorrow. The day after that at the latest."

"Do you think they'll deny me bail?"

"Unfortunately, yes. The prosecutor is bound to point out that you have the money and the means to disappear for good."

Poe didn't respond. I hadn't wanted to tell him that, but I also didn't want to give him false hope.

"Mara's a good attorney. I know she'll do everything she can. There's something else you have," I said.

"What's that?"

"Me."

"I do, don't I?"

"I better get to it. I don't want you spending a second longer in here than you have to."

I leaned forward and kissed him.

"Happy anniversary," Poe said.

I didn't respond because I was afraid I might break.

"There's something for you at the house. It's in my office. I intended to wrap it but didn't get the chance," he said.

"What is it?"

"You'll have to wait and see tonight when you find it."

I stood.

I walked across the room but stopped at the door. I turned back to Poe.

"This will be over soon. I promise."

"Alana, find the gift. It's important to me."

"Okay. I'll look for it as soon as I'm home."

I left him and headed back to Captain Price's office. Shaw intercepted me right as I was about to walk through the door.

"Were you just talking to my suspect?" he asked.

I ignored him and entered the office. Shaw followed me inside.

"I know you're married to the guy, but this is my case."

Captain Price looked up at us from his desk.

"You can't expect me not to get involved," I said.

"That's exactly what you're going to do," Price said.

"What about the phone? Were his fingerprints on it?"

"I don't have to answer that," Shaw said.

"They weren't, were they?"

"We're not going to try the case in my office," Price said.

"His case is full of holes. We all want the truth. All I'm asking is to help."

"That's not happening, Alana. I can't have the wife of a murder suspect working the case."

"I'm not asking for it to be official. Give me some time off. Let me prove to you he didn't do it. You owe me that."

"You're right. I do owe you, but you're not taking time off, and there's no way in hell I'm letting you investigate this under any circumstances," Price said.

"Don't make me do this," I said.

"Do what?"

"I can't just stand by and do nothing. I can't."

"You have to, Alana. Leave it up to his attorney. Let her do the investigation."

"I'm sorry, but I won't do that."

Price turned to Shaw.

"Would you give us a minute?"

Shaw hesitated. Then he left the office.

Price walked across the room and shut the door.

"Poe didn't do this. He's not capable of it."

"We both know that's not true," Price said.

I knew immediately what he was referring to. Poe had learned the identity of my attacker. Of course, now I realized how he'd figured that out, but he'd attacked the man in the middle of the night. He didn't kill him, nor did he even try, at least I don't think he did. Instead, he broke every bone in the man's hands. He didn't break them as much as he'd pulverized them. He'd told me Foxx's presence was the only thing that had stopped him. Price had figured most of this out. He'd confronted Poe about it. Poe hadn't denied attacking the man, nor did he confirm it. I'm not sure why Price didn't arrest Poe. Maybe he didn't think he had the evidence. Maybe it was my friendship with Price, and he'd put himself in Poe's shoes. Either way, I owed Price big.

I didn't relish where this conversation was headed.

"You never know how someone is going to respond to pressure. It makes people behave in unpredictable ways. I read those messages between them. She was leaning on him hard."

"You don't even know if that phone belonged to Poe."

"So you're convinced he didn't have an affair, either?" Price asked.

"He wouldn't do that to me."

Price looked away.

"I'm sorry for putting you in this position," I said.

"Then don't do it."

"What would you do if it was your wife who'd been arrested?"

"I think you know the answer to that question."

"So why ask me to sit on the sidelines?"

"Because you have to. You'll jeopardize this entire investigation if you're involved, whether you're on leave or not. I'm sorry, but I can't have it any other way."

This point had been in the back of my mind since I'd started the drive to the station from my home. I knew what his take would be, and I also knew it was really the only position he could possibly have.

I walked over to the captain and put my badge on his desk. I then placed my service weapon beside the badge.

"Don't. I won't accept your resignation. I know how much you love this job."

"I do, but I love my husband more."

I turned from the captain and walked out of his office. I halfway expected him to call after me, but he didn't. Shaw was leaning against the wall outside Price's office. I didn't know if he'd overheard the conversation, but he probably had. Either way, he didn't say anything to me as I passed.

I walked the rest of the way down the hall and through the lobby of the station. I was out of the building before I truly realized what I'd just done. I got a sick feeling in the pit of my stomach that only got worse with each step I took. I was halfway back to my car before I remembered it technically wasn't mine. It belonged to the department. I'd driven it for years, but now I needed to find another way home.

I didn't want to go back into the station, even to pack my personal items at my desk. I couldn't stand around and have everyone looking at me, either. I was sure Shaw had already started the gossip train, and I didn't want to be there when it finally hit the lobby desk.

I continued through the parking lot and walked a few blocks to a shopping plaza down the street. Ironically enough, it contained a sushi restaurant that Poe and I enjoyed. I walked up to the restaurant and stood under the awning to get out of the hot sun. I did a quick internet search on my phone for a local taxi service and was about to call them when my phone rang. It was Foxx.

"Hey, Foxx."

"Have you found out what the hell is going on?"

I filled Foxx in on a few of the details of the case.

"All right, I'm on my way there now."

"You're coming to the station?"

"Of course. I want to help."

"How close are you?"

"I should be there in another ten minutes or so."

"Do me a favor and swing by the shopping plaza down the street. I'm outside a sushi restaurant. I'll be waiting for you here."

"You're having lunch?" Foxx asked.

"No. I came here to get away. I just quit my job."

"You did what?"

"I'll tell you about it when you get here."

I ended the call before he could say anything else.

Foxx arrived in less than ten minutes. He pulled up to the curb, and I climbed onto the passenger seat of his SUV.

"How's he holding up?"

"You know him. He's tough."

Foxx drove off and headed back toward Kaanapali.

"I don't understand any of this. How the hell did his fingerprints get inside that apartment, and what about the phone?" he asked.

"Someone has set him up. That's the only explanation I can think of."

"Who would want to do that?"

"Maybe it's related to a previous case he was involved with."

"Have any of those people gotten out of jail?"

"I don't think so. They all got long sentences, but I'll have to check."

"What are you going to do now, especially since you're not a cop anymore?"

"You don't have to be one to solve these cases. Poe proved that. Where is Ava by the way?"

"Hani has her. I called her shortly after you left the bar."

"Does she know about Poe?"

"Yeah, I told her. Was I not supposed to?" Foxx asked.

"It's fine. I'm surprised she hasn't called me."

"I told her not to. I said she should wait for you to contact her."

"She actually listened to you?"

"I'm as surprised as you are. Why did you quit? I don't understand."

I told Foxx what happened in my captain's office. It still didn't feel real. I'd been a cop for almost fifteen years, and now my career was over. Everything was happening so fast. I tried my best to calm my mind, but my thoughts were coming a million miles per hour.

Foxx drove me home. It was usually a drive I enjoyed. The scenery was breathtaking, but I couldn't see any of it. I couldn't stop picturing Poe sitting in that interrogation room. I knew what was to come next. He'd be fingerprinted and photographed and tossed in a cell. I wanted to stop it all. I wanted to shout to Foxx to turn the vehicle around and head back to the police station so I could free Poe and bring him home. But I couldn't.

We finally got back to our neighborhood. Foxx lived just down the street. I saw Hani's car in my driveway. That wasn't the only car there. My mother's was as well.

34

Chapter 5
I Told You So

Perspective: Alana

Foxx parked in the driveway behind my mother's car. It surprised me because I somewhat expected him to slow down and tell me to jump out the window so he wouldn't run the risk of being spotted by Hani or my mother. He had a terrible relationship with both of them. Did I blame him? Yes and no. My family can be difficult to get along with, but he was just as much at fault. He never should have fooled around with Hani if he didn't want it to be serious. He was a good father to Ava, but his relationship with Hani had only gotten worse in the last few months.

Foxx turned off the ignition and opened his door.

"You're coming in?" I asked.

"You don't want me to?"

"It's not that. Of course, you're welcome."

"I won't cause a scene. I promise."

It wasn't him I was worried about.

We walked up to the garage, and I punched in the code on the control panel that opened the door. We walked past Poe's BMW and up the stairs that led to the door that opened to the kitchen. We entered the house and saw Hani and my mother sitting on the sofa in the family room. My mother had Ava in her arms. Hani stood and walked quickly to me.

"Is Poe all right? When is he coming home?" she asked.

Hani hugged me before I had a chance to respond.

"They've charged him with murder," Foxx said.

"How is this happening? I don't understand. Poe would never hurt anyone," Hani said.

"They think he killed some woman named Brooklyn Van Kirk. We both met her on a case about a year ago," I said.

"This is the one where you were attacked?" Hani asked.

"Yes, and I just learned Brooklyn knew about it, at least she knew the guy who did it."

"That's why they think Poe killed her?" Hani asked.

"No."

"They think Poe had an affair with her. They said he murdered her to keep the truth from coming out," Foxx said.

I shot Foxx a look that probably would have knocked him over if he'd actually been facing my way. Instead, he was looking in the direction of my mother. Maybe he was wondering what her reaction would be. There was no reason to guess. It was as predictable as the sun coming up in the morning.

"An affair? What proof do they have?" Hani asked.

I hesitated because I really didn't want to get into the details of the case then.

"Did you speak with Poe? What did he say?" Hani continued.

Unfortunately, they needed to hear the story at some point, and I doubted I'd get them to leave without telling them everything.

I walked into the family room and sat across from my mother. Hani sat down on the sofa beside her. I filled them in on everything that had happened from the time I got to the house and saw the forensics team to my meeting with Poe at the police station and finally my decision to resign from the police force.

"I can't believe you quit. Poe does this, and now you have to lose your job?" my mother asked.

"Mother, please," Hani said.

"Just a minute, Mom. What do you mean by 'Poe does this?'" I asked.

"I think it's pretty obvious, Alana," Foxx said.

He turned to my mother.

"I don't appreciate you talking about him like that," he continued.

"I'm sorry. I don't remember asking for your opinion. Why are you even here? This is a family matter."

"A family matter? That's my kid you're holding. Now all of a sudden I'm not a member of the family?"

"You and Hani aren't married. So, no, you technically aren't a member of this family."

"You're a real piece of work, Ms. Hu, but I'm guessing you already know that."

"It would be best if you'd just leave so I can talk to my daughter in private."

"In private? Really?" Foxx asked.

"No, mom, maybe you should leave," I said.

She turned to me.

"I know you think he's your friend, but he's not. He's Edgar's friend. You can't tell me he didn't know about this affair with this Brooklyn girl. I'm sure he helped cover it up."

"I didn't cover up anything, and there was no affair," Foxx said.

"You're still covering for him now? Well, you're a loyal friend. I'll give you that."

Foxx turned to me.

"I'm sorry, Alana, but I do think I better leave. I promised you not to make a scene, and I don't think I can keep that promise if I don't get the hell out of here."

"You don't have to leave," I said.

"I do. I'll call you in the morning. I want to help figure this out."

"Thanks for giving me a ride."

"It's not a problem. Call me anytime. I mean it. I'll be there."

"I know you will."

Foxx exited the house.

My mother turned to me after hearing the door shut behind Foxx.

"You can go to work tomorrow and ask for your job back. Just tell them you got overly emotional. I'm sure they'll understand given the circumstances. Anyone would overreact like that."

"What do you care if I keep my job or not? You always hated me being a cop. I figured you'd be happy I finally left."

"It's true that I haven't liked you doing that job. It's too dangerous, but you need a way to support yourself, especially now."

"Look around you, Mom. You think I'm going to have trouble paying the bills? We have plenty of money."

"No. Your husband has plenty of money."

"You're incredible. You really are. Not that this is any of your business, but Poe put me on every one of his bank accounts after we got married. I have access to all of it."

"You think you do, but how do you know there aren't accounts he's kept secret from you?"

"I'm not going to get into this argument. You either believe Poe's innocent, or you believe he's guilty. But I'm not going to play your 'I told you so' games."

"You think I'm enjoying this? I'm hurting for you. This is the last thing I wanted to happen."

"Just to be clear. You think he's guilty?" I asked.

My mother didn't respond.

"I can understand you believing he had an affair, especially after what happened to you, but I can't for the life of me guess why you think he's capable of murder," I said.

"What's that supposed to mean?"

"Come on, Mom. You know exactly what it means."

"So now you're going to try to hurt me. Is that what you're doing? You're hurting so you want others to hurt, too?"

"That's not what I'm doing. I'm trying to make a point. You haven't liked Poe from the beginning because he reminds you too much of Dad. They both came from wealthy families. They both came to the island and married a local girl, and now you're convinced he's going to leave me just like Dad left you."

"I'm surprised at you, Alana. I didn't think my daughter had such cruelty in her."

"I'm not trying to be. I'm trying to get us past this hang-up you have. Poe isn't like Dad, not in every way that really matters. He isn't going to leave me."

"He's not? Looks like he just did."

"Now who's being cruel?" I asked.

"The sooner you accept this, the better."

"Maybe you need to leave, Mom, before this gets any uglier."

Hani looked over to me.

"What are you going to do next?"

I appreciated her attempt to shift the subject, but I didn't think it would make much of a difference. Family lines had just been crossed. They'd actually been obliterated, and I knew we'd never be able to go back.

"I need to build a case for his innocence. It's not really that much different from any other assignment I've done dozens of time. It's just now I'm trying to prove the opposite. I need to take the evidence piece by piece and try to break it apart."

"Do you think you can do that?" Hani asked.

"I do. Poe said he met you the day Brooklyn was killed. He said you met him in the parking lot of a Home Depot."

"Yes, I remember that, and I'll testify whenever you want me to."

"I need more than your word. Try to find anything you can that proves you were there. If you have text messages to Poe setting up the meeting, then send me those."

"I also have my work calendar, and I can ask my clients to say that I met with them at those times."

"Good. I appreciate your help."

"What about the store? I bet they have cameras in the parking lot. I'm sure they recorded the whole thing," Hani said.

"That's on my list, too. I want to overwhelm the prosecutor. Maybe she won't be swayed herself, but she's bound to know a jury will be moved by a mountain of evidence showing that Poe was framed. That's what it's going to come down to, showing the prosecutor that she can't get past reasonable doubt."

"So you do have your own doubts about him. You don't need to prove he's innocent. You just need to show that he might not be guilty," my mother said.

"No, Mom. I just know how this game is played. No prosecutor wants to lose a case. It makes them look bad, and it hurts their chance at promotion. Piper Lane is no different. She's an ambitious person. She doesn't take a case unless she's sure she can win it. I have to make her think she might have backed the wrong horse."

Hani turned to our mother.

"Come on, Mom. We should get going. Alana needs time to think, and I need to get Ava home."

Hani took Ava out of her arms. The baby stirred but thankfully didn't start to cry.

My mother stood.

"I'm sorry, Alana. I really am."

"Sorry about which part? About Poe being arrested or how you talked about my husband?"

She didn't answer me. Instead, she turned and walked through the kitchen and headed out through the garage.

"Don't worry about her. You know what she's like," Hani said.

"That's easier said than done."

"For what it's worth, I believe Poe. He practically worships you. There's no way he would do this."

"Thanks."

"Do you know what I would give for someone to feel that way about me?"

I saw the pain in her eyes. Then I looked down at Ava. I knew Hani felt so lonely, and that was probably the main reason she's thrown herself so hard into her new career. I felt bad for not spending more time with Hani. I made a mental note to change that, but it would need to wait. Poe needed me more now than anyone else did.

"Thanks for coming over. It meant a lot."

"Call me if you need something. I don't want to bother you, but if you need help, I'm more than willing."

"I know you are."

I walked Hani outside and stood beside her vehicle as she strapped Ava into the car seat. I said goodbye again and waved as she backed out of the driveway.

I was about to turn to go inside when I started to cry. My mother's words had cut me deeply, despite all of my efforts to keep them from affecting me. She had a way of knowing where all the soft spots were. It was something I'd known about her for a long time.

Poe wasn't immune from those attacks either, but he'd taken them all and never once returned the hostility. Did that matter to her? Not one bit. She was utterly convinced that he was guilty of every charge she'd ever accused him of, and nothing he or I could say would ever change that.

Chapter 6
The Desk

I walked back into the house and headed for our dining room where we kept a small beverage refrigerator for our beer and wine. I opened it and immediately saw the six Purple Haze beers. Poe said he'd bought the beer for home but hadn't had any of them yet.

If he'd only had the beer at Harry's, the person who took the beers that ended up in Brooklyn's recycling container must have been inside the bar at the time Poe was having the drink. They couldn't have relied on getting lucky by randomly pulling three empty beer bottles out.

I assumed the waitresses or bartenders would toss the empty bottles into a trash or recycling can behind the bar. Someone, presumably the bar-backs, would take those cans to the back where the larger containers were located. That would still mean there were a ton of new bottles on the top portion of those larger containers.

It made more sense for the person to grab the bottles just after they were placed in the smaller recycling bins. That most likely meant one of two possibilities: Someone was pretty good at sneaking behind the bar without the bartenders or anyone else noticing, or the person who pulled those three specific Purple Haze bottles was a waitress or bartender. If that was the case, why would someone at the bar want to help frame Poe? Had he gotten into an argument with them? Had someone paid the waitress or bartender to take them?

I made a mental note to ask Poe if he remembered what night he might have had those beers. Poe and Foxx had extra security cameras installed inside and outside the bar after a violent incident over a year ago. I could always ask Foxx to review the security footage for that particular night, if Poe could remember which one it might have been, and see if he could spot who might have taken those beer bottles.

I closed the beverage refrigerator and tried to figure out what to do next. I remembered what Poe had told me in the interrogation room. He asked me twice to find my anniversary present in his office. It seemed like a silly request given the circumstances, but there must have been a reason for him wanting me to find it.

I walked upstairs to his office. I searched the top of his desk, but I didn't find anything that looked like a gift to me. There were a few receipts from a local hardware store and some receipts from a variety of restaurants. I checked the name of each restaurant and remembered going to those places with Poe. There were also some thumb drives that I assumed Poe had used for his photographs. His Canon 5D camera was on the desk as well, along with two lenses and a card reader.

His laptop was there. It wasn't password protected, despite me telling him a million times to do it. I opened the internet browser and logged onto his email account. It had a password since the software forced him to do it, but I knew the information so I was able to access his files. I scanned through several days' worth of emails. He hadn't sent an email in that time, but he had received several sales and marketing emails. I opened his trash folder and saw several other marketing emails he'd already deleted. Those had been deleted over a week ago, so it was apparent he didn't use his email very often.

I opened the desk drawer and saw my anniversary gift: a tiny jewelry box. I opened the box and saw the diamond earrings inside. They were beautiful, but that's not what really got my attention.

Poe had told me in the interrogation room that he hadn't opened his desk drawer in weeks. In fact, he hadn't hesitated a second when I asked him about it. I found the sales receipt for the earrings. He'd bought them that morning, so why did he tell me he hadn't been inside the drawer? Had he forgotten that he'd put them in the drawer and instead thought he'd left them on top of the desk? I didn't think that likely. It made more sense that he'd hide them in the drawer since they were a gift and our anniversary was still a few days away. I didn't regularly go into his office, but he never keeps the door shut, and his desk is in full view of the doorway that we walk by every night to go to our bedroom.

I pulled out my cell phone and called Mara Winters.

"Good evening, Alana. How are you holding up?"

"It still hasn't sunk in yet. Do you have anything new to report?"

"Unfortunately, no. Did you get a chance to speak with Edgar today?"

"That's actually why I was calling. I'm hoping you can clarify a few things for me."

"I hope so. What did you want to know?"

"When Detective Shaw mentioned the cell phone found in Poe's office, what was Poe's reaction?"

"He said it must have been planted. He also asked Shaw why he'd be so careless to hold onto the phone if it had really been his."

"Just to confirm, Shaw said the phone had been found in Poe's office desk drawer."

"I believe so."

"Did Poe have anything to say about that?"

"Not that I remember."

"Poe didn't say that he hadn't opened that drawer in weeks?"

"No. I would have remembered that. Is that what he told you?"

"Yes."

"What's the significance of that?"

"Maybe nothing. Did Shaw show you or Poe the transcripts of the phone messages?" I asked.

"Not during the interrogation, but I received them afterward."

"Anything jump out at you?"

"Yes, but I may be overanalyzing it."

"What is it?"

"I'm sorry to have to say this. I know how sensitive all of this is."

"Just say it. I need to know."

"Brooklyn Van Kirk mentions your name in several of the text messages. In some of the other messages, she uses the term 'your wife.'"

"What's the context?"

"She demands to know if he's going to leave you. Then things turn more confrontational over time, and she threatens to expose the affair."

"How long do these messages go back?"

"About four or five months."

"How often are the text messages exchanged?" I asked.

"Some days have several messages back and forth. Then it goes a few days with nothing and then another group of texts."

"When was the last message sent?"

"The night before she was killed. Ms. Van Kirk says she's going to see you at the police station and expose the affair and the pregnancy. She didn't get a response, and she sent several messages repeating the threat."

"You said something jumped out at you. What was it?"

"Over the course of the four to five months, there are a handful of instances where she used the name 'Poe.'"

"That's his nickname," I said.

"I'm aware of that, but who uses someone's name in a text message unless they're referring to a third party. I'm guessing you've sent hundreds, probably even thousands of text messages to Edgar. Have you ever once used his name? You don't because there's no need. He knows you're talking to him, and you're not going to waste time by typing extra letters."

I knew what she was implying. They had to make sure the police knew it was Poe.

"It was sloppy, but maybe they couldn't resist doing it. Potential proof of a setup in my opinion," Mara continued.

"Can you send me those transcripts?"

"They gave me hard copies, but I can scan them and email them to you."

"Can you do that tonight? I know it's getting late."

"It's no problem."

"Thank you."

I ended the call with Mara. She'd given me conflicting opinions on Poe's potential affair. She'd said the topic was sensitive, which I don't believe she'd have said if she thought the affair didn't happen. On the other hand, she indicated that the text messages gave some reason to believe the whole thing might have been a setup. She was clearly on the fence as to whether or not Poe had really been with Brooklyn. Was I? If I was being totally honest with myself, I didn't want to think about it.

I walked downstairs and went into one of the front rooms that we used as a library of sorts. There was also a small desk where Poe kept the computer for the home security system. He'd spent a small fortune upgrading the system after my attack. He'd had extra cameras installed around the exterior of the house so that every square inch was covered. Every window in the house, including the ones on the second floor, had wireless sensors. There was no way anyone could get near or in the house without us seeing it.

The cameras recorded twenty-four hours a day. Poe had the footage going to two different sources, which was way overkill but was also indicative of how much he worried about my safety. The footage went to a hard drive, which was stored on the desk in our library. It was also backed up to a cloud service operated by the security company.

I sat down at the desk and logged onto the laptop that controlled everything. I opened the alarm system software and pulled up the footage from the day before Brooklyn was killed. If the last text message exchange had happened on that day, then the phone would have had to have been planted in his office after that.

It took me a few hours to go through all of the various cameras. I watched them up to the point that the police arrived to take Poe into custody. I only saw four people on the cameras during those days before the arrest. There were numerous points that Poe and Ava appeared on the camera. Hani was also there when she came by the house to pick up Ava. I saw her vehicle drive up the driveway. She got out of the car and walked to the front door. Poe let her inside the house and then she reemerged with Ava just a few minutes after that. I was the fourth person to appear on the footage when I returned from work at night.

I also reviewed the footage from the day Brooklyn Van Kirk was killed. I saw myself leave early that morning. Poe left the house shortly after that. He didn't return for a few hours, but when he did, I saw him remove Ava from the car.

I knew Poe would often pick up Ava from Hani's house, and he would take her around the island on various sightseeing adventures. I always found it a bit silly since she was only one, but I also knew he really enjoyed driving her around. It was more than likely that the few hours that elapsed on the security cameras was taken up with one of those driving trips.

Unfortunately, the security footage established two things: No one came to the house to plant the phone inside Poe's office, and Poe's absence from the house that particular morning gave him more than enough time to murder Brooklyn, at least in the eyes of the police.

I thought back again to my conversation with Poe. He'd been very quick to say he hadn't been inside his desk drawer for weeks, only now I knew that wasn't true. He'd lied to me, yet he'd told me to do something that guaranteed he'd be caught in that lie. Had he gotten sloppy because he was undoubtedly stressed out and tired? Maybe. I just wasn't sure.

Chapter 7
Not Guilty

Perspective: Poe

How many of you have spent the night in jail? I'm guessing most of you haven't. I alluded to an earlier time when I'd been arrested. I'd found a suspect who'd committed suicide over the guilt he'd felt for murdering a rival. The detective in charge had a rather low opinion of me. I'm assuming he still does. He was highly annoyed that I'd gotten involved in the case. He was also jealous of my relationship with Alana. It turned out he'd been carrying a torch for her for years. I'm sure that's an old and out-of-date way of saying he had feelings for her, but I'm no longer hip, if I ever was to begin with, and I don't know the new vernacular.

This detective never got the courage to act on his feelings for Alana. I don't think it would have mattered, anyway, as Alana had zero interest in the guy. In fact, I don't believe her opinion of him could get any lower.

Anyway, he arrested me for murdering the guy who'd clearly killed himself. The murder weapon, a gun, was in the dead guy's hands, and his prints were the only ones on it. There was also the guilty confession the guy had recorded on his cell phone moments before shooting himself. The detective knew I didn't do it, and it was a clear-cut case of abuse of authority. Did that mean the detective received any type of disciplinary action? Of course, he didn't. It was all chalked up to an innocent misunderstanding and the detective's exuberance of wanting to solve a horrible crime. I was encouraged to let bygones be bygones.

I spent two nights in jail, but I was never worried about it. Maybe that sounds weird. After all, I was behind bars, but I never thought for a second the charges would stick. I was more annoyed and pissed that the detective had gotten the upper hand on me, but I knew it was only a matter of time before I was released. As I looked back on that incident, I realized just how stupid I'd been. Innocent people get convicted every day, even when there's little evidence against them. I'm sure you already knew that, and you're probably assuming I was pretty naïve. I was, and I believe I mentioned that in the beginning of this tale.

I'm by no means a hardened person now. I mean how hardened can you get when you live in a house on the ocean? But I know a lot more about life than I did back then, and I'm smart enough to know when to be scared. I knew I hadn't killed Brooklyn, but I also knew they'd put together enough evidence against me to easily convince a jury that would be desperate to make someone pay for the murder of a young pregnant woman.

If I had to guess, I'd say I might have gotten fifteen minutes of sleep that night. I couldn't stop thinking about the conversation with Shaw the day before. He'd been convincing, and I got the impression that even Mara had started to question my innocence by the end of the interview. I went over everything he'd said about a million times, and I thought I had a pretty good idea of what was going on. I just didn't know why, and I had no idea how I'd prove my theory, especially since I was stuck inside a cell.

I assumed they'd come get me at some point to take me to the courthouse where I'd be given a chance to enter my plea. I'd come to the conclusion that Alana was right when she predicted they'd deny me bail. I tried to mentally prepare myself for the anger and disappointment that was undoubtedly coming my way when I officially heard the judge tell me I wasn't going anywhere.

A police officer eventually came to get me sometime in the morning. Instead of taking me to court, he took me back to the same room where I'd been interrogated the previous day. I entered the room and saw Shaw and Mara seated around the table. There was a third person as well. She looked about Mara's age, maybe forty-five, and she had short black hair and dark eyes. None of them stood when I entered, not that I expected them to, and they didn't even say anything as I walked across the room.

The police officer led me over to the table, and I sat down beside Mara. I was determined not to be the first person to speak. I thought that would show some kind of weakness or nervousness on my part. The room was silent for several long moments. Finally, the new woman spoke.

"Mr. Rutherford, my name is Piper Lane. I'm with the District Attorney's Office."

She paused as if she were expecting me to say something in return. I didn't.

"We got the lab results back on that hair found on your clothing," Piper Lane said.

"What hair?" I asked.

"It was found during the search of your home. There were two hairs. Testing confirms they're from Brooklyn Van Kirk."

"You said they were found on Mr. Rutherford's clothing. This was the clothing he was wearing when you arrested him?" Mara asked.

"No. The hairs were on a men's extra-large t-shirt in the clothes hamper in the master bathroom," Shaw said.

"Why didn't you mention this yesterday?" Mara asked.

"We wanted to get the test results back first," Shaw said.

Neither Mara nor I responded, and the room went quiet again. Brooklyn's hair in my house, as well as a secret phone with messages to and from her. My fingerprints on beer bottles in her kitchen, and an eyewitness neighbor who swore she saw my car in Brooklyn's parking lot. They'd been thorough.

"The DA has authorized me to offer you a deal. Plead guilty to second-degree murder and we'll recommend to the judge a term of twenty years."

"Second-degree? How did you come up with that?" Mara asked.

Piper Lane turned to me.

"Maybe you didn't go over there with the intention to kill her. Maybe you just wanted to talk to her. I'm guessing she made more threats to you, and you lost control."

"Is that how you see it?" I asked.

"The DA wants to close this," Lane said.

"The husband of a well-known detective. I'm sure this looks bad for everyone," I said.

"It's a good deal. I personally don't think you deserve it. You'll be out before you're sixty. Meanwhile that girl's dead."

"Doesn't seem fair, does it?" I asked.

"No, it doesn't."

"I'm in here, and the person who really strangled Brooklyn is walking around free. Does that bother you?"

Shaw smirked, but I didn't turn to look at him.

"This deal is going to last another sixty seconds," Piper Lane said.

"Twenty years," I said.

The lawyer and I looked at each other. I didn't see any nervousness in her eyes, not that she had anything to be nervous about, but it meant one thing to me. She wasn't in on this.

I looked at Mara. I couldn't read her expression, either.

"What do you think?" I asked.

She paused, and I turned back to Ms. Lane before Mara had a chance to answer.

"I'm going to say no to your plea deal. I'll see you in court today or tomorrow or whenever it is you're going to drag me in front of the judge."

"We're not offering this deal again. It's now or never."

"If I say no to this, then you're going with first-degree murder?"

"That's right."

"I'll take my chances."

Shaw turned and motioned for the police officer who'd remained by the door to come get me.

"I do have one question," I said.

Lane held her hand up, and the cop stopped walking.

"What is it?" she asked.

"You said it was an extra-large shirt. What specific shirt was it?"

"A UVA shirt, dark blue."

"University of Virginia, my alma mater."

I turned to Mara.

"Please let Alana know that."

Mara nodded.

"You're not getting away with this Rutherford. I never lose," Piper Lane said.

I ignored her comment and stood.

The cop took me back to my cell. I was probably there a few more hours before they came for me again. This time they took me to the courthouse. There was a weird mix of pleasure and pain as I stared at the blue sky above me on the short drive over. I longed to be in my backyard, swimming and laughing with Ava. We'd be there when Alana would walk through the gate and smile at us. Then she'd go inside and change and eventually come back outside to the pool. We'd spend hours lounging around and staring at the ocean. All that and more had been taken from me, and I had no idea if I was going to get it back.

The police officer parked at the side of the courthouse and took me through a door that led to a hallway and a small room where I waited another hour or so for my time before the judge. I saw Alana and Foxx when the cop escorted me into the courtroom. I nodded to them both as I was led over to a wooden table. They were about three rows back from me. I turned and looked at Piper Lane, who stood behind another table beside mine. She glanced back at Mara and me but didn't say anything. She turned away and went back to organizing her papers. I looked behind her and saw Detective Shaw a few rows back.

"Is this when you tell me I should have taken that plea deal?" I asked Mara.

"No. We'll beat this."

"Do you really believe that?"

"Yes, I do."

"You didn't look so sure back at the station."

"I don't make impulse decisions. You should know that about me by now."

"What's changed in the last few hours?"

"It's taken me a while to process your reaction to all of this."

"What do you mean?"

"An innocent person would be freaking out right now. They'd be screaming over and over again about how the police had nabbed the wrong person."

"And a guilty person?"

"Guilty people have one of two reactions. I've seen it a million times. They either completely fall apart and confess to everything…"

"Or?"

"Or they become very calm. Nothing rattles them, no matter how much evidence is presented. They're too cautious about giving anything away."

"So that must mean you think I'm guilty."

"Today I realized there was a third option. This is like a poker game with you, or maybe chess. Yes, that's a better comparison. You're studying the board. Looking at all the pieces."

I turned and looked at Alana.

"Based on your analogy, would that make Alana the queen?"

"The queen is the most powerful piece on the game."

"Did you tell Alana about the shirt?" I asked.

"Not yet, but I will. Want to clue me in on why a UVA shirt is so important?"

"Alana will let you know."

"I assumed as much. Just so you know. It's usually best not to keep information from your attorney."

"You'll know soon enough. Of course, I could be completely wrong about all of this."

My hearing began, and the charges were read. Piper Lane went over the evidence, and the judge asked me how I intended to plead. Mara answered for me: Not guilty. Lane then did as predicted when she pointed out my wealth and ability to escape the island and disappear for good. I didn't think it was as easy as she made it seem, but I hadn't really thought about escaping anyway.

The judge agreed with her and denied me bail. The whole thing was over as fast as when I'd been arrested in my own house. I was getting run over by the system, and the speed at which it was carrying me to a lifetime sentence was startling.

Alana and Foxx walked up to me as one of the courthouse guards pulled me away.

"Foxx, tell her about the phone call I got the day after the wedding. She needs to know."

I saw Alana's confused look. She turned to Foxx, and then I was dragged out of the room.

Chapter 8
The Phone Call

Perspective: Alana

"What was he talking about?" I asked.

Foxx looked around the courtroom. I followed his gaze and saw Piper Lane walking toward Mara.

Foxx turned back to me.

"Not here. Later."

I walked closer to Mara since I didn't want to miss their conversation. I couldn't hear what she and Piper were talking about, though. They shook hands and then Piper looked over to me. She hesitated a moment and then walked over to the wooden boundary that separated the lawyer's area from benches where the audience sat.

"How are you holding up?" she asked.

"How do you think?"

"This isn't personal, Alana. I'm just doing my job."

"You're going to owe him an apology. Everyone is."

Piper didn't respond. Instead, she gave me this sad expression that bordered on pity and walked away. I turned back to Mara who was walking over to me.

"That went as expected," I said.

"Your conversation with Ms. Lane or the hearing?"

"Both. What did she tell you?"

"She asked me if I thought Edgar would reconsider the plea deal."

4096

"I wasn't aware one was even on the table."

Mara told me about the District Attorney's offer for Poe to plead guilty to second-degree murder in exchange for a shorter sentence.

"I hope you both told her what she could do with that offer."

"Edgar rejected it, as I'm guessing you could have predicted."

"I'm surprised they'd even offer a deal. I know Piper pretty well. She seems sure of herself."

"There's something Edgar wanted me to tell you," Mara said, ignoring my statement. "They found Brooklyn Van Kirk's hair on one of his shirts. Did you know about that?"

"I heard something about it yesterday, but the test results hadn't come back yet."

"They confirmed the hairs belonged to her. Edgar said to tell you they were on his UVA shirt. Is there some significance to that?"

"Yes. It's my shirt now."

"What do you mean?"

"I would often wear it to bed when we started living together. I sort of took ownership of the shirt. He hasn't worn it in months. In fact, I just put it in my dresser now."

"They found the shirt in the hamper. Do you have separate hampers for your clothes and his?"

"No. We use the same one."

"So the hairs could have transferred from one of his shirts to the UVA shirt."

"It could have, but I doubt it. They saw an extra-large shirt and just assumed he'd been the one wearing it."

"They?"

"Whoever planted that evidence. Maybe one person. Maybe more than one."

"Do you have a theory as to why someone would want to frame him?"

"Not yet, but I'm working on it."

I could tell by the neutral look on her face that she wasn't convinced he'd been framed. Did that bother me? Not really. I knew she'd do a good job of defending him either way, and I'd rather have someone on our team who made their own judgements and didn't just blindly follow what others thought or said.

"I need to get back to the office. Let's touch base later today," Mara said.

"Of course. I'll talk to you later."

Mara left, and I walked back to Foxx who was now standing near the door that led out of the courtroom.

"About that phone call," I said.

"Let's go outside. I'll tell you everything."

Foxx and I left the courthouse and made our way over to his SUV. He'd picked me up that morning despite me telling him that I intended to drive myself to the hearing. He insisted on taking me. Now I wasn't sure if I was about to regret that decision since he'd obviously kept something from me. Poe had, too, and I tried to brace myself for whatever revelation was coming.

We climbed inside the vehicle, and I turned to him.

"What's going on? What phone call was he talking about?"

Foxx hesitated.

"You heard Poe. He specifically asked you to tell me."

"Poe got a call the morning after your wedding."

I didn't remember him getting a call that morning, but that didn't mean one didn't come through. He'd rented one of the suites at the hotel so we didn't have to make the long drive home after the reception. We'd slept late the next morning and spent the afternoon on the beach after brunch. It had been a great day. He certainly hadn't mentioned a phone call, though.

"Who called him?"

"The guy didn't give a name. It probably wouldn't have mattered if he did. There's no way he would have given his real one."

"What did this person want?"

"He offered Poe a job."

"A job?"

"He said he'd been impressed with how Poe figured out that smuggling ring last year. Poe told him to get lost."

"I don't understand. This guy was with law enforcement?"

"No. He was the real guy in control of the ring. Koa was just the local guy running this one part of it. Poe thought the smuggling ring might be in multiple countries."

Koa was the name of the guy who'd been arrested for a crime ring that Poe discovered. He was now behind bars in a Maui prison.

"What did the guy say after Poe refused to work for him?" I asked.

"He told Poe that he'd have to kill him. Then he hung up the phone."

"You didn't think this was important to tell me?"

"Poe swore me to secrecy. He didn't want you to know."

"Why in the world wouldn't he tell me?"

"He didn't want you to worry, He said he didn't think there'd be anything the police could do to protect him."

"You mean there wasn't anything I could do. I've got news for you both. I'm not some helpless little female you two need to protect. I've been a cop since before either of you moved to the island."

"I'm sorry, Alana, but he's your husband. He should have been the one to tell you, not me."

"You're right. He should have."

"Put yourself in his shoes for a minute. You'd barely survived that attack. He didn't want anything upsetting you. Then he gets the call the day after the wedding. What was he supposed to do? Ruin that moment?"

"It's not about ruining a moment. It's about being honest with me, and someone threatening to kill him is a lot more important than lounging around some resort."

"He never lied to you."

"Don't try to get him off on a technicality. Withholding information is the same as lying in my book."

"I'm not trying to argue the point. He just didn't want to put anything more on you."

"It's been a year since then. He sure as hell could have told me at some point."

"I actually asked him about that a while ago. He said he thought it was just an empty threat."

"Why would he think that?"

"He said he didn't even think the guy lived on the island. He said the guy was just trying to scare him."

"Did he say why he didn't think the guy was on Maui?"

"No. I just figured it was some hunch he had. You know how he gets those. Why do you think he wanted me to tell you now?"

"Because he thinks this is somehow connected to the murder of Brooklyn Van Kirk. I found out the other day she was the one who told Poe the name of the person who attacked me and killed Brooklyn's boss. Poe must think her murder might have been revenge for revealing that information."

"Why would someone wait an entire year to kill her?"

"Maybe it took them that long to figure out Brooklyn's role in all of this."

"So they killed her for her betrayal and then framed Poe for breaking up the smuggling ring?"

"Maybe. But why not just kill Poe, too? Why go through the trouble of setting him up?"

"Does Mara know about all of this?" Foxx asked.

"No, and I don't want to tell her yet."

"Now who's holding back information?"

"You can't tell anyone about this phone call. Promise me that."

"Why don't you want his attorney to know? She has to prepare a defense."

"It's bigger than his trial. I just need a little time to figure this out."

"How can it be bigger than his trial? We have to get our boy out of jail."

"Don't you see? Poe put it all together, but he couldn't tell me about it because he knew our conversations were being recorded."

"What are you talking about?"

"The jail. There are cameras everywhere. Everything is being monitored, and if it isn't, it's being captured and someone will just review it later."

"I would think you'd want to tell the police about this. They know Poe's role in breaking up that ring. Now you can prove motivation for the frame job."

"They did a good job. They really did."

"Who did?"

"The burner phone is the most damning piece of evidence. It was found in the desk drawer in Poe's office. Poe claimed in his first interview that he hadn't been in that desk in weeks, only that wasn't true. He'd literally been in the desk just a few hours before the police found the phone when he put my wedding anniversary gift inside it. I checked. There's not much inside that drawer. If the phone had been inside it, he would have seen it. He didn't say that, though. He kept quiet about it."

"Why? It might have helped prove he didn't do it."

"Not really. They would have just said he was lying about it. Or worse, they would have realized that he knew."

"Knew what?"

"That the police put the burner phone in the desk when they conducted the search."

"The police? Wait a minute."

"It makes sense. You don't conduct a smuggling ring of that magnitude without some form of police protection."

"You mean having a dirty cop on the payroll?"

"Among other things."

"A cop planted that burner phone?"

"And put the hair on the old t-shirt," I said. "After my attack, Poe upgraded the security system at the house. There are cameras everywhere now, and they never stop recording. I searched through those camera files for the last two weeks. No one but family members come anywhere near our house. If Poe didn't put the phone in his desk, than the only other option is a cop."

"Let's say you're right. How do you figure out which cop put it there?"

"It might have been more than one. Maybe one person was a lookout while the other planted the evidence."

"How many people were on the search? Did you see when you went back there?"

"I don't have an exact count, but it wouldn't be unusual for a dozen or more people to conduct a search of a house that size."

"This is crazy, Alana. You know that, don't you?"

"It's not as far-fetched as you think."

"How did they get Poe's car and also the beer bottles in that girl's house?"

"I don't know yet, but I'm working on it."

"Are you going to take any of this to your old department? Is there anyone there you can trust?"

"Better if we keep this between the two of us right now."

"Okay. What are you going to do now?" Foxx asked.

"You set Poe up with that auto mechanic. Right?"

"Yeah. He was a friend of a friend."

"I need his information. It's time he and I had a conversation."

Chapter 9
The BMW

Perspective: Alana

Foxx said he didn't want to just tell me the name of the car mechanic. He wanted to personally drive me to the guy's shop, and he suggested we head there at once.

I wasn't sure I wanted him to go with me at first, mainly because I didn't know how this would all go down with Foxx there. He can be an emotional person. Sometimes that has its advantages, but usually it doesn't. I didn't want him losing control, especially considering how much was on the line. Then again, I wasn't so sure I could control myself, so maybe it would be a good idea if he were there to protect the owner from me. Of course, I could have gotten this all wrong, and Poe had simply made a mistake when he said he didn't remember ever driving to that apartment complex.

The auto shop was a few miles from the airport in a section of town crowded with small businesses and shops that catered to locals. I drove up to the small white building with the name "Perkins' Auto Repair" in large blue letters above the door. There were two open bays, and I could see they both had cars inside. We parked in the tiny gravel lot, and Foxx turned off the ignition.

"How do you want to handle this?" Foxx asked.

"Not sure. We don't even know he's responsible for the car being at that apartment."

"He had it for two months. Who else would it be?"

I didn't have an answer, and I had no idea what I was going to do if the owner or one of his employees hadn't been the one to drive to Brooklyn's place.

We climbed out of the car and immediately heard the loud whooshing sound of one of those hydraulic guns that mechanics use to loosen lug nuts. Foxx followed me inside the lobby. There were several shiny wheel rims hanging on the wall behind the cash register.

"I think that's Perkins," Foxx whispered to me, and he motioned toward a man in his fifties behind the cash register.

The guy had short gray hair and a thin build. He looked like he was just a few inches taller than me.

We had to wait a few minutes for Perkins, or at least the person we thought was Perkins, to finish helping his customer. He handed the lady a credit card form which she signed. He then stapled it to a printout of her repairs and handed the paperwork to her. She thanked him and walked past us on her way out of the shop.

"Can I help you two?" Perkins asked.

"Yes, we're looking for Dylan Perkins," I said.

"That's me. What can I do for you?"

"I'm Detective Alana Hu with the Maui Police Department. Is there someplace we can have a private conversation?"

I didn't have a badge to flash, and I hoped he'd just accept that I was with the cops.

"What's this about?" Perkins asked.

"Maybe out back. I don't think you want to have this conversation in earshot of your customers."

Perkins hesitated a moment. Then he led us through the garage and out a back door. We followed him to a wooden picnic table that had a few soda cans and a metal coffee can filled with cigarette butts on top. I thought he was going to sit on one of the benches. Instead, he stayed standing and turned back to us.

"Now can you tell me what's going on?"

I reached into my jacket pocket and removed a small photograph, which I handed to Perkins.

"You worked on that car about a year ago."

He looked at the photo.

"Yeah. I remember. Z3 convertible. It was a real mess. Owner drove it into the ocean."

"He was forced off the road," Foxx said.

Perkins shrugged his shoulders.

"Doesn't matter to me how it got there. Took a while, but we got it back in good shape. What does this have to do with anything?"

"When you work on cars, do you or your employees ever drive the cars home?"

"Never. Sometimes we test drive them around town, but we don't ever take them home. We either leave them in the garage or we park them back here."

I looked around us and saw several cars parked in the grass. The grass was kind of high, and I wondered how long the cars had been there. They looked more like cars ready for the junk yard than cars waiting to be worked on.

"How secure are they back here without a fenced-in yard? Have you ever had any stolen?" I asked.

"No problems. You can't see the cars from the road, either."

"I'm sure people know they're back here."

"Maybe, but we haven't had anyone mess with them. Look, I don't know what's going on, but I haven't done anything wrong. The guy brought the car in. I fixed it and gave it back to him. End of story."

"You never drove it to an apartment complex?" I asked.

"No. I drove it a few blocks around here to test everything out. That was it."

"Here's the thing. The owner always kept it inside a locked garage. The only time it was out of there was when you had it. I don't think you're being honest with us. I think someone took that car out of your shop, and I think you know who."

"I'm gonna have to ask you both to leave."

"We're not going anywhere. Answer the lady's question," Foxx said.

"I fixed the car and…"

"Tell her who took it," Foxx yelled, and he slapped his hand against the picnic table.

It made such a loud smack that I almost jumped. Perkins certainly did.

"Get out of here," he said after recomposing himself.

"Not until you tell us who took the car," Foxx said.

"What's the problem?" a male's voice said behind us.

Foxx and I both turned and saw one of Perkins' mechanics standing several feet away. He held a large wrench at his side.

"It's all right, Tom. They were just leaving," Perkins said.

"No, it's not all right. You haven't told us what we need to know," Foxx said.

"You heard him. Get out of here," Tom said.

"This doesn't concern you. Go back to work," Foxx said.

Tom got this look in his eyes that I've seen a million times before. There's a switch that goes off in some people when they're about to attack. All reasoning goes out the window and rage takes over their brains.

The mechanic held up the wrench and charged Foxx. Foxx is a huge man, and people always underestimate his speed. He was a football player for the Washington Redskins, though. Even the big men in professional football are several times faster than the average guy.

Foxx stepped to the side just as Tom swung the wrench at his head. It missed by just a few inches, but now the mechanic was completely off balance. Foxx punched him in the gut, and Tom dropped to the ground. He started coughing as he tried to suck air back into his lungs. Foxx stood over him and looked like he was about to hit him a second time.

"That's enough!" I yelled.

Foxx picked up the wrench and tossed it several feet away. It landed just a few feet from one of the junk cars.

I turned back to Perkins.

"Tell us what happened."

Perkins looked at Foxx, who by now looked like he was about to lift one of the broken-down cars and toss it at Perkins.

"This guy came to me. Asked if he could borrow the car for the day," Perkins said.

"He just showed up at your garage? Did you know him?" I asked.

"Never met him before. He said he'd seen me working on the car and admired it. Said he wanted to test drive it."

"Why would you let him? You didn't own the car. You couldn't sell it to him."

"I told him all that, but he was insistent. He said it was always his dream to drive something like that."

"So you lent him the car?"

"Yeah."

"Did he pay you?"

Perkins nodded.

"How much?" Foxx asked.

"Five K."

"He paid you five thousand dollars to drive the car?" I asked.

"It was all in cash."

"So you knew this wasn't about some dream to drive a nice car. There had to be something else to it."

Tom the mechanic struggled to his feet.

"Stay down," Foxx said, and he pushed him back toward the ground with his foot.

"He had the money in an envelope. I couldn't say no."

"Yes, you could have."

"What would you have done if he didn't bring the car back?" Foxx asked.

Perkins said nothing.

"He would have called the police and said the car had been stolen. That way his insurance would have covered the car or Poe's would have. Meanwhile, he still gets the five grand, all tax free," I said.

"I'm sorry. I know I shouldn't have done it," Perkins said.

"How long did he keep the car?"

"Just a few hours."

"Did he ever come back to your shop and ask to take the car again?"

"No. I never saw him after that."

"Did he tell you his name?"

"No."

"What did he look like?" Foxx asked.

"Hawaiian guy. Average build. Maybe in his late thirties or early forties."

"Here's what you're going to do. I'm going to give you the name of a local attorney. I want you to call her today and set a time to go to her office. You're going to tell her everything you just told us. In return, I'm not going to arrest you."

"Why are you even interested in any of this? What did that guy do when he had the car?"

"He helped frame someone for murder."

I took the photo of Poe's car back and handed Mara's business card to Perkins.

"Call her now. I want to watch you do it."

We followed him back to the lobby and watched as he dialed Mara's number and set an appointment to see her that afternoon. Foxx informed him that he'd be checking in with Mara that evening, and he'd be terribly disappointed if he heard that Perkins hadn't gone. Perkins didn't respond, and I thought the odds were pretty good that he'd make it to Mara's. Foxx's display had been a powerful one. Poe had told me that Foxx was an accomplished fighter. It wasn't like I didn't believe him, but I'd just never seen it firsthand. He'd dropped that mechanic like it had been nothing at all.

We walked back to my car and climbed inside.

"Hopefully he won't call the cops," I said.

"I'm sorry. I know how much that job meant to you."

I didn't really have a reply. Foxx was right. It had meant everything to me, but it was nothing without Poe.

Chapter 10
Purple Haze

Perspective: Poe

If I ever get out of this place, I'll be tempted to write a memoir about it. Being in jail is much like going to the DMV, only you know you're probably never going to get out of there. You spend most of your time looking around the room and trying to figure out what the deal is with everyone else. Of course, they're looking at you in much the same way.

I tried to entertain myself by creating back stories for the various people. I didn't know any of their names, nor did I want to. That didn't stop me from creating names for them, though. There was Eddie, who I'd decided had robbed a bank to pay for the dental procedure he desperately needed. The guy looked like he was missing the majority of his teeth, although I tried not to get too close to him for a full examination.

There was also Frank. I guessed he was in there for some pornography-related issue. Decorum fully prevents me from elaborating any more on him.

The third guy I named was Donovan Kensington III. He undoubtedly had committed a financial crime. Maybe a Ponzi scheme that had bilked his friends out of millions. The guy was dressed in the God-awful orange jumpsuit like we all were, but he somehow had a way of looking down at us all.

Finally, there was Butch. He was the leader of some motorcycle gang, and he'd started a bar brawl when some drunk tourist made fun of him for ordering a tropical drink with an umbrella in it. Butch might be a tough guy, but he couldn't resist the taste of fruity mixed drinks.

Yeah, I know what you're thinking. Poe is already losing it after being in jail for just a few days.

My little creative exercise was broken when I was told I had a visitor. When I got down to the room, I saw it was Foxx and not Alana. The officer led me to the table where Foxx was sitting. I sat across from him.

"Not who you were expecting?" Foxx asked.

"It's not that."

"I understand. I really do."

I knew Foxx did, and I also knew that's why he was here. He knew better than most how much these visits can mean.

"I spoke with Alana just before I came over here. She told me to let you know she's going to see you soon. She had someone she had to meet with this morning."

"Did she say who?" I asked.

"No."

"Is she making any progress trying to get me out of here?"

"I don't know. She's keeping everything pretty close to her."

I knew Foxx wasn't being honest with me because he'd looked away when he'd made that statement. It was his obvious tell, and it's not something I'd ever let on that I knew. So why hadn't he told me what Alana was up to? Was it because it was bad news? Maybe.

"You look tired," I said.

"I've been up all night going over security footage at Harry's."

"Why?"

"Alana checked your refrigerator at home. She said all the Purple Haze beers are still there. That means the beers had to have been taken from our bar."

"You were looking for someone who might have lifted them from out back?"

"Yeah. I went over the receipts since we started stocking that particular beer. I only found four with the NC code on them."

I knew what Foxx was getting at. NC referred to No Charge. We told the bartenders and waitresses to enter that charge code if the drink or meal was on the house. It was mainly used for inventory purposes so we could track the inventory to what was being bought by customers, even if the drink had been on the house.

This was due to a bartender we fired about six months ago. We discovered the guy had a habit of giving away the bulk of his drinks. It was a common tactic by bartenders to increase their cash tips at the expense of the owners. They'd give the drink away and ask the customer to show their appreciation for their generosity. The customer would tip far more than they normally would. It was a good deal for the customer because they still got the drink for less than they would ordinarily pay, even with the increased tip. Of course, it was a terrible deal for Foxx and me.

We confronted the bartender when we found out his little plan. Foxx fired him on the spot, which pissed me off because I wanted to be the one to fire him. After that, we implemented the NC policy. The code also applied to Foxx and me whenever we ordered something for ourselves.

"Was there one person who gave me those beers?" I asked.

"No. There were three different servers."

"Who was it?"

"Kiana, Molly, and Tommy. The first receipt had five beers on it. I think that was the night I introduced the beer to you. I'm pretty sure I had a few with you. Someone would have had a hard time figuring out which beer bottle was yours and which was mine if they'd taken them that night."

"What about the other transactions?"

"Each one had one beer on the receipt. I looked at the time on the receipts. They were all around lunch time."

That made sense since I often came by Harry's that time of day. I'd go over the accounting with Foxx, and we'd often have lunch together. I'd drink one beer at the most. I'd leave most of my evenings free for Alana. If I did go to Harry's at night, I'd usually bring Alana with me. I'd usually order a Manhattan in the evening. I tended not to order that stiff drink during the day, though.

"Three lunch receipts equals three empty beer bottles. Did those three transactions also have three different servers?" I asked.

"Yeah. Kiana gave us the beers on the first night, and she also gave you the beer on the first lunch. Tommy served you on the second lunch, and Molly served you on the third one."

"Do any of those people have issues with me?"

"Not that I know of, but they wouldn't have told me if they did. It didn't have to be them, though. I was thinking about that on the way over here. It could have been someone else who was also working those same days. I'll check the schedule when I get back to the bar."

"Does the staff know what's happened to me?"

"Everyone on the island knows. It's all over the news."

"What are people saying?"

"They tend to stop talking when I walk by them. I think they know what I'd do to them if I caught them badmouthing you."

There was a long pause in the conversation, and I watched as Foxx casually looked around the room. He turned back to me, and his voice got softer.

"I don't think for a second that you'd ever hurt that girl."

"I appreciate that. I feel like there's a 'but' coming next."

"Nobody's perfect, even you."

"I never claimed to be."

"I know you didn't."

"What are you getting at?"

"That girl was a beautiful woman, and we all make mistakes."

"Is this your way of asking me if I had an affair with her?"

Foxx didn't answer me. He didn't have to. We both knew what he was getting at. There was a part of me that was offended by his uncertainty, but I also got why he was asking. Human beings often behave in unpredictable manners, even when we think we know everything there is to know about someone and how they act. That was a lesson I'd certainly learned during these investigations. We all think we're intellectual creatures. We're the top of the food chain, but we're still animals at our core beings. We still let our emotions control us, at least some of the time. I wouldn't be the first man to stray in his marriage, even with a woman as beautiful as Alana.

"Is this just your doubt asking, or is there some other reason?"

"Kiana came to me last night. She said Molly had mentioned something to her," Foxx said.

"What was it?"

"She said Molly told her that she'd overheard you arguing with a woman on your cell phone during one of your lunches. She got the impression it wasn't Alana."

"Did she say why she didn't think it was Alana?"

"I asked Kiana that, and she said Molly didn't tell her."

"What were we supposedly arguing about?"

"Molly heard you tell this person not to threaten you."

"You believe this story?"

"I'm not saying I believe it."

"What are you saying?"

"I'm asking you if I need to have a conversation with Molly and tell her to keep her mouth shut. This is none of her business."

"Don't say anything to Molly. I don't know what she thinks she heard, but no one has threatened me lately, at least not until I got here. This may surprise you, but the people in here aren't exactly model citizens."

"Don't joke, Poe. This is serious."

"I know it's serious. I didn't cheat on Alana. I'd tell you if I did. Does Alana think I did? Does she have doubts like you?"

"You know Alana. She's insecure."

Foxx was right. Alana was a ten, in every way that can be measured, but she acted like she had no idea she was. I didn't know why that was for the longest time. Then I met her mother. The woman had Alana and her sister convinced that a man's entire reason for being was to betray women. I knew Alana realized on an intellectual level that it wasn't a true statement. If you hear something every day for years, though, there's still a small section in the back of your mind that believes it, no matter how hard you try to push it away.

"Has she been talking to her mother?"

"Yeah. Luana and Hani were at your house when I dropped Alana off the other night," Foxx said.

"I assumed as much. Did you talk to Luana?"

"Yeah, and it went about as well as you can guess."

I laughed. As much as my mother-in-law got to me, she affected Foxx a thousand times more.

"We ought to put her on your case. She'd have this thing wrapped up by lunch time."

"Are you kidding me? She probably thinks I'm guilty."

"Maybe."

"Maybe. There's no doubt about it. By the way, how's my dog?" I asked.

"Are you serious? You're in jail, and you're asking about that damn dog of yours?"

"How is he?"

"I'm watching him. Alana asked me to because she wants to be free to investigate your case."

"Are you taking him on walks or are you just letting him out the backyard?"

"What different does it make?"

"He needs his exercise. I try to walk him at least three to four times a day."

"He can run around the backyard. You're insane. You know that, don't you?"

"I just thought of something. I know I told you not to say anything to Molly, but maybe that was bad advice. Let her know that you had your doubts about me and Alana."

"Why?"

"See what she knows. Either she's lying about me for some reason, or she just misunderstood a conversation I was having. I want to know which one it is."

Foxx and I spoke for a few more minutes before the police officer came to take me back to my cell. You may not believe this, but our conversation was a brief escape from this place, at least in my mind. It almost felt like we were back at Harry's.

Chapter 11
Under the Banyan Trees

Perspective: Alana

It killed me not to go see Poe that morning, but I assumed he'd support my decision if he knew what I was trying to do instead. I needed information. There was only one person I thought would give it to me, and it was a slim chance at that.

I sent a text fairly early in the morning and asked Captain Price to meet me at the Banyan Court Park in Lahaina. It was a favorite place of Poe's, and he'd often meet with people there during his investigations. The site was in a fairly crowded part of Lahaina, which was one of the major tourist spots on the island. It was easy to get lost in the crowd and go unnoticed. I'd hoped one of his spaces would bring me luck. I could certainly use a bit of it.

The Banyan Park was also just down the street from a café where I knew the captain often stopped for a morning coffee and a Danish pastry. His house was on the outskirts of Lahaina, and the café was an easy detour versus the places in Kahului that tended to get very busy in the mornings.

I didn't get a reply to my text, but I decided to head to the park anyway. It wasn't all that far from my house, and I was getting a little stir crazy pacing the floors. At the very least, the drive and the walk around Lahaina would give me fresh scenery and maybe a better chance to collect my thoughts and figure out a game plan.

I parked a short distance away from the café and walked down Front Street. I arrived at the Banyan Park but didn't see Price anywhere. There were just a few tourists walking around this time of day. Most were looking at those little books that list the various shops and restaurants in the town. A few other people were taking photographs of the massive trees.

I checked the time on my cell phone. I was about ten minutes early. I also noticed I still hadn't received a reply to my text. I sat on one of the benches that overlooked the massive trees to give Price a chance to swing by, although my gut began to tell me he wasn't going to show.

I decided to call Mara to see if she'd made any progress on her end. I slipped my phone out of my pocket and dialed her number. She answered on the second ring.

"Good morning, Alana."

"Sorry to call so early."

"It's no problem. I'm already in the office."

"I was just checking to see if that car shop owner came to see you yesterday."

"Mr. Perkins. Yes, he was very forthcoming. How did you get him to talk?"

"A friend of mine convinced him."

"Say no more. I had planned on calling you soon. I discovered something interesting last night."

"What is it?"

"I must have looked at that photo of Edgar's car outside the apartment complex a million times before I noticed an interesting detail. Brooklyn Van Kirk's apartment complex is located in Kihei. According to the detective, the neighbor took the photo because she thought the storm clouds had an interesting pattern to them."

"I remember hearing that. It was a B.S. excuse."

"Sure, but it might also save us. Kihei has over two hundred and seventy days of sun a year. The photo does show rain clouds, though."

"How does that help us?"

"Because we can potentially narrow down the day the photo was taken."

"The data on her cell phone should tell us that."

"True, but I'm still having a hard time believing she chose to take the photo on the exact same day the car was taken from Mr. Perkins."

"Did Detective Shaw indicate when the photo was shot?" I asked.

"No, but I asked Mr. Perkins if he remembered what day the BMW was borrowed, if that's the best word to describe their transaction."

"Could he remember that far back?"

"Not exactly, but he deposited the cash the next morning. He said his neighborhood had a burglary that same week, and he was worried about keeping so much cash around. I had him log into his bank account from my office to find the date of the deposit. I then compared the weather reports from the day before when Edgar's car was taken. It did rain in Kihei that same day."

"What about the weather on the surrounding days? Did you think to check that?"

"I did. Sunshine for over twenty days before and several days after. There's also no report of rain for the two weeks before Brooklyn Van Kirk's murder. I think we can make a convincing argument that Edgar's car was only at that apartment complex for one day, probably just a hour or so. If he'd been having this long-term affair with her, the car would have been seen multiple times and probably by multiple people. I know it's not a Ferrari, but it's still a noticeable model."

"Were there any reports of other neighbors seeing the car?"

"Not that Detective Shaw brought up. I think he would have said something if he had more witnesses. If that neighborhood is like mine, they'll have at least a few busybodies."

I knew what Mara was getting at. Poe and I had two people on our street that took notice of everything. Nothing escaped these people.

"Do you know the name of the neighbor who took the cell phone photo?" I asked.

"No, but they'll have to give it to me in discovery."

"Hopefully I'll have that information here shortly."

"How?" Mara asked.

"If this meeting happens. I'll give you a call later. Good work on the photograph. That was clever thinking."

"Thank you. Talk to you soon."

I ended the call with Mara.

"What photograph are you talking about?"

I turned when I heard the voice behind me. It was Captain Price.

"I wasn't sure you'd come," I said.

"I wasn't going to. Then I drove by and saw you sitting here. What made you come out here when I didn't respond this morning?"

"Hope and a little bit of desperation."

"And you know I sometimes go to that café down the street."

"Sometimes? Maybe a little more often than that."

"Is that your way of saying I need to ease off those pastries?"

"Not at all."

Captain Price walked around the bench and sat down beside me.

"What did you want to talk about?"

I hesitated a moment. I knew what I wanted to ask, but I still wasn't sure the best way to convince him of my argument.

"Have you rethought your resignation?" he asked.

It was interesting that his train of thought had gone there first when it hadn't even crossed my mind. I'd resigned myself to the notion that I wasn't ever going to be a cop anymore.

"Is there anything new in the investigation?" I asked.

"I'm not going to talk about that."

"We're out of the office."

"That doesn't change anything. You know that."

"There's something I discovered yesterday. I want you to know about it."

"You should take it to Shaw. He's handling the case."

"I assume it will eventually get to him."

I told him about my conversation with Perkins, and Mara's discovery that the cell phone photograph had most likely been taken on the exact same day the car was taken from the auto shop.

"You believe this Perkins?" Price asked.

"Why would he lie? It makes him and his business look bad if it's true."

"I don't see how this negates the evidence. Sure, it's the same day, but coincidences happen, even if you don't want them to."

"His car is there just one day, actually just a few hours, and it's the same time some neighbor decides to take a photo of storm clouds. That's more than a coincidence."

"That was always just a small piece of evidence. It doesn't explain the phone in your husband's office or the victim's hair in your bathroom."

"No. It doesn't, but you have to admit it's a compelling fact. Someone didn't pay a lot of money to take a BMW on a joyride for a few hours. There's lots of high-end cars you can rent on this island. This person also had a very specific destination in mind, and it happened to be Brooklyn's apartment building."

"You wanted me to come here just so you could tell me about a car?"

"No."

"This is where you ask me for the huge favor that's almost certainly going to be illegal."

"I'd like the name of the woman who took the cell phone photo."

"I can't give that to you."

"You have to tell Poe's lawyer the name. Mara Winters has the right to cross examine her."

"Only you want a crack at her first."

"Something like that."

"That's all you want?"

"Not quite."

"I didn't think so," he said.

"Mara reviewed the bank records of the auto shop dealer. They show he received a cash payment for letting the car be borrowed. I'm betting the neighbor received a similar cash deal for taking that photo."

"You want me to get a warrant to access her bank records?"

"Yes."

Price shook his head.

"Unbelievable. You really thought I would agree to that?"

"I'm not asking you to do it for me."

"If not you, than who? Your husband? I've got news for you, Alana. I'm not exactly a fan of Edgar Rutherford."

"You've never said anything like that before."

"Why would I? Your personal relationship is none of my business. If he makes you happy, so be it, but the guy's been crossing the line ever since he got to our island. Hell, he's destroyed that line so many times, I've lost count."

"Our island? I don't remember you being born here."

"I've been here for over thirty years."

"Look, I'm not trying to argue with you."

"No. You just asked me here to make an illegal request. I should have arrested your husband after he beat the living hell out of that guy. Then maybe Brooklyn Van Kirk would still be alive."

"The guy who put me in the hospital and almost killed me? What would you have done if it had been your wife?"

Price didn't respond.

"I'll take your silence as your answer, and for the record, I want the bank records so I can find the truth. I thought that's what all cops wanted."

"If you wanted access to these types of things, then you never should have quit your job."

"You didn't exactly give me a choice."

Captain Price stood.

"The name of the neighbor will be given to your husband's attorney in due time. Please don't contact me again, at least not until this case is concluded."

He started to walk away when I called out to him.

"There's something else."

Price stopped and turned back to me. I stood and walked over to him.

"I wasn't going to say this, not until I had more evidence."

"Say what?"

"That phone wasn't in Poe's desk drawer until the police conducted the search. He'd gone into that desk just a few hours before to hide my anniversary gift."

"And you believe him?"

"Of course, I do. I wouldn't be standing here talking to you if I didn't."

"You're accusing a member of my department of a serious crime."

"I am, and I don't do that lightly."

"This is his theory or yours?"

"It's both of ours."

"You know how many times criminals blame the cops for planting evidence. You've been accused of that yourself if I remember correctly."

"I do know, and sometimes they're right. Not always, but sometimes."

"I'm sorry, but I'm playing this one by the book. If you have evidence of something, have your attorney present it, or contact Detective Shaw and have him follow up. Please don't call me again."

Captain Price turned away and left the Banyan Court Park.

I'd taken a gamble by talking to him, and I'd lost.

Chapter 12
Harry's

I had no way of knowing whether Captain Price would keep my suspicions to himself. He was clearly angry with me, and I assumed there was a good chance he'd go directly to Detective Shaw. My only hope was that he'd cool down by the time he got to the office. The drive between Lahaina and Kahului was a long one. Maybe he'd come to the conclusion that it was better to be cautious than automatically write off the possibility that he had a dirty cop in his department.

I looked at the time on my phone. It was still early, probably too early for Foxx to have gotten back from his meeting with Poe. I decided to drive to Kahului myself. Both Poe and Hani had said they'd met each other in the parking lot of the Home Depot so Poe could get Ava. I knew Hani would make a good witness at Poe's trial, but she was his sister-in-law and juries usually assume a family member will lie for another. I needed proof of their meeting.

I parked in the back of the lot, which had almost no cars in it. It made sense that Poe and Hani would meet around here. It was right by the road, and there would have been no reason for them to drive closer to the store where the parking lot was decidedly more crowded.

I climbed out of Poe's BMW and looked around the lot. I may have forgotten to mention this before, but I don't actually have my own car. The department provided me with a vehicle, but now that car was sitting in the parking lot at the police station. They'd almost certainly had assigned it to someone else by now.

There were several light poles in the parking lot. I spotted at least three security cameras on a few of them. They were pointed in various directions, so it seemed likely the entire lot was covered.

I entered the store and walked over to the service desk. I introduced myself as Detective Alana Hu and asked to see the manager. I assumed there was little chance the store would call the office to verify that. I'd also gotten dressed in my business suit that morning, which had been my usual wardrobe for work. Most people on Maui were dressed in casual attire. Show up in business wear and they almost always assume you work for the government.

The manager came out, and I explained to him that we were searching for images of a car that had been used in a recent murder. Of course I was looking to prove the exact opposite of that, but I figured he'd be more willing to help if he thought he was helping to solve some salacious crime.

He led me to the offices in the back of the store and helped me go through the security cameras. I already knew the morning and the general timeframe of the meeting between Poe and Hani. I asked him to pull up the cameras in the rear of the parking lot. It took less than ten minutes of searching to find the right video. Poe was the first to arrive. I saw his SUV pull into one of the outer spaces. He stayed in his vehicle until Hani arrived. Then he climbed outside and walked over to her car. She handed him Ava. They spoke for about a minute and then Poe walked back to his vehicle where he strapped Ava into the backseat of the SUV. He climbed behind the wheel and drove off. The entire meeting lasted less than three minutes.

I pulled a thumb drive out of my suit pocket and asked the manager if he'd copy the video for me. Before he did that, I rewound the video and stopped it on a frame that clearly showed Poe and Hani talking to each other. I printed that freeze frame to a color printer that was attached to the computer that controlled the security system. I also took a photo of the frame with my cell phone. The time stamp of the encounter was clear to see on the upper right corner of the image. They'd met at 10:05 in the morning.

I thanked the manager for his assistance and walked out of the store to the

BMW. The security footage proved Poe was telling the truth, but it wouldn't be enough to clear him. There would have been plenty of time for him to have committed the murder and still make it to the meeting with Hani. I needed to prove he was at Baby Beach before that, and I thought I knew a way to get that done.

I searched my contacts for the phone number for Abigail Ford, who was the cop who'd told me about the forensics team finding Brooklyn's hair on the t-shirt. I dialed her number.

"This is Ford."

"Abigail, this is Alana."

There was a pause on the phone.

"Are you there?" I asked.

"Yes. Sorry. I'm just a little surprised to hear from you."

"I'm sure. I guess you heard I resigned."

"I heard. There's a lot of people upset about that, including me. I wish you weren't gone."

"Thanks. That means a lot to me."

"What can I do for you?" she asked.

"I'm trying to establish where my husband was at the time of the murder. He says he was at Baby Beach that morning around 8:30. I know there are several traffic cameras that would have caught him driving through Kahului on his way toward the beach. He owns a tan Lexus SUV. I can text you the license plate number."

"You want me to go through the traffic cameras for you?"

"Yes. I'm sorry to have to ask you to do that."

"Did you ask Shaw and he said no?"

"I haven't asked him. Not yet."

"Why not?"

"Abigail, he's completely convinced that Poe killed that girl. He's not going to take the time to go through those cameras."

"I think you're selling him short. I really don't think he's trying to railroad your husband."

"Will you search the cameras for me? I really need to get this done."

"I'm sorry, Alana, but I can't. You know what they'd do to me if I got caught."

I didn't answer her. Yes, I knew what they'd do, and I knew I was asking for a big favor. But that's what you sometimes ask of friends, isn't it?

"Please call Shaw and ask him. He'll probably surprise you and search the traffic cams," she continued.

"All right. I'll talk to you later."

I waited for her to say goodbye, but she didn't. The phone call got disconnected a second later.

I made a mental note to tell Mara Winters to formally request copies of the traffic camera footage. They wouldn't be able to deny her access to it, but they'd probably drag their feet in the process. They could delay her getting that footage for weeks if they wanted.

I started the car and drove back toward Kaanapali. I stopped in Lahaina and headed for Harry's. I saw Foxx's SUV as I pulled into the parking lot. It was beyond ironic that he and I had become such close friends over the last few years. Sure, he was husband's best friend, but my first encounter with Foxx had been when I'd arrested him for murder. He'd completely forgiven me, at least I thought he had. If he hadn't, he'd done a hell of a job of acting the part. He'd been here for me in a big way after Poe's arrest, and the people I'd spent thousands of hours working beside had turned their backs on me. Everyone talked about work colleagues as being one big family. It was all garbage. There was no other word to describe it.

I parked the BMW and walked into the building. It was mostly empty at this time of the morning. I saw Kiana behind the bar. She was busy stocking the various small refrigerators with beers. She looked up at me as I walked toward her.

"Hello, Ms. Rutherford. I'm so sorry for what's happened to Mr. Rutherford."

Despite our best efforts, Kiana insisted on calling Poe and I by our last name even though we were all around the same age. Poe was her boss, and she wasn't going to drop that formality. I'd also told her that I hadn't taken Poe's last name, but that didn't matter either. I was Ms. Rutherford to her, and I was certainly okay with that.

"Thank you, Kiana."

"I want you to know I don't believe he ever could have done those things."

"That means a lot to me."

"Mr. Foxx is in the back. I assume that's why you're here."

"Yes. He went to see Poe this morning. I came by to see how the visit went."

I headed into the back room where Foxx and Poe's shared office was. It was really more of Foxx's office than Poe's. Foxx worked at the bar full time. Poe was usually only here a few hours a week. He was an equal financial investor, but he was more responsible for the books than the actual day-to-day running of the business. They were both okay with that arrangement, and it had been the plan since the beginning. I also thought it was the good intention of not mixing too much business with friendship. There needs to be a line somewhere, and it's always tricky trying to figure out where that should be.

Foxx was sitting in front of their security system and looking at the video monitors. He turned to me when I walked in the room.

"Hey there, I'm just looking at this footage again."

"What are you looking for?" I asked.

Foxx told me how he'd spent the previous night going through all of the receipts where a Purple Haze beer was comped and then comparing the dates on those receipts to the security footage.

"How you found anything interesting?"

"Nothing, but I'm thinking more and more that it had to be one of the three employees who served those beers to Poe. I can't find any footage of someone going through the recycling bins or the trash cans out back, and I've gone through everything twice."

He told me the names of the three employees: Kiana, Molly, and Tommy.

"Have you had a chance to talk to them yet?" I asked.

"No. I'd planned on calling you later this morning to see if you wanted to be a part of that. How did your meeting with your old boss go?"

I told Foxx about Price's rejection of my request, as well as Abigail's refusal to go through the traffic cameras for me.

"Doesn't surprise me. Everyone's going into butt-covering mode right now," he said.

"I didn't expect it from Price. I really didn't."

"Sometimes people can surprise you. It sucks, but it's the truth."

"He said something else that I'm having a hard time processing."

"What's that?"

"He said that he'd never liked Poe. I had no idea he felt that way."

Foxx looked away.

"What?" I asked.

"It's nothing."

"You look like you know something."

"It's best if I stay out of this one. It's between you and him."

"Have you even met Captain Price?"

"Briefly. He came by the hospital during your surgery, but he spent most of his time speaking with Poe outside the waiting room."

"You obviously have an opinion of him. What is it?"

"It's not my opinion."

"Then whose is it?"

"No one's."

"Did Poe say something to you? Did he and Price get into an argument that I don't know about?"

"Not that I know, but Poe doesn't like the guy."

"Why not?"

"It's not that big of a deal. I don't think it has anything to do with Poe getting framed."

"What is it? Tell me."

"He said Price kept referring to you as 'our girl.' Poe didn't like it."

"Our girl?"

"Yeah. Poe said it really bothered him. He said he let it go the first time, but then Price said it several more times."

"It's just an expression. I don't think it means anything."

"Maybe not."

"Did he confront him about it?"

"Not that I know of."

"I still don't see what the big deal is about the use of the words 'our girl.'"

"You're not Price's girl. You're Poe's girl."

"I'm sure Price knows that."

"Then why did he keep saying what he was saying? Was he trying to piss Poe off? Was he trying to make him jealous?"

"Jealous of what? There's absolutely nothing going on between Price and me," I said.

"Maybe he wants to change that."

"That's crazy. He's at least twenty years older than me, and he's married."

Foxx laughed.

"First of all, older guys often chase younger women, and since when did being married stop certain people?"

"Doesn't matter. He's never done or said anything inappropriate."

"That doesn't mean he's not thinking about it. You're a good looking woman, Alana. Poe and I were just talking about that this morning."

"You were talking about how I looked?"

"Not like that."

"Like what then?"

"We were just saying that we think you sometimes don't realize the impact your beauty has on guys around you. Makes perfect sense to me that Price won't help you free Poe. He wants him out of the picture."

"This is all nonsense."

"Believe what you want to believe. Maybe I'm wrong, but maybe I'm not."

"Let's get back to these three employees of yours. I saw Kiana out there. When are Molly and Tommy scheduled to come in next?"

Foxx looked at his watch.

"Molly should be here soon. Do you want to talk to Kiana now?"

"Sure. Let's grab her before Molly arrives."

Foxx and I left the office and walked back to the bar. Kiana had finished stocking the refrigerators and was now wiping down the bar.

Foxx and I sat on two barstools, and she walked over to us.

"Did you two want anything to drink?" she asked.

"No. We just wanted to ask you a few questions," Foxx said.

"What about?"

"This may seem a bit odd, but do you remember serving Poe a Purple Haze beer?" I asked.

"I'm not sure. Maybe. Sometimes he'll order a beer at lunch but not lately. He usually orders a Diet Coke when he's watching Ava."

"What about at night? Do you remember serving him one then?" Foxx asked.

"I don't think so. He always asks for a Manhattan when he's here at night."

"When you guys pick up the customer's empty bottles, what do you do with them?" I asked.

"We put the bottles in a recycling bin behind the bar. There's a separate can for the trash."

"Who takes the bin out back once it's full?" I asked.

"It depends. It's usually just whoever is available. I try to take it out once it reaches the half-full mark because it gets pretty heavy. I can't keep up on the weekends, so the bin is almost always overflowing. I usually ask one of the guys to take it out back then."

"You normally ask Tommy?" Foxx asked.

"Sometimes. Just depends who is behind the bar at the time."

"Have you ever seen anyone separate the bottles?" I asked.

"What do you mean?"

"Maybe someone who might take certain bottles out of the bin and put them somewhere else."

"Why would someone do that?"

"So you've never seen someone take any specific bottles out of the bin?" Foxx asked.

"No. We just take the entire bin out back and dump it."

"Now this is a sensitive question, but I want you to be honest with me. Have you ever heard Poe get into an argument with someone, maybe on the phone?" Foxx asked.

Kiana hesitated.

"You should tell her," Foxx urged.

"Tell me what?" I asked.

Kiana turned to me.

"Molly said she overheard him yelling at someone about a week or so ago. He told someone on the phone that they shouldn't threaten him."

"Did Molly say who he was talking to?" I asked.

"She said she didn't know."

"Did she hear anything else?"

"No. If she did, she didn't tell me."

"Have you heard anything yourself or was it just what Molly told you?" I asked.

Kiana shook her head.

"I've never heard anything strange. He's usually talking to Mr. Foxx or he's with you."

"Okay. Thanks Kiana. Please don't mention this conversation to anyone. All right?" I asked.

"I won't say anything."

Foxx and I stood and walked to one of the booths in the back of the bar. He told me that Kiana had said the same thing to him late last night in regards to Molly's comment about Poe's phone call. I didn't have a chance to make a comment because Molly came in a second later. Foxx called out to her and asked her to come over. We repeated the same questions about the beer bottles. She said she didn't remember serving him any Purple Haze beers, nor did she have any idea who might have taken select bottles out of the recycling bin. I then asked her about the phone call she supposedly overheard.

"I didn't hear Poe saying anything like that."

"You didn't overhear a telephone call with him?" Foxx asked.

"I've seen him use the phone, but he never made a comment about someone threatening him."

"It's okay, Molly. You're not in any kind of trouble. If you heard something, we need to know about this. A crime has been committed, and we're trying to figure out what really happened," I said.

"I'd tell you if he did, but he didn't."

"So what did he say?" Foxx asked.

"I've seen him make several calls from here, but I don't really pay much attention to it. It's none of my business."

"You swear you didn't overhear him tell the person on the other end of the phone not to threaten him?" I asked.

"No. Never."

"Okay. Thanks for your time," I said.

Molly slid out of the booth and walked over to the bar. She said hello to Kiana and then she put her purse behind the bar and started to put her apron on.

I turned to Foxx.

"Can you walk me outside?"

"Sure."

Foxx and I left the bar, and we walked over to the BMW.

"What do you make of that?" I asked.

"She's lying. She told Kiana she overheard something. She either made that part up, or she's lying to us when she said she didn't hear anything."

"Maybe Kiana is the one lying."

"What would she have to gain?"

"It would take the heat off her and put it squarely on Molly. Think about it. Kiana takes the three beer bottles, then tells you Molly is casting doubt on Poe. It's a pretty simple tactic."

"I don't know, Alana. Kiana really likes Poe. I just can't see her doing something that would hurt him."

"Does she even know it hurt him? Maybe she thought it would be easy money, just like the guy at the auto shop," I said.

Foxx didn't have an answer.

"Let me know when Tommy is coming in, and I'll drive back up here."

"What are you going to do now?" Foxx asked.

"I need to call Mara and ask her to request copies of the traffic camera footage. I'm trying to prove that Poe was on the other side of the island when Brooklyn Van Kirk was murdered."

"I'm going back inside and look through that footage one more time. Maybe Kiana or Molly will get nervous after we talked to them, and they'll let something slip."

"Thanks, Foxx. I appreciate everything you're doing."

"It's no problem. Poe would do it for me. Hell, he has done it for me."

I said goodbye to Foxx and watched as he walked back into the bar. I reached into my pocket and pulled out my cell phone. I was about to look up Mara's number when my phone rang. It was actually Mara.

"I was just about to call you," I said.

"We got the name of the neighbor who claims she saw Edgar's car outside the apartment. I was about to call her to set up a meeting. Would you like to be a part of that?"

"Do me a favor and hold off. Send me the name, though. I need a day or two to get background information on this lady."

"You don't want to talk to her today?" Mara asked.

"No. Not yet. We're going to get one good shot to catch this lady in a lie. I want to be prepared."

Mara and I spoke for a few more minutes. I told her about the security camera footage I copied from the Home Depot, and I asked her to make a formal request for the traffic camera footage from the intersection of Hana Highway and Airport Road since Poe would have had to drive through there on his way to and from Baby Beach. I left out my discussion with Foxx and two of the servers at Harry's. We still had no definitive proof that the bottles had even come from there, although I tended to believe Foxx's theory.

I ended my call with Mara and climbed into the BMW. I pushed the top back on the convertible for the drive back home. I looked at the bar one more time before putting the car in reverse. Did I believe Kiana or did I believe Molly? One of them was lying but which one?

Doubt crept back into my mind where all of my insecurities tended to live. I couldn't push the question away. Had Poe really had the conversation where he told someone not to threaten him? Had Molly overheard that remark and denied it because she either didn't want to hurt me or she simply didn't want to get involved in the personal life of the man who owned the bar where she worked?

No, I couldn't accept that Poe would lie to me. I wouldn't accept it.

I backed out of the parking space and was about to put the car in drive when my phone pinged. It was the text from Mara. There was a name along with an apartment number: Genesis Riley, Apt. 3C.

Well, Ms. Genesis Riley, I was about to learn everything there is to know about you.

Chapter 13
Genesis Riley

Perspective: Alana

It took me about an hour to drive from my house in Kaanapali to the apartment complex where Brooklyn Van Kirk was murdered. The complex was a couple of blocks back from South Kihei Road and consisted of three buildings that together formed the shape of the letter C. The soft green paint job was badly faded and in desperate need of a facelift. There was a small parking lot in the middle. It would have been impossible for someone to have missed Poe's car if it had been there on multiple occasions as Shaw had said.

Mara Winters had given me Brooklyn's address, so I was able to quickly find the unit. It was located on the ground floor of the middle building. I pulled out my phone and opened up the photo of Poe's car in this lot. I compared the position of the BMW and saw it had been parked directly in front of Brooklyn's apartment.

I looked around the lot and saw a few cars currently parked here that also corresponded to the cars in the photograph. I then compared the angle of the photo and saw where the person who shot it must have been standing. I knew Genesis Riley lived in unit 3C. I spotted her unit on the top floor.

I walked across the lot and headed up the exterior staircase to reach the third floor. I walked down the hallway and did another comparison to the photograph. It looked like it was the same spot. I was about to knock on the apartment door when something jumped out at me. This wasn't the right spot, after all. The hallway had a black metal railing that ran the length of the building. The support beams ran from the floor to the ceiling, and there was a decorative metal piece that ran just below the roof line.

I looked at the photo again. It was a wide shot that showed most of the parking lot. I could see the roof in the photo, and there was no decorative metal piece. I walked over to the railing and leaned across it to try to see to the second floor. The vantage point wasn't good, so I had to walk back down the hallway and take the staircase to the second floor. I walked onto that hallway and looked at the roof. There was no decorative strip. I compared it to the photo again. This was definitely the spot where the photo was taken.

I headed back to the third floor and knocked on the apartment door. I pulled my jacket back as Genesis opened the door. I had a fake badge on my waist, and there was no way she wouldn't be able to see it. Many cops have convincing fakes since losing the real one can be a major fiasco and require hours of paperwork and a butt chewing from your supervisor. No one really looks at them closely anyway. I'd turned in my real one to Captain Price, but I still had the fake one. Was I worried about getting caught impersonating an officer? Not really. How was Genesis going to prove it?

"Ms. Riley, I'm Detective Alana Hu. I was hoping you could answer a few of my questions regarding your neighbor, Brooklyn Van Kirk."

"I already spoke to that other detective."

"Yes. It was actually Detective Shaw who asked me to come out here. He's busy with other aspects of the case, and he needs some follow-up information from you. May I come in?"

Genesis hesitated a moment. Then she stepped back and allowed me to enter.

So, what does someone named Genesis look like? I guessed her age at around thirty years old. She had long, dirty blond hair and pale eyes. She was my height, around five-foot-five, and she was a little on the skinny side.

She led me over to a sofa that matched the outside color of the apartment building. I wasn't sure if that was an intentional decorating move on her part, but the furniture looked old and beat up. She'd either bought it at a yard sale or had dragged it around with her on multiple moves.

Genesis sat down on the sofa, and I sat on a matching chair beside it. The chair creaked, and I felt a hard spring jam into the back of my legs.

"What is you want to know?" she asked.

"I know you took the photo that showed the BMW in the parking lot. What made you realize it might have belonged to the person who'd been going to Ms. Van Kirk's apartment?"

"Like I told that detective, I'd seen him and his car several times."

"About how many times?"

"At least a dozen."

"When did he come by this complex? Was it during the day or night?"

"All sorts of times."

"You saw him and the car both during the day and at night?"

"That's right."

"Did you get a good look at the guy, or was it tough to see from up here on the third floor?"

"I saw him a couple of times when I'd get back from work."

"So you were still in the parking lot?"

"Yeah."

"And he was either arriving at or leaving her apartment?"

"Yeah."

I reached into my suit pocket and removed a piece of paper. I unfolded it and showed her the photograph.

"This is the man. Correct?" I asked.

Genesis took a long look at the photo.

"Yeah, that's him."

"Good."

I folded the photograph and slipped it back into my pocket.

"I can't tell you how fortunate we were that you took the photo of that storm cloud. It's really the only proof we have that he'd come to her apartment."

"Yeah. It was lucky."

"When did you take the photograph that day?"

"It was in the afternoon. I don't remember the exact time."

"Had you just gotten home or had you been off that day?"

"It was when I got back from work."

"You work at a shop down the street, Maui Sand and Surf Shop?"

"Yeah."

"How long have you worked there?"

"A couple of years."

"Is it a good place to work?"

"It's all right."

"Pays the bills, though. Doesn't it?"

"Barely. Maui's an expensive place to live."

"It is. Most people have more than one job, but I'm sure you know that already. Where else do you work?"

"Just there. I used to wait tables at night, but I haven't done that in a while."

"Why is that? You get tired of it?" I asked.

"Something like that. It was tough. I was on my feet all day at the shop and then I'd head to the restaurant and work another five or six hours."

"I'm sure your back was killing you, too."

"Every day."

Genesis laughed.

"So you quit the restaurant job because you got tired of it and not for another reason?"

"What does this have to do with your investigation?"

"I'm glad you asked that. I checked with your landlord. You'd be surprised what people will tell you when you're a cop. Sometimes people freak out and they refuse to talk at all. Other times people tell you everything. Your landlord fit into the second category."

I paused and waited for my words to sink in. I'd interviewed enough people in my time as a detective to know when someone was nervous. Genesis certainly was. The lack of eye contact. The hands rubbing each other. The stiff shoulders. It was all there.

"He said your rent here is around sixteen hundred a month, which is pretty close to average for Maui. I bet that's pretty tough to pay just working at a shop that sells t-shirts, baseball caps, and beach towels."

"I get by."

"I doubt that. I'm sure it was pretty hard even when you were working at the restaurant, too. Tourists don't tip that well. They spend all their money on the airplane tickets and the hotels. Not much left for the waiters. It's not fair, but that's the way it is. They come to the island and expect to be treated like royalty. Then they leave lousy tips."

"Tell me about it."

"I get it. That's why you started changing the tips on those credit card forms. I used to work at a restaurant, too. I know how it works. You swipe their credit card, and the machine prints out a receipt. After they sign it, you go back to the machine and enter in how much they tipped. It's not hard to change the amount. Maybe you put a one in front of the five, and a five dollar tip suddenly becomes fifteen dollars. Do that enough times and you have a pretty good night. The tourists are long gone before they get their monthly statements. They probably charged enough meals during their vacation that they don't realize they got overcharged at your restaurant. Unfortunately, if you do that scam enough times, you're going to eventually get caught. That's what happened. I spoke to your old manager. He confirmed you were changing the tips, and he fired you a few months ago. I'm guessing word got around, and you couldn't find a new waiting job. Nobody wants a thief to tarnish the reputation of their restaurant."

"He didn't call the cops because he couldn't prove a damn thing. He just let me go because he didn't like me."

"Oh, I don't know. I suspect he could prove it. He had the credit card receipts, and I'm sure some of the customers you ripped off would have been more than willing to email him their copies to show the discrepancy. But that's a lot of work for him to do. Much easier to just terminate your employment."

"That's why you're here? You want to arrest me for credit card receipts?" she asked.

"No. I'm going to arrest you for obstruction of justice and making a false report to the police."

Her eyes grew wide, and I knew I'd gotten her attention.

"I see your phone on the table over there."

Genesis turned and verified she'd left it on the table beside the sofa.

"You didn't take that photograph of the parking lot. Someone else took it," I said.

"That's not true."

"It's not even from the correct floor. That photo was taken from the second floor. Why would you walk downstairs to take it when you have a better vantage point from up here?"

"I noticed those storm clouds when I was walking up the stairs, so I stopped to take it."

"Okay, but why walk the entire length of the hallway to shoot it? Why not take it from the staircase?"

Genesis didn't respond.

"Here's something else. I spoke with your manager at the surf shop. She said you were working the day that photo was taken."

"I was, but I'd just gotten off work."

"Not true. I have the weather data from that day. I compared it to your work schedule. You were off that morning, but you worked the afternoon and the evening shift. Kihei had sunshine in the morning when you were home. The storm rolled in that afternoon. You'd been at work for over two hours by then."

I paused and waited for her to say something. She didn't.

"Your landlord said you were two months behind on your rent. That's probably because you'd lost your waitress job. He said he was about to toss you out when you paid the back rent and also the current month's rent. That's almost five thousand dollars. How did you come up with that kind of money? You make sixteen bucks an hour at the shop. How did you manage to work three hundred hours in one month? I did the math, Genesis. It doesn't add up. You doing something else for that money?"

"I didn't do anything wrong."

I reached back into my suit pocket and removed a second piece of paper. I opened it up and held the paper out for Genesis to see.

"I got a warrant for your bank records. You wrote a check for the rent. It's listed on here. So is a large cash deposit. Where did you get that cash?"

"I didn't do anything wrong," she repeated.

"Someone else took that photo and sent it to you. They paid you to lie to the police and say you did. You never saw that car. You sure as hell didn't see Mr. Rutherford going into her apartment."

"I did see him."

I pulled the photograph out of my pocket again.

"This isn't even a photograph of the right guy. Rutherford has dark hair. This guy is a blond. I scanned the photo out of fashion magazine."

"I didn't take a good look at that photo before. Now I see it's not the same person."

"You're still going to stick to your story?"

"I took that photo. I swear."

"I don't have time for this. Let's go."

I stood and walked toward her.

"Where are you taking me?"

"Genesis Riley, I'm arresting you for obstruction of justice and making a false report. You have the right to remain silent."

"Wait. Wait. Wait."

I stopped talking but stood in front of her.

"You don't understand. I can't just say I didn't take that photo."

"Why not?" I asked.

"They'll kill me if I talk."

"Who threatened you?"

"I never even met the person. I don't even know their name."

"An innocent person is in jail right now because you wanted an easy payday. You're not going to get away with this. Stand up."

Genesis hesitated again.

"On your feet. Let's go."

She started to cry.

"I got a call one night at the shop. They told me they were going to send me a photo. They said all I had to do was tell the cops that I took it. That was it."

"When did you get the cash?"

"After I talked to that detective. They left an envelope on top of my back tire. It had the five grand in it. I didn't even see who left it. They said to tell that cop that I saw a tall white guy with the girl. That was it. I did exactly as they told me."

"You never personally saw the BMW or the guy, did you?"

"No."

"Let's go."

"Hold on. I thought you wouldn't arrest me if I told you the truth."

"I'm not taking you to the station. We're going to see a lawyer. You're going to tell her everything you just told me. You're also going to need her help when you confess to what you've done."

"What about the guy who called me? He's going to kill me when he finds out I talked to you."

"The police can protect you."

Genesis stood. It took all of my strength not to knock her back down. Her lies had helped frame Poe, and she didn't give a damn.

I grabbed one of her arms and escorted her to the door.

By the way, I'm guessing you're wondering how I got the search warrant to gain access to her bank statement. I didn't. They weren't even her records. They were mine.

Chapter 14
The Sun through the Trees

Perspective: Alana

We left the apartment complex, and I drove Genesis to meet with Mara in her office. I simply didn't trust her to go on her own. I could tell she was experiencing real fear, and I knew that was a powerful tool that could sway her to turn around and head home. She could even decide to leave the island for good.

Mara's office wasn't that far from the police station and the prosecutor's office. I hoped to convince her to present our evidence of witness tampering after she heard Genesis' story. Mara's assistant led us back into her office. I gave Mara a brief rundown on Genesis wanting to change her testimony. I then told her about the threat she'd received if she ever decided to come clean.

Mara assured Genesis that she'd try to smooth things out with the police. We both knew Genesis hadn't lied about Poe's car because she was afraid. She'd done it for money, plain and simple. I didn't think it likely the police would decide to forgive and forget, but I also knew why Mara had tried to reassure her.

She asked Genesis to wait for her in the lobby since she wanted to speak with me in private. I was a little nervous since I was still worried Genesis could change her mind at any moment and make a run for it.

After Genesis walked back into the lobby, Mara shut the door behind her. "How did you convince her to tell the truth?"

"It took some doing, but I presented her with a few inconsistencies between what she'd said and what I'd learned about her, such as her work schedule showing she couldn't have been there when the photograph was shot."

"And that's all it took?" Mara asked.

"That and a few other things. What difference does it make? She's admitted to her role in this frame job."

"Come on, Alana. You know it makes all the difference in the world. Did you lead her to believe you might still be with the police department?"

I hesitated.

"You did, didn't you?"

"Yes, and I'm well aware of the risks."

"Once she gets to the station, it's going to take her all of sixty seconds to learn you're not a cop anymore. They could arrest you for impersonating a police officer."

"Yes, they can."

Mara sighed.

"What would you have me do? I'm not going to have Poe spend another night in jail, not if I can help it," I continued.

"All right, but maybe it's best if you don't come with me."

"That won't matter. If they're going to arrest me, then they'll arrest me, whether I'm there or at home."

"You don't seem bothered by it."

"I am bothered by it, but I can't do anything about that now."

Mara and I left her office and walked into the lobby. Fortunately, Genesis was still there. Mara asked her to ride with her so they could go over the best way for Genesis to present her story to the prosecutor. I decided to follow them in my own vehicle.

We were halfway to the prosecutor's office when my phone rang. I didn't recognize the number, and I almost let it go to voicemail.

"This is Alana Hu."

I heard a recording saying the call was from the local jail. Poe's voice came on a few seconds later.

"Hey, it's me. Where are you at right now?" he asked.

"Driving to meet with the prosecutor. That's why you called me, to find out where I am?"

"Sorry, I'm just excited. I need you to go home. There's something I want you to check out."

"It's going to have to wait."

"It can't."

"You realize we're trying to get you out of jail."

"I remembered something about that day Brooklyn was killed. This could clear me if I'm right."

"This something is at the house?"

"Yeah. It's in my office."

"What is it?"

"My camera. I'd completely forgotten I'd taken the photos. I only snapped a few before my swim at Baby Beach. I deleted a couple of them right after I took them. I'm really hoping there's at least one left."

"What does this have to do with anything?"

"The metadata. It should all be there."

We spoke for a few more minutes as Poe walked me through what he needed. I ended the call after telling him I'd be by to see him later that day.

I knew the meeting with Piper Lane would be in excellent hands with Mara, even if I wasn't there, and if Poe was right about the photograph, then it could be the one piece of information that would tip the scales in his favor.

I made a quick U-turn at the next stop light and drove back toward Kaanapali. It took me almost two hours to make the trip home, grab his camera and laptop, and then head back to Piper Lane's office. I'd called Mara on the way there and asked her to stick around so I could help her present the final evidence. She was understandably confused as to my reason for driving away. I told her I would explain everything in person.

I finally got to the prosecutor's office after fighting traffic all the way back. The lot was jammed with cars, and I had to park in the back row. I grabbed my leather bag and climbed out of the car. I saw Mara outside by the lobby door as I approached the building.

"I was just about to call you," Mara said.

"How did everything go with Genesis?"

"As well as could be expected. She repeated everything she told you and I. I'll admit I was nervous. People often change their stories once they get here. The office can be intimidating."

"Did Piper say whether or not she's going to charge her for making a false report?"

"She didn't."

"Where is Genesis now?"

"She's still in there. Ms. Lane called Detective Shaw over. They're probably trying to figure out who sent Genesis that photograph."

"Does this mean Poe is in the clear?"

"No. Piper kept talking about the burner phone and the victim's hairs found in your house. They're not budging on the murder charge. So, why did you go back to your house?"

"I found something that might change their mind."

Mara and I went into the building and were taken back to Piper Lane's office. I didn't see Genesis or Shaw in there.

Lane was sitting behind her desk, and she stood as we entered.

"Detective Hu, good to see you again. It is still Detective, isn't it? At least that's what you told Ms. Riley."

I ignored her dig, and Mara and I sat down on two stiff chairs in front of her desk.

"Mara said you had something to show me," Lane continued.

"I assume Mara told you about the meeting I had with Mr. Perkins. He's the one who owns the auto shop that repaired my husband's car."

"Yes. He claims he lent the car out for an exchange of cash. Ms. Winters has submitted some so-called evidence that the photo taken of the BMW outside of Ms. Van Kirk's apartment was shot on the same day the car was taken from the auto shop."

"So-called evidence?" I asked.

"Weather reports aren't exactly definitive proof of anything. You know as well as I do that the weather on this island can change in a split second. Just because some report says it was sunny on a given day, it doesn't mean there weren't storm clouds that briefly blew through the area."

"No, it's not definitive proof, but it goes a long way to creating reasonable doubt with a jury. Ms. Riley admitted she didn't take the photograph. She lied for financial gain, and Mr. Perkins has given us a definitive time when the car was out of his possession. Perkins also helped frame an innocent man for money. The jury will want to punish those two, and they'll do so by finding Mr. Rutherford not guilty," Mara said.

Lane didn't respond.

"There's more," I said, and I reached into my bag.

I removed a folder and placed it on the desk in front of me.

"The medical examiner's report indicates Brooklyn Van Kirk was murdered between seven and ten in the morning. Do you acknowledge that?" I asked.

"That's what the report says."

"I would routinely leave for work around seven-thirty each morning. I'll testify that Poe was still at our house that morning when I left."

I opened the folder and removed several pieces of paper. I divided the papers into two sections and handed Piper Lane one of them. I slid the other matching copies to Mara.

"My sister works as a wedding planner. I've included a printout of her work calendar. It shows she had a series of meetings that same day Van Kirk was murdered. I've included copies of her emails to these clients to verify the times of those meetings. You'll also see a copy of the text message exchange between my sister and my husband that show she arranged to meet him in the parking lot of Home Depot at ten that morning. She asked him to watch her daughter for the day."

"That still gives your husband at least an hour to have detoured to Kihei to murder Ms. Van Kirk," Lane said.

"No, it doesn't."

I reached back into my bag and removed a small laptop, the camera card from Poe's Canon camera, and the compact flash card reader.

"This card is from Poe's DSLR camera. He told you he went to Baby Beach for a swim before his meeting with Hani."

I plugged the card reader into the USB port and powered the computer on.

"What he failed to remember until this morning is that he shot a few photographs right after arriving at the beach. He'd noticed the sun bursting through the leaves of a cluster of palm trees. He wasn't happy with the shots so he deleted most of them. Fortunately, there was one shot left," I said.

I opened the folder for the camera file and double-clicked on the image. It was a shot of the palm trees with the sun behind them. I hadn't had time to check the file before leaving the house. I prayed the metadata information Poe said was on here would be correct.

"This is a pro-level camera, and it puts all sorts of information on each photo file, much more than the data a cell phone camera puts on a photo. This metadata includes the camera's aperture, the shutter speed, and the focal length of the lens. It also lists the time of day and the GPS coordinates of where the camera was when the photograph was taken," I continued.

I turned the computer around so both Mara and Piper Lane could see the metadata display beside the photo of the palm trees.

"I'd encourage you to type these coordinates into your computer. I'm certain you'll find they match the coordinates for Baby Beach," I said.

Piper Lane didn't move for her computer. She just studied the data on the screen.

"The time on that file also verifies Poe was telling the truth about where he was. It would be impossible for him to have driven to Kihei, then go to Baby Beach to take that photo, then go to the parking lot to meet my sister. There simply wasn't enough time."

I reached back into the folder and removed two final printouts.

"Here's a still frame from the security camera footage at the Home Depot. It's also time stamped. Those two people are Poe and my sister. You'll also notice the two vehicles behind them. Those are their two SUVs."

"I made a request to the police department to check the traffic cameras around that area, but that request was ignored. There's a camera on Hana Highway that I'm sure will show Mr. Rutherford's vehicle coming from the Baby Beach area and heading toward Kahului where his meeting with Hani

Hu took place. I have no doubt the times will all synch up," Mara said.

I expected Lane to finally say something, but she didn't.

"Ms. Hu has proven that it was impossible for Mr. Rutherford to have been in Kihei at the time of the murder. I formally request that all charges filed against Mr. Rutherford be immediately dropped and a public apology from this office be released today. You arrested the wrong man, Ms. Lane. There's no way a jury will convict once we present this evidence. We now have far more than reasonable doubt, burner phones or not. Detective Shaw rushed to judgement, and he's failed to follow-up on several discrepancies. Pin this one on him. He deserves it. You're going to go through a lot of time and expense to bring Mr. Rutherford to trial, and you're going to lose. Do you really want this loss on your record? Do you really want the media attention?"

Lane turned to me.

"I'm sorry, Alana. I'm truly sorry."

"I don't want to hear it. I want my husband out, and I want him out now. Not tomorrow. Not tonight. Now."

Piper Lane reached for her desk phone. It was over.

Chapter 15
I'd Almost Given Up

Perspective: Poe

The door to my cell opened, and I saw a male police officer standing in the doorway. I didn't recognize him.

"What's going on?"

"You're being released. The charges have been dropped."

He somewhat growled those sentences, and I got the unmistakable impression he didn't agree with the decision. I knew I wouldn't get anything else out of him, so I didn't bother asking why they were letting me go. I supposed it didn't really matter. I was leaving this God-awful place. Hopefully, it would be for good.

It took another hour for them to process me out. I got my personal clothes back, and I exited the jail. It was nearing sunset by the time I left the building. There was one person waiting for me, and I'm sure you can guess who it was. She was standing at the end of the sidewalk, and she was the best thing I'd seen all week.

I walked up to Alana.

"I knew you'd do it."

"Did you really?" she asked.

"Who is better than you?"

I hugged her close to me, and I didn't let her go for several long moments.

I turned and took a last look at the jail. I wanted to flip them the bird, but I also didn't want to give them another reason to lock me up. Is the bird illegal, though? It was better not to take any chances.

We walked over to my BMW, and Alana held out my keys.

"Want to drive?" she asked.

"Actually, I think I'd prefer to sit on the passenger side if that's okay with you."

We climbed into the car, and I leaned the seat back, which wasn't very far considering how small the interior is. Alana drove us out of Kahului, and pretty soon we were traveling down the coast with the top down on the car.

It was a route I'd taken a thousand times in the last few years, but I'd never grown tired of the view. One of the interesting things about Maui was how the color of the water seemed to change depending on what side of the island you were on. The water was a deep blue on this road toward Lahaina and Kaanapali, and the setting sun seemed to enhance the richness of the blue even more. It was perhaps my ideal color, and it never ceased to amaze me in its beauty.

"Do you want to stop somewhere like Harry's?" she asked.

"No. Let's just go home."

"We do have one stop we need to make, but it will be a quick one."

"Where's that?"

"You'll see."

I didn't argue the point. Instead, I closed my eyes for a several long seconds and felt the warm breeze wash over my face. I was free. My incarceration hadn't lasted that long. I was one of the lucky ones, but it was still long enough to fill me with a sense of dread and hopelessness. I hadn't been completely honest with Alana outside the jail. I did have faith in her abilities, but I'd almost given up.

We drove past Lahaina and continued on to Kaanapali. Alana turned into our neighborhood, but we still hadn't made the unknown stop she'd mentioned before. She made a quick turn into Foxx's driveway.

"There's someone in there waiting for you."

"Is this some kind of surprise party?" I asked.

"No. Just a party of one. He's been down here for the last few days. I'm guessing he's ready to come home, too."

I climbed out of the car and walked to the front door. I punched in the door code to unlock it. I heard the little guy's barking a second later. I opened the door, and Maui the dog rushed out. He did his little dance and jumped all over my lower legs. I thought he might give himself a heart attack. I picked him up and carried him back to the convertible.

"Foxx has been watching him for me. I knew I wouldn't have time running all over the island."

I got into the car, and we made the short drive back to our house. I remembered all of the cop cars and the forensics van parked in front of the house. The only vehicle I saw in my driveway now was my SUV.

The driveway was wide enough for Alana to drive around the SUV. She opened the garage door with the remote and made the sharp turn inside. The three of us got out and climbed the short staircase into the house.

Alana tossed the car keys onto the kitchen counter and turned to me.

"There's something we need to get out of the way first."

"What's that?" I asked.

"If you ever keep something from me like that threatening phone call, I'll lock you up myself."

I thought it best not to point out she wasn't a cop anymore. It had to be a sensitive topic, and I didn't need to incite her anger anymore.

"I think you know why I kept it a secret."

"I'm not helpless, Poe."

"I know you're not, but you didn't see yourself on that floor. I did, and I've never felt so helpless in all my life. I didn't want you anywhere near that case ever again."

"Keeping me in the dark isn't going to make it go away. I could have helped."

"What could anyone have done?"

"Someone messes with you, they mess with me. We're supposed to be a team," she said.

"You're right. I made a mistake, and I'm sorry. By the way, I see you're wearing the diamond earrings I bought you."

"Don't try to change the subject. You're not getting off that easy."

"They do look nice. You have to admit it."

"They do. Don't they?"

Alana laughed.

"You're out. You're really out," she continued.

I walked over and kissed her.

"Did anyone ever tell you how amazing you are?" I asked.

"It's been a while."

"Then let me say it. You're amazing. Thank you."

"What do you want to do now? Are you hungry? I'm sure the food in there sucks."

"I know it's not our anniversary yet, but let's go upstairs and celebrate early."

Alana smiled, and I followed her to the second floor. Our lovemaking was slow and tender that night. Afterward, we laid on our sides and just looked at each other. I took in every inch of her body. I ran my fingers through her hair and stared into her eyes. I could never get past those dark eyes. They just seemed to see every part of me, both the good and the bad, and yet she still wanted to be with me. She was so beautiful, and I couldn't believe she was mine. I couldn't believe how much she'd changed my life. They'd tried to take all of that away from me, even though it had just been temporary.

We eventually got dressed and made our way downstairs. We walked outside to the backyard. We sat around the pool and listened to the waves break against the shore. Maui the dog raced around the yard. He seemed intent on inspecting every inch of it as if he fully expected to discover someone or something had invaded his space while he'd been away. Everything must have checked out okay because he trotted back over to us and plopped down on the cement patio beside our chairs.

"I think he's glad to be back," Alana said.

"He's not the only one. I haven't even asked you yet what the deciding factor was. What made them let me go?"

"Fear."

"What do you mean?"

"The prosecutor was terrified of losing the case. She has promotions on her mind, and she wasn't about to have a big X against her record. We presented her with so much evidence that I knew she'd let you go. Never underestimate some government employees' unwillingness to put themselves out there."

"Do you think there's a chance they'll charge me again?"

"I don't know. I doubt it, but there's still that cell phone and the victim's hair to deal with."

"Does anyone know what we think happened?"

Alana told me about her conversation with Captain Price and how she'd tipped our hand to the fact that we thought a corrupt officer had planted the evidence.

"Will they make another move for us?" I asked.

"They have to know we haven't uncovered their identity yet. My guess is they'll wait and see what we do next."

"I never even got that far in my thinking. It's hard to plan move number two when you don't know if you'll ever get out of that cell."

"Me neither. All my attention was on getting you out."

"What do you want to do now? How can we go after these people if they're cops? We don't even know how many of them there are."

Alana didn't respond. I felt guilty for pointing out the weak points in our plan, if we even had one. They were obvious, and speaking them out loud could only serve to bring us down.

"I was so sure I'd put it all behind me. I didn't want any part of this," I said.

"Put what behind you?"

"These cases. I always saw them as me matching wits with someone else. Even when I was in danger, it still felt like some kind of game. That changed when they tried to kill you."

"So what do you want now? Do you want to just walk away?"

"It wouldn't work, even if it was what I wanted. But I don't want that anymore. Not now."

"What's changed?" she asked.

"They tried to take what's ours. No one does that and gets away with it."

"We don't have much to go on."

"We probably have more than you think. Let's go over it piece by piece."

"Well, we know someone borrowed your car from the auto shop. Presumably, he's the same man who took the photo of your car outside Brooklyn's apartment. He's probably also the person who texted Genesis the photo and paid her to lie to the police."

"Maybe not. Maybe he's just the grunt doing the physical work. I doubt he's with the police, either. There's no way he'd run the risk of someone seeing his face."

"Genesis claimed that she never met anyone in person. She didn't even talk to them. It was all by text message. There's also the beer bottles to follow up on. Someone from Harry's took them, and they had to meet the person in order for them to get the bottles."

"Maybe not. They could have just left them at some predetermined place and time. I'm assuming you didn't find out who took them?" I asked.

"No, but I think there's an easy way. I mean it would be easy if I had the legal authority to check their bank records. We know Perkins and Genesis both got thousands to help frame you. The man or woman who took those beer bottles probably got paid, too."

"What about Brooklyn? One of her friends must have known something. Detective Shaw told me the text messages between Brooklyn and the phone they planted went back for months."

"Mara told me they accused you of regularly giving her money every month. That was probably payment for sending those text messages. They'd been planning this frame job for a while."

I could see why Brooklyn had wanted to get back at me. I'd forced her to reveal the name of the man who attacked Alana. I knew she probably resented me for that. Once the false relationship had been established, they no longer needed her around.

My phone rang and I looked at the display. It was Foxx. I didn't want to talk with anyone but Alana at the moment, so I let the call go to voicemail. Less than thirty seconds went by, and Foxx called again. I answered this time.

"Hello."

I expected him to say congratulations for getting out of jail, and I assumed he'd invite me to Harry's to celebrate. Instead, he said something I'd hoped to never hear again.

"Poe, there's been a murder."

"Who?"

"Molly. Kiana just found her."

Chapter 16
Molly

"Where's Kiana now?" I asked.

"She left Harry's a little while ago. Molly didn't show for work yesterday or today, so Kiana went to check on her. Her place is just a few blocks from the bar."

"Are you still at Harry's?"

"Yeah, but I'm heading to Molly's house. Kiana's pretty upset."

"Send me the address. I'll meet you there."

I ended the call and turned to Alana.

"What's going on?" she asked.

"Molly's been killed. She worked at Harry's as a waitress."

"I know. I talked to her a couple of days ago. Where was she found?"

I told her what Foxx had told me. My cell phone buzzed a moment later. I looked down at the phone and saw Molly's address on the display.

"Foxx is on his way to her house now. He said Kiana's pretty torn up."

"I'm sure."

We took Maui the dog inside, and I grabbed the car keys off the kitchen counter. It only took about fifteen minutes to get to her house. I knew Molly had always walked to the bar, but I didn't realize just how close she'd actually lived. The house was tiny. From the outside, it looked like it couldn't be much bigger than one or two rooms. It was painted in a faded light blue. There was thick brush on one side and another tiny house on the other.

Three police cars were parked in front of her house, and their blue and red flashing lights created swirls of color on the officers and neighbors standing in the street.

We did a slow drive past the house, and I parked my convertible a couple of houses down. Alana and I got out of the car. I didn't see Foxx's SUV, so I assumed he'd walked over from Harry's.

We walked slowly over to the crowd. I was nervous just being around these police cars. It was a feeling I'd never experienced before.

"Poe."

I turned when I heard my name and saw Foxx walking toward us. He slapped my shoulder with his large hand.

"It's good to see you out. I'm sorry this is how we're meeting. I'd planned on having a party for you at Harry's."

"Thanks. I'm sure we can have that at some point. Where's Kiana? Is she okay?" I asked.

"She's being interviewed by the cops."

Foxx pointed toward Molly's house, and we saw Detective Shaw speaking with Kiana by the curb. He turned as if he'd actually heard Foxx's words. He stared at us for a long moment. Then he turned his attention back to Kiana.

"Do you have any other details?" Alana asked.

"No. She just said she'd found Molly dead. I got here a few minutes before the cops arrived."

"Did you go in the house?" Alana asked.

"No, but I saw Molly from the porch. Her body's just a few feet from the open door."

"Could you tell how was she killed?" I asked.

"Someone cut her throat. There's blood everywhere."

"She probably opened the door, and the person immediately killed her," Alana said.

I looked around the area. There were a couple of street lights, but they were mostly obscured by tall trees which made the area pretty dark. It was a fairly narrow road that ran into a dead end. There wasn't much reason to drive down this way unless you lived here or were visiting someone. It would have been easy for some intruder to kill Molly in her doorway and get away completely unnoticed.

"You said she hadn't shown for a couple of days. Did she call in sick or something?" I asked.

"No. She just didn't show up. We were pretty busy too, so she really left us short-handed. By the time things slowed down, it seemed like a moot point to call her."

"This was the work shift after we spoke with her?" Alana asked.

"Yeah. The next day."

"I'm guessing you talked to her about the Purple Haze beer bottles?" I asked.

"She said she didn't know anything about them. She also denied overhearing a conversation you had where she'd originally claimed you told someone not to threaten you," Alana said.

"You specifically asked Molly about it, and she said she didn't say that?" I asked.

"Yeah. If she was acting, she did a pretty good job. She seemed genuinely confused as to why we were asking that," Alana said.

"Were you thinking Kiana might have lied about it then?" I asked.

"The thought crossed my mind," Foxx said.

"What are you doing here?"

We turned at the sound of the male's voice and saw Detective Shaw walking toward us.

"This is a crime scene. You can't be here," he continued.

"The victim was an employee of ours. I think it makes perfect sense that we'd be concerned and want to know what happened," Alana said.

"An employee of ours? I didn't realize you owned a piece of that bar, too."

"What's mine is hers," I said.

"What happened here?" Alana asked.

"It would be inappropriate for me to talk about that with a civilian."

"Okay. Fine. Play it that way," Alana said.

"Don't interfere. I'm warning you."

Shaw turned from us and walked back to the house.

"Let me guess. He's the guy who arrested you," Foxx said.

"Yep," I said.

"Do me a favor, Foxx. Try to get Kiana's attention. See if you can bring her over to our car," Alana said.

We walked back to the BMW while Foxx headed closer to the house.

"So Shaw picked up this case. How bad is this for us?" I asked.

"I'm not sure, yet. But it makes sense he'd get it. It has to be connected to the murder of Brooklyn Van Kirk."

We waited by my car for several minutes. Foxx came back first, and he was followed shortly after that by Kiana. Her eyes were swollen, and I could tell she'd been crying.

"I'm sorry for what happened to Molly. I know she was your friend," I said.

Kiana didn't say anything. She just looked back at the house. I didn't know if she was reflecting on her relationship with Molly or if she was worried the police would see her talking to us. Speaking of the police, I hadn't seen Shaw since he'd told us to leave. He was probably in the house.

"How did you find her?" Alana asked.

Kiana turned back to us.

"I walked over here after work. I knocked on the door, and it opened some. It must not have been completely shut. That's when I saw the blood on the floor."

"When was the last time you saw or spoke to Molly?" Alana asked.

"It was a couple of nights ago at work."

"Did you and Molly speak about your conversations with Alana and me?" Foxx asked.

"No. She never said anything about it."

"Kiana, I was told Molly said she'd overheard me having an argument with someone on the phone, but she denied that when Alana and Foxx asked her about it. Do you know why she would have done that?" I asked.

"I have no idea. She told me that. I didn't make it up."

"No one's accusing you of that. We're just trying to figure out why she would make up a story like that. Did she not like Poe? Did she ever criticize him?" Foxx asked.

Kiana looked at me.

"It's okay if she did. We're just trying to figure out the truth," I said.

"She didn't talk about you much. She never said anything bad."

"Were you two close? I know co-workers can sometimes become good friends," Alana asked.

"We were friends but not best friends."

"What did you two talk about at work?" Alana asked.

"Stuff like where she was from, how she ended up on Maui. Things like that."

"Where was she from?" I asked.

"Seattle. She said she got tired of the dreary weather, and she wanted something completely different. She'd also broken up with her boyfriend, and she wanted to start over."

"Do you know if Molly had money problems? Did she ever complain about not being able to pay the bills?" Alana asked.

"Sometimes, but everyone complains about those things."

"Did she say anything in the last few weeks about getting some money?" Foxx asked.

"No. I think she would have mentioned that."

"About that conversation you had with Foxx and Alana, are you sure you never saw her taking any beer bottles from the bar?" I asked.

"No. Why does everyone keep asking me about the bottles? Is someone stealing from the bar?"

"It's nothing like that," Foxx said.

"Then what is it?"

"Someone helped frame me, Kiana. They took three bottles I handled at the bar and gave them to someone else. They wanted to make it look like I was somewhere I wasn't."

"You think Molly might have done that?"

"That's what we're trying to figure out. If there's anything you heard or saw, anything odd that Molly might have said, we really need to know," Alana said.

"She seemed fine to me."

"Even after we spoke with her the other day? She didn't seem nervous at all?" Foxx asked.

"No. She was fine."

"Did she have any roommates?" I asked.

"No. She lived alone. She told me her boyfriend sometimes stayed with her, but I think he has his own place."

"Have you met him? Do you know his name?" Alana asked.

"He's come to Harry's a couple of times. His name's Pika. I don't know his last name."

"He's Hawaiian?" Alana asked.

"Yes. I think he grew up on Oahu but moved here several years ago."

"Do you remember if he's tall or short?" Alana asked.

"He was average height. Maybe a few inches taller than Molly."

I watched as Alana turned and looked at Foxx. I didn't know what that look meant, but I was sure I'd find out later tonight.

We thanked Kiana for answering all of our questions. I felt bad for the interrogation of sorts, especially after what she'd found inside the house. I'd found bodies before during some of my investigations. They aren't something you can ever forget.

Foxx offered to walk Kiana back to Harry's, and she happily accepted.

Alana and I stood beside the BMW and looked at the house again. We watched as the paramedics carried Molly's body out on a stretcher. I thought back to the conversation we had beside the pool in our backyard. I'd expressed a desire to get out of this dreadful game. There was no chance of that now. Someone had been murdered, and I knew it was because of me and the case that had fallen apart earlier in the day.

That brought up some interesting questions. Molly hadn't shown for work two days in a row. Had she been dead that long, or was this something that occurred just a few hours ago? Was her death the result of her getting spooked by Alana's questions? If so, she must have known who told her to take those bottles? She had to have called them and warned them that Alana knew something was up. It had been a fatal mistake on Molly's part since I doubted there would have been any way Alana could prove she'd taken the beer bottles short of a confession. She could have kept her mouth shut, and maybe nothing would have happened.

I turned to Alana who seemed as affected as I was by the sight of Molly's body being lifted into the back of the ambulance.

"You seemed to have a reaction when Kiana said the boyfriend was a Hawaiian."

"It was an interesting coincidence. Of course, that may be all it is."

"Why did you ask what size the guy as?"

"Perkins said the guy who came by his auto shop to take your car was a Hawaiian. Perkins described him as being of average height and weight."

"That is interesting," I said.

Chapter 17
An Envelope Full of Cash

Perspective: Poe

Alana and I waited around the area for another hour or so to see if Molly's boyfriend would show up, but he never did. We drove back to our house and walked upstairs to the bedroom after receiving another enthusiastic greeting from Maui the dog. I'd only been gone a couple of hours this time, but he still acted as if he hadn't seen me in months.

I was beyond exhausted at this point, and I spent the final minutes before falling asleep thinking about everything that had happened that day. I'd started out the morning waking up in a jail cell. Now I was back in my own bed. I should have been in a state of excitement and euphoria, and a part of me was. But mostly I couldn't stop thinking about Molly. I hadn't known her that well. Sure, I'd spoken to her numerous times over the last year, but our conversations had never gone beyond the polite comment about work or some mundane topic like the weather or some sports score on the TV above the bar.

I didn't see how her death couldn't be related to the failed attempt at pegging Brooklyn's murder on me. Molly had helped frame me, at least that was the prevailing theory. The more I thought about it, the more convinced I became that she knew the name of the person who framed me or at the very least their face. It didn't make sense that the person would feel the need to kill her if she didn't have any way of identifying them.

Of course, I could have gotten all of this wrong. Molly's death simply might have been the result of a robbery. I didn't think that was likely, but it was a possibility I had to consider.

I rolled over to thank Alana again for everything she'd done to get me out of jail. She was already fast asleep. I closed my eyes and was asleep myself within seconds.

It felt like I had only been out for a couple of hours when Alana's cell phone woke us both. She always kept hers on the nightstand, which is probably not the best place to keep it if you want a full night's sleep, but her job required her to be reachable twenty-four hours a day. Yeah, she wasn't a cop anymore, but I guess old habits die hard.

Alana reached for her phone while I looked at the time on the digital clock on my nightstand. It was already seven in the morning. We were both usually up about an hour or so before now, so we must have been even more tired than we realized.

Alana answered the phone. I only heard her end of the conversation, and the only thing I could gather from it was that someone wanted to meet with her that morning. She ended the call as I swung my legs off the bed. I always needed to do that in slow motion since Maui the dog often slept on the floor beside the bed, and I didn't want to bring my two hundred pounds down on top of the little guy. He had his own bed on the other side of the room, but he rarely used it.

"That was Price," Alana said, as she placed her phone back on the nightstand.

"Price as in Captain Price?"

"Yeah."

"What did he want, especially at seven in the morning?"

"He asked if I'd be willing to come see him at the office this morning."

"I hoped you told him he was more than welcome to come see you at your office."

"And where exactly would that be?" she asked.

"Our swimming pool. I could put a nice desk out there for you. Let him see how great you're doing."

"A desk by the pool? What do you think he wants?"

"What do you mean? You know exactly what he wants. He wants you to come back to work."

Alana stood and walked into the restroom without commenting on my prediction.

I looked down just in time to see Maui the dog conduct a graceful roll onto his back so I could rub his chest. It was part of our morning ritual that I'm sure he'd missed while staying with Foxx. I tended to treat the dog like he was my child, whereas Foxx saw him for what he really was: a dog.

Alana walked out of the bathroom but stopped in the doorway.

"Do I even want to go back?" she asked.

"I don't know. Do you?"

"He really pissed me off the way he talked to me."

"How did he talk to you? You never really told me."

"I knew I was asking for a big favor, but I thought we had a friendship of sorts."

It was a common mistake people made. We all often confuse working relationships, even friendly ones, with being a true friend of the other person. Yeah, we might see them at the occasional holiday party or you might regularly have lunch with them, but that's a far cry from being there for the person when they're having a crisis. Price had turned his back on Alana. He'd turned it on me, too, but I had no illusions that we were friends. I didn't even know if the guy liked me or not.

"In Price's defense, he was in a tough spot," I said.

"And we weren't? If I'd been told that I might have a corrupt cop, I wouldn't just dismiss it."

"How do you know that's what he did?"

"Because I saw his reaction with my own eyes. He pretty much just shrugged his shoulders and walked away."

"Try to remove Price from the decision."

"How can I? He'd be my boss again."

"Sure, but how often do you really interact with him?"

"I'd see him on a daily basis."

"Yeah, but what is the percentage of time you actually spend with him? Five percent of your day?" I asked.

"Maybe not even that much."

"I remember when I had that architecture job, there were a couple of guys that I just couldn't stand. They were real douchebags."

"How did you handle them?"

"Whenever I knew I was going to have to interact with them, I made it a little game. I made the point of the meeting to not get upset by them. It was a test of my self-control."

"Did it work?"

"Not really. I still hated them."

"So why are you suggesting it to me?"

"Because you're smarter than me, and you might be able to pull it off."

"Maybe."

"Maybe to being smarter than me or the pulling it off part?"

"Not sure. Probably both."

I laughed.

"You're undoubtedly smarter than me."

"I just don't know what to do."

"I know it hasn't been that long, but have you missed the job yet?" I asked.

"Not until last night. I couldn't stand not being able to go into that house and see what was going on. It pissed me off to no end that Shaw could and I had to stay on the street."

Alana didn't need to tell me that for me to realize that's how she'd felt. Her frustration had been written all over her face.

"You've generally liked Captain Price until all this went down. Don't let one interaction taint your entire relationship with the guy."

"It's not just that," she said.

"What else could it be?"

Alana didn't answer me.

"Did something happen that you're not telling me about?" I asked.

"He made a comment about you. It really surprised me."

"What was it?"

"He said he didn't like you."

I laughed again.

"Why is that funny?" she asked.

"Because I'm surprised that's all it was."

"Why are you surprised?"

"I could have told you months ago that he didn't like me."

"How? You hadn't even meant him until the hospital."

"Because of what I'd been doing since coming here. I'm sure I was a pain in the butt of the department. They only let me get away with it because of my relationship with you. They probably would have personally escorted me to the airport if you weren't here."

"Foxx thinks Price is jealous of you."

"Wait a minute. You and Foxx have talked about this?"

"I saw him after the conversation with Price. He said you were the one to bring it up."

I didn't respond.

"Well, did you?"

"I might have said something," I admitted.

"You might have? You either did or you didn't. I don't believe for a second you don't remember."

"I was probably just being paranoid."

"What was it about him that you didn't like?" she asked.

"I don't know. It was the way he looked at you."

"How did he look at me?"

"The looks lasted a second or two longer than they should have."

"That's silly. How long is someone supposed to look at someone else?"

"I wasn't timing him or anything, but I got the impression he was admiring you versus just looking at you as part of a conversation."

"He made it personal, Poe. He refused to help and then he insulted you."

"Here's my take on it all. You love that job. You told me it's all you ever wanted to do. Don't let Price or anyone else for that matter keep you from doing what you enjoy. What time are you supposed to meet?"

"He asked me if I could see him before nine."

"Wonder what the rush is."

"His day's usually pretty packed."

"Go see what he has to say. Maybe he'll apologize to you."

"I don't know."

"What's it going to hurt? Maui and I will be back here hanging out."

I saw Alana look past me toward the dog. I turned and looked at him, too. He was on his back with all four legs sticking up in the air. He seemed to realize we were staring at him, so he rolled over and starting racing around the room.

"I wish I could be in such a good mood every morning," Alana said.

"Yeah, we should both take life lessons from the dog."

"What are you doing today?"

"I know what I'd like to do, but I don't know if there's any way it's going to happen."

"What's that?"

"I'd like to meet with Molly's boyfriend. What was his name? Pika or something?"

"I think it was Pika."

"I have no idea how I'm going to find this guy. There's your reason to go back to being a cop. You can get information so much easier, and you can share it with me."

Alana smiled.

"So nice of you to tell me your true motivation."

"Go see Price. Hear what he has to say and follow your gut instinct. It won't ever steer you wrong."

"I don't know about that. My gut told me to stay away from you."

"Stay away from me?"

"Some charming rich guy from the east coast? Nothing but trouble."

"First of all, I'm sure I was nowhere near charming, and you had no idea I had money."

"So why did I say yes to your dinner invitation?" she asked.

"It was my body. Pure and simple."

"Oh my God, how did I know you were going to say that?" she asked.

"I'm nothing if not predictable."

"Are you kidding? You're the most unpredictable person I've ever met."

"Well, that in itself is a form of predictability. Figure out what a normal person would do and then assume I'll do the opposite."

Maui barked once. I wasn't sure if that was his way of agreeing with me or if he was simply letting me know he had to go outside to use the bathroom. I decided it was probably best to assume it was the latter.

"Come on, Maui. Let's go outside."

I grabbed my swimsuit on the way out of the bedroom. Maui the dog dashed down the stairs and ran for the sliding glass door in the back of the house. I stripped off my t-shirt and underwear and slipped on my swimsuit.

I walked to the back and opened the glass door. Maui ran into the backyard. I closed the door behind me and walked over to the swimming pool. Morning swims had become one of my favorite activities since moving to Maui. I didn't have a pool in Virginia, and the idea of swimming in the gray waters of the Chesapeake Bay and Atlantic Ocean never quite appealed to me. I much preferred the clear salt water pool in my Maui backyard. I dove into the pool and swam several laps. I alternated between swimming underwater and on top. It was a great way to wake up in the morning and also stretch the muscles of my back, shoulders, and neck.

I eventually climbed out of the pool and sat on one of the patio chairs that overlooked the ocean. Maui was busy running from one corner of the yard to the other. I wasn't exactly sure what he was chasing, but he seemed intent on catching it. Most of the time, I had the sneaking suspicion that he was just trying to impress me by putting on a show. Perhaps he was trying to demonstrate his diligence at guarding and patrolling the property.

Alana came outside after taking a shower and changing into one of her work suits. I was a little surprised to see the outfit. It wasn't like I thought she'd go to the Price meeting wearing shorts and flip-flops, but I didn't think she'd show up as if she was ready to get back to work. I thought she might try to make Price grovel more.

I hugged and kissed her goodbye. After she left, I swam several more laps in the pool. Then I made my way back into the house. I changed into shorts and a t-shirt. I brought Maui back inside. I got my phone so I could listen to music while I ran three miles through the neighborhood. The neighborhood isn't that big, so I usually just lapped it several times. I didn't want to risk getting hit by an inattentive driver if I ran alongside the main road.

I was just starting mile number two when my phone rang. I intended to let it go to voicemail, but I saw it was Foxx calling.

"Hello."

"You okay, buddy? You sound a little winded."

"I'm jogging."

"Oh, that explains it. Listen, I need you to come up to Harry's right now. I have someone I think you'd like to meet."

"Who is it?"

"His name's Pika. Ring a bell?"

"I'll be there as soon as I can."

I ran back to the house and changed into a fresh pair of shorts and another t-shirt. I texted Foxx as I walked to my car to let him know I was on the way to Harry's.

I walked into the bar and found Foxx standing beside Kiana. There was no one else in Harry's, and I assumed Pika had already left.

"Sorry. I got here as fast as I could. How long ago did he leave?" I asked.

"He's still here," Foxx said.

I looked around the bar a second time since I assumed he'd been tucked into one of the booths, and I just hadn't seen him the first time. I still didn't see anyone, though.

"Where is he?"

"He's in the office. He's not going anywhere."

Foxx's tone seemed to suggest there might have been a bit of a confrontation between the two of them.

"Don't tell me you forced him back there."

"No. I just implied he might regret leaving before you got here."

"Why is he even here?"

"He came to talk to me. He wanted to know if anything strange had happened at the bar the last time Molly was here," Kiana said.

"I'm assuming he knows about Molly," I said.

"I guess the police told him last night. He's really torn up."

I looked toward the closed door of the back office.

"Want me to go back there with you?" Foxx asked.

"No, why?"

"We think the guy helped frame you. I'd be pretty pissed if I were you."

"I'll be fine."

"Call if you need help. I have no problem holding him down."

"I'll let you know."

I walked to the back of the bar and went inside the office. I found a nervous-looking Pika sitting on the chair in front of Foxx's desk. I couldn't judge his height since he'd stayed seated when I'd entered, but he was of average build, just like Perkins' description.

"Nice to meet you, Pika."

I wasn't sure why I'd just said that since it really wasn't nice to meet him. The guy had taken my BMW in an attempt to frame me for murder, if Alana and Foxx's theory was correct, that is.

I walked around to the other side of the desk and sat down on Foxx's leather chair.

"I'm sorry about Molly. I understand you were her boyfriend."

Pika said nothing. He just looked at the floor.

"How did you hear about her passing?" I asked.

He looked up at me.

"I went over to her house last night when I couldn't get a hold of her. The police were still there."

"Did they interview you?"

"Some detective did. I don't remember his name."

"Shaw."

"It might have been."

"When was the last time you spoke with Molly?"

"I don't know what's going on here. Why do you want to know about any of this? I told your buddy out there I'm going to call the cops as soon as I get out of this bar."

"Why don't you call them now?"

"Because he took my damn phone."

I somehow managed not to laugh. Foxx was a determined guy. That was one of his many attributes I admired.

"Let me ask you one question first. Then I'll tell you why I'm interested. All right?"

Pika nodded.

"Did you go to Perkins Auto Shop about a year ago and pay the owner cash to borrow a BMW convertible for a few hours?"

I saw his eyes widen.

"I'll take that as a yes. I'm the owner of that BMW. That's why I'm interested."

"You can't prove anything."

"I don't have to."

"I didn't steal the car. I brought it back."

"How much did they pay you to take my car to that apartment complex?"

Pika said nothing.

"I thought you were interested in figuring out what happened to Molly. I'm pretty sure this is all connected."

"Why should I talk to you?" he asked.

"You're right. You don't have to talk to me. Maybe you should go to the cops. Did you tell Detective Shaw about your part in all of this?"

Pika looked down at the floor again.

"My wife works with him. She's at the station now."

I pulled my phone out of my pocket and placed it on the desk in front of me.

"I can call her right now if you'd like. We can set up a time to speak to Shaw."

Pika still didn't respond.

"You didn't tell him anything about this. I wouldn't have. You know it puts you in a bad light. Hell, they might even try to pin her death on you."

"You can go to hell. I had nothing to do with her murder."

"If you say so, but here's what I think happened. You got greedy and wanted all that money for yourself."

"You're just making wild guesses. You don't know what happened."

"I know you paid that auto shop to take my car to that apartment in Kihei. Then you took a photograph of it with your phone. You took the shot from the second floor when you should have taken it from the third floor."

I could see the look of surprise on Pika's face.

"You see I know a lot more than you think I do."

"We didn't know what it was for. What would you have done? Someone offers you a ton of money to drive a car someplace. You going to turn that down?"

"How did it happen? Who hired you?"

"Molly never even met the guy," Pika said.

"How did he get in contact with her?"

"She came home from work one night and found an envelope partially hidden under her doormat. She opened it and found a thousand dollars inside. She got a text the next morning. Someone asked her if she wanted to make even more money. They told her about taking your car to the apartment complex."

"Did she know why this person wanted that done?"

"No. It seemed like easy money."

"Did she even ask?"

"Would you have? She didn't want to risk the job going away."

Time for a little side note. The older I get, the more and more convinced I become that humans are basically selfish jerks. They don't mean to be. Well, some of them probably do, but most don't. It's in the DNA. They just instinctively become self-centered. They're that way as kids when they demand the toy for themselves. It only becomes worse and worse as they get older. Most people don't ever stop to think how their actions affect others. They just plunge right ahead, consequences be damned.

Molly had to know the BMW was my car. She'd seen it in the parking lot of Harry's a thousand times. She also clearly knew the Purple Haze beer bottles were mine, yet she probably didn't give two seconds of thought that somebody might be wanting to frame me for a crime.

If that thought did cross her mind, then she certainly pushed it away as quickly as she could. All she thought about was that money. It's the only thing she cared about. Did I blame her for that, especially since most people would have done the same thing? Hell, yes, I blamed her. Just because humans as a group can be despicable, it doesn't mean I give individuals a pass.

I also want to point out that I don't think she deserved to die for the part she played in putting me behind bars. That probably goes without saying, but I just wanted to qualify that so you don't think less of me.

"Tell me how it all went down. When did you find out about the money?" I asked.

"The same night she found it by her door. I came over to the house, and she showed me the envelope."

"Did you ever see the text messages?"

"Sure. I stayed over that night, so I was still there in the morning when the first message came through."

"Do you know if she kept the messages on her phone?"

"No, she deleted them."

I made a mental note to ask Alana to try to get Molly's phone records, if she decided to go back to the department, that is.

"Was taking the BMW the first job?"

"Yeah, she asked me to do it. She was scared to go over there herself."

"How did you get the money to pay off the owner?" I asked.

"The person left the money in another envelope. They said they'd hurt Molly if she tried to run off with it. She gave me the cash, and I took it with me to that auto shop. More money came a few days after I did the job. That was our payment."

"And you texted the photo of my car at that parking lot to whoever gave you the money?"

"No. I sent it to Molly so she could do it. We didn't want the person knowing that she'd brought me in."

"Do you still have the photo on your phone?"

"No. I deleted it right after I sent it to Molly."

"What happened after you got paid for the car job?" I asked.

"We didn't hear anything else for a long time. We figured it was over. No one seemed to get hurt, so we didn't think it was that big of a deal."

"Then the person contacted you about the beer bottles?"

"Yeah. It was maybe a year later."

"Was the message about the bottles from the same phone number?"

"I'm not sure. I didn't ask Molly about that. The guy asked her to grab a few bottles that you'd handled."

"Did Molly tell you specifically that they were my beer bottles?"

"She said it was her boss. I figured it was the other guy."

"You mentioned a few times that it was a 'he' who contacted Molly. How do you know it was a male?"

"Because Molly saw him."

"She did? When?"

"She secretly recorded the guy the last time he left the envelope under her door. She hid one of my surf cameras in the tree."

"Please tell me you got a good recording of his face."

"No, but we could tell it was a guy."

"Do you still have the video?"

"Yeah. I've got the card on me now. I've been trying to figure out whether to go to the police with it."

"Why wouldn't you?" I asked.

Then I realized Molly wasn't the only one who'd put themselves first. I'm sure she'd told him she'd figured out the significance of the beer bottles and the BMW after my arrest. She probably felt guilty about it, but she was probably even more worried that their part could potentially expose them to their own problems with the law.

"There's no reason for you to get involved if you don't want to. Show me the card. I can even copy it to the office computer. I'll make sure it gets to the police. No one will know it came from you."

Pika hesitated a moment. Then he reached into his pocket and pulled out the card. He'd already inserted it into a mini USB reader since those action cameras have cards that are smaller than your pinky nail.

He handed me the card, and I inserted it into the USB port on the office computer. The camera folder popped up a second later, and I dragged the contents folder over to the desktop. Those camera files are designed to play on any computer, so I didn't need any special editing software to play it. I double-clicked on the file and saw a wide shot of Molly's front yard.

"The guy shows up about thirty minutes into the clip," Pika said.

I clicked on the timeline of the video file and eventually found the right section. I watched as a person dressed in jeans and a dark sweatshirt walked into the frame. It was night, so the footage was already dark and underexposed, but I could still make out the image. The person had the hood of the sweatshirt pulled over their head. The camera had been placed in a tree beside the house, so I was getting an extreme profile shot of the front porch. Unfortunately, the person never turned toward the camera, so I couldn't get a glimpse of their face or even their hair.

I understand why Pika said the person was a male, though. They looked tall and had broad shoulders. It almost certainly wasn't a woman. I watched as the guy put the envelope under the doormat and walked away. I pulled the USB drive out and handed it back to Pika.

"That's not going to help the cops much, is it?" he asked.

"No, but it will help some, knowing they're looking for a male."

Pika stood.

"I'm sorry for what happened to you. For what it's worth, Molly was really upset when she heard you'd gotten arrested."

There were a million things I could have said in return, but I said nothing. I just nodded.

Pika turned from me and exited the office. I thought about walking out with him and asking Foxx to return his phone. Instead, I decided to let Pika figure out how to get it back.

I looked back at the video image on the office computer. I played the clip and froze the video as the guy stood on Molly's porch. He may as well have been a ghost for all that I could make out. I had next to nothing, expect for the confirmation that Molly and her boyfriend had played a part in my incarceration.

I looked at my watch. It had been a couple of hours since Alana left for the police station, and I wondered why I hadn't heard from her yet.

Chapter 18
Anger

Perspective: Alana

I found myself driving to the police station with no idea what I was going to say or do once I got there. I've always relied on my gut instinct. Maybe everyone does, but my gut seemed to have taken the morning off. I tried to think through the reasons for going back to work, as well as the reasons for just doing my own thing, whatever that might be.

I debated whether or not I could do the investigative thing with Poe, but I wasn't even sure if that's something he wanted to do anymore. He'd given it up after we got married. I knew he was about to dive back into it, but that had more to do with clearing his name than anything else. Would he continue it after that? I didn't know, nor was I sure I'd want to be a private investigator since I'd spent a career doing things on an official level with the power and authority of the law behind me.

My mother has always accused me of being a prideful person, so the thought crossed my mind several times during the drive that I was just being stubborn at not jumping at the chance to be a cop again. Speaking of my mother, I was still pretty pissed off that she hadn't called to apologize for how she'd leapt to the conclusion that Poe was guilty.

I knew she'd heard he'd been released. I made it a point to tell Hani, and Hani's incapable of keeping anyone's secrets but her own. Still, I'd heard nothing from my mother. Was I surprised? A little, but maybe I shouldn't have been. I still hadn't told Poe what she'd said about him. He was a patient guy, especially where she was concerned, but this could easily push him over the edge. I wouldn't blame him, either. She'd been nothing but ugly to him since they first met.

Back to my meeting, or at least the drive to my meeting with Captain Price. I mentally wrote the pluses and minuses to going back to work. The positives far outweighed the negatives, so why didn't I feel this overwhelming desire to say yes? Maybe it was way more than pride.

Then I realized I was also probably being arrogant. I didn't even know the real reason Price had asked me to come to the station. Maybe he just intended to apologize for doubting Poe, but he could have easily just done that over the phone.

I still hadn't come to any kind of conclusion by the time I arrived. I parked Poe's SUV and made my way toward the lobby. I didn't think I could just walk back to his office, especially since I didn't work there anymore, but I found Captain Price waiting for me in the lobby when I opened the door.

"Good morning, Alana. Thank you for coming to see me."

I nodded. I didn't know why I suddenly felt like he had the upper hand, nor did I know why I felt nervous.

"Let's go back to my office," he continued.

I followed Price to his office. I stopped counting the number of people who stared at me and didn't bother saying hello or good morning or any kind of greeting one might give someone after working with them for years. I began to feel like people were looking at me as if I had some contagious disease. It's amazing how many people pretend to not know you exist when they fear being cordial to you might somehow hurt their career.

Price held his office door open for me and then shut it after we'd both entered. There were two chairs in front of his desk. He sat on one of them instead of the large leather chair behind his desk. I sat on the other.

"I'm sorry for not calling earlier," he said.

I didn't respond.

"How is your husband doing?"

"How do you expect?"

"I know you're angry with me, and you have every right to be. I'm sure you think I turned my back on you."

"The thought crossed my mind."

"I couldn't appear to be helping you. You know that."

"Well, that's the crux of our disagreement, isn't it?"

"What do you mean?"

"I never asked you to do anything dishonest. What I asked for, what I still think was a perfectly reasonable and reasoned request, was for you to help me discover the truth."

"You're better than you think, Alana. You're also more resourceful. Did it ever occur to you that I knew you didn't need my help? There could be no charge of impropriety if I'd given you access to resources you shouldn't have had in the case."

"That's unworthy of you," I said.

"How so?"

"Complimenting me as a reason to justify your inaction."

"If you say so. That doesn't mean it isn't the truth."

I don't know what got into me. Actually, I do know. It was anger. I realized at that moment in Price's office that I no longer cared what he thought of me. Whatever kind of relationship we'd had, it was now gone. I never cared for taking sides, but sometimes you have to. On one side there was Captain Price and his office politics. Poe was on the other. There really was no contest. The nervousness I'd been experiencing a moment ago completely fled.

"Can I ask why you wanted me to meet with you?"

"Isn't it obvious?" he asked.

"No, it isn't."

"I'd like you to come back to work. I never officially accepted your resignation, so you still always had your job."

"Hedging your bets in case Poe might have actually been innocent?"

"No. I just didn't have the heart to tell them to process your paperwork. I'd hoped you'd change your mind."

"Let me ask you something. I requested the department release a statement officially clearing my husband of the murder charges. We've done that for others who were proven innocent. That didn't happen in Poe's case. Why?"

"He was released within one hour of your meeting with Piper. Have you ever seen anyone out that fast?"

"But why not the public apology? Is it because you're not convinced he didn't do it?" I asked.

Price didn't respond.

"I assumed as much."

"I can't get past the phone and the victim's hair on his clothing."

"It was my shirt."

"That doesn't mean it didn't start out on his and transfer to yours in the clothes hamper. You know that's possible."

"Are you planning on charging him again?"

"That depends."

"On what?"

"On what new evidence comes to light. Shaw is still working the case."

"Shaw is sloppy. He failed to follow up on several things that would have shown Poe didn't do it."

"Try to remove your relationship from the equation. What would you have done if you'd found that evidence against him?"

"I would have arrested him, but I wouldn't have stopped investigating. Shaw quit searching the moment he had my husband in handcuffs. He got lazy. Maybe he was always that way, and I just didn't realize it."

"Maybe he's just not as good as you. Had you ever considered that?" Price asked.

I said nothing.

"Come back to work. I want to give you the Molly Randolph case."

"I assumed Shaw would get that one. I saw him at the scene of the crime."

"You were there last night?" he asked.

"Of course. She worked for my husband. Another one of his employees found her body. He was understandably shaken."

"Shaw doesn't have to be the lead on this."

"Why wouldn't he?"

"Because it might be connected to the murder of Brooklyn Van Kirk's."

"Might be? How is it not? Molly Randolph helped frame Poe."

"That's not proven."

"Not yet, but it's only a matter of time before it comes out," I said.

"Wouldn't it be a thousand times easier if you had the department's resources behind you? You want to prove his innocence beyond a shadow of a doubt, come back and do it."

"What about Shaw? How's he going to react to you giving me the Randolph case?"

"He'll just have to get over it."

I hesitated a long moment. Price's argument was a good one, and it had been the number one reason I'd arrived at for being a cop again.

I guess I could rightfully accuse myself of taking the easy way out. I decided to postpone the real decision for a later date. I'd come back to nail the person who framed Poe. Then I would decide whether to stay indefinitely or quit the job for good.

"What happens when this case ultimately spills over into the Van Kirk investigation? And it will. Will you tell me to back off?" I asked.

"No."

"Then you have a deal. I'd like to start now. I don't want to waste any more time."

"I assumed as much. You already came dressed for work."

Price smiled. I didn't.

"Does Shaw have any idea this is happening?"

"Not yet. I'm going to meet with him next. There's one more thing, although I hesitate to bring it up."

"What is it?" I asked.

"It's Beverly. She's sick."

Beverly was his wife. She was a wonderful woman, but I hadn't seen her in months.

"What's wrong?"

"She has breast cancer. She's been undergoing treatment for a while. She didn't want to talk about it. She didn't want people fussing over her. I don't want to go into too much detail. I know she wouldn't want me to, but things are not going well. I'm going to be taking more time off to spend with her."

"I'm so sorry."

"I wanted you to hear it directly from me since I'm sure it's only a matter of time before it gets out. You know how this office is. Gossip travels at the speed of light."

Price hesitated.

Then he said, "The other day, in the park, I regret what I said about Poe. This isn't an excuse, but I'd been up all night with Beverly. Sometimes I think her treatments are worse than the actual disease."

"Please let me know if there's anything I can do. Is Beverly up for visitors?"

"I'll ask her. I know she's always been very fond of you."

"Please give her my best."

"I will."

I stood.

"Alana, be careful. If someone in this office did plant that evidence..."

His words trailed off, but I got the point. A dirty cop was one of the most dangerous kinds of criminals. They knew your procedures and processes. They wouldn't be easy to catch, and they wouldn't go quietly. They'd already made the decision to betray their brothers and sisters. They wouldn't hesitate to kill one, too.

I walked toward the door when Price called out to me.

"Aren't you forgetting something?"

I turned and saw Price had moved to behind his desk. He opened one of the drawers and pulled out my badge and service weapon.

"These belong to you. I think you'll need them," he continued.

I walked to his desk, and he handed me my badge and gun.

"Thank you."

"Tell your husband I'm sorry. I'll tell him myself when Beverly starts feeling better, and I have time to come over. I'd like to do it in person."

"Of course."

I left his office and walked back to my desk.

I sent Poe a text along the way: Gone back to work. Will call later today. I have a plan.

My phone pinged a few seconds later: Ok. Saw Molly's bf. He confirmed payment for bottles.

I stared at the phone's display. She'd been proven guilty, but we'd already assumed as much. She paid for her betrayal with her life.

I felt terrible for doing so, and as much as I needed to start on the Molly Randolph case, I needed to do something else first. I needed to see our IT department.

Chapter 19
Beautiful Memories

Perspective: Poe

I left Harry's and drove back home. I'd copied the video file to a data DVD in Foxx's office, so I grabbed my laptop off the coffee table after greeting an excited Maui the dog. I inserted the DVD into the laptop and copied the file to the desktop. I played it once more. I'm not really sure why since I'd already watched the clip about ten times at Harry's. It wasn't like I was going to see something new, and I didn't. Still, there was something satisfying about seeing the image of the guy that probably had set me up. He was real, and we now had proof.

I decided to shift gears a bit and concentrate on the murder of Brooklyn. Perhaps I could gather a few pieces of evidence from both Molly's and Brooklyn's cases, and together they would complete the puzzle.

I thought back to a conversation Brooklyn and I had in the photography gallery that had belonged to her employer, Gabriel Reed. She'd admitted that most of their work had consisted of wedding photography and not the high-end commercial and landscape photography they liked to promote.

Her old boss had a great collection of Canon cameras and lenses, and I remembered Brooklyn telling me she didn't have the money to start her own photography business after her employer had been murdered. I suspected at the time that Brooklyn would eventually decide to swipe Gabriel's pro gear. It wasn't like her boss had any relatives who would come looking for it.

I logged onto the internet and did a Google search for Brooklyn Van Kirk.

I also entered the key words "wedding photography" and "Maui." I got several hits. I chose the top link which took me to a website for Van Kirk Photography. It certainly wasn't the most creative of business names, but it did the trick.

Unlike her boss, Brooklyn hadn't tried to fool the public into thinking she was a high-art photographer. All of the images on the website focused on weddings and family and couple portraiture, most of which had been shot on a beach or under some cluster of palm trees. It made sense. If you run a business, you should always go where the money is. People came to the island for vacations and weddings, and I imagined a good photographer who knew how to market him or herself could probably make an okay living catering to those clients.

There was a behind-the-scenes page on the website. I clicked on it and immediately recognized many of the same images that I'd seen on her boss's old website. Brooklyn had done a decent job of selecting the photos that showcased her and not Gabriel Reed. I could see where she'd also cropped the images at odd dimensions, which was probably an attempt to eliminate her former boss altogether.

I then compared the weddings that were featured in the behind-the-scenes photographs with the shots under the page labeled "weddings." Something interesting jumped out at me. Almost all of the weddings could also be seen in the behind-the-scenes section. It was easy to tell since the wedding couples were prominently featured in the images.

There were multiple possibilities for this. The first was that Brooklyn had created her website just before she first started her photography business. She didn't have any of her own images since she'd spent all her professional time working for someone else. She had to use her old boss's work to populate her website. Maybe she just hadn't bothered updating the site, even though she'd been on her own for almost a year. The second possibility was that she knew her photography work wasn't that great, so she was using his work to trick clients into hiring her. The third possibility was that she was a good photographer, but she hadn't gotten much new work.

I clicked on another page labeled "videos" and found several short clips of various weddings. I played a few minutes of one of the videos. The work was quite good. It was well shot and edited. There was a link at the bottom of the video page that stated Van Kirk Photography had partnered with a company called Beautiful Memories Video Productions. On a side note, it was hard to believe a company that could produce such nice videos would have such a terrible business name.

I clicked on the link for Beautiful Memories, and it brought me to their website. There were more samples of wedding videos, as well as a few hotel and resort marketing videos and commercials for local businesses like restaurants and bars.

I went to the contact page and saw they were located in Lahaina. I closed my laptop and turned to the dog.

"Well, Maui. I'll be back in a little while."

I walked into the garage and hopped into the BMW. I pushed the top back so I could enjoy the sun on the short drive. There was nothing quite like feeling the sun on your face when you've just spent a week in jail.

I actually passed Harry's a couple of times while searching for Beautiful Memories. I finally found the business tucked into the back corner of a shopping plaza that catered to tourists searching for - how should I say it - more affordable gifts? The stores mostly sold t-shirts that would shrink three sizes after washing them, miniature hula dancers for your car's dashboard, and little wooden figures with oversized male genitalia. Yes. You read that correctly. That one was quite an odd gift that I'd actually seen in many stores across the island. The wooden guy wears a little barrel, and his you-know-what pops up when you take the barrel off of him. I'm not sure why someone would want to fly all the way to Hawaii, only to return with that item, but to each his own.

Fortunately, the shopping plaza had a large parking lot, and it was free. I pulled into the lot and made my way to the video shop. I debated whether to make up a story about wanting a commercial for Harry's or whether I should just come out and say why I was there. I decided honesty is the best policy. Actually, it wasn't that. I just didn't want to waste time.

I entered the shop and saw a variety of large photographs on the wall that

featured the video cameraman doing his thing at different weddings. It was kind of ironic because he was using the same model of Canon camera that I had. The 5D shoots both stills and video. I just never use the video feature.

"Can I help you?"

I turned at the sound of a man's voice and saw a guy about my height and weight walk from behind a partial wall in the back of the shop. He had short blond hair and wore a black t-shirt with the name "Beautiful Memories" in white letters across the front pocket.

"Yes. I'm looking for the owner."

"That's me. I'm Ted Anders."

"I'm Poe. Nice to meet you."

We shook hands.

"How can I help you?" Ted asked.

"I was wondering if I could ask you a few questions about a business partner of yours: Brooklyn Van Kirk."

Ted's facial expression immediately changed. His warm smile turned into a look of sadness.

"Are you with the police?"

"No, but I'm investigating her death."

"You're a private investigator?"

"That's right. I knew Brooklyn a while ago, but we fell out of touch."

"How did you know her?"

"I met her through her old boss, Gabriel Reed."

He seemed to accept my vague reasoning for conducting an investigation, for which I was grateful.

"I can't believe what's happened to her. I heard they caught the guy who did it, at least they thought they did. I think he might have just gotten released."

"He did. They let him out yesterday. How did you find out about her death?" I asked.

"The guy who runs the shop next door. He told me as soon as I got back."

"Got back from where?"

"My dad had heart surgery, so I was back on the mainland for a couple of weeks. Brooklyn was killed while I was away."

"I saw on her website that you guys had a partnership of sorts. Is that correct?"

"Yeah. We tried to feed each other work. If she booked a wedding, she'd recommend me for the video and vice-versa. We even offered clients package deals."

"How has business been?"

"Not great. I'm probably going to have to give this place up."

I'd wondered as I'd driven over to his shop why he'd felt the need to have a store front. It wasn't like people would walk by and just decide to book a video shoot at the last minute. Furthermore, if you were having a wedding on Maui, wouldn't you book all your vendors before you even left to fly to the island? You're certainly not going to wait until you land and then go searching through some low-end shopping plaza for a wedding videographer.

I looked at the large photos of Ted shooting video.

"Did Brooklyn shoot these images of you?"

"Yeah. We did a few jobs together. She shot these then. She was cool."

"Did Brooklyn work out of her home or did she have a gallery somewhere?"

"I think she did most of her stuff from her apartment. Sometimes she'd come here if we did the job together or if she just wanted to get out of her place. It wasn't super close for her, though."

"Do you know how business was for her?"

"She was slow, too. She always complained about money. I know she said for a while that she was trying to save up money to go to California."

"What part?"

"I think San Diego."

"Did she have friends or family there?"

"I don't think so. I think she was more attracted to the weather. She said she thought it would be a lot like Maui."

I didn't think San Diego would be that much cheaper than living on Maui. I thought it might even be more expensive. I also wondered how much work a wedding photographer could get there.

"You said she talked for a while about leaving. Did she stop talking about that?"

"Not really. I just didn't talk to her much these last few months," he said.

"Did you guys stop working together?"

"You could say that. I called her for a few jobs, but she said she wasn't interested."

"Really? Had she given up photography?"

"She didn't say so. She just said she wasn't interested in doing the jobs."

"That's pretty strange. She was desperate for money and then she was turning down work?"

The truth was, though, that I didn't find it strange at all. I'm sure you don't either. We both know she was probably getting money to help set me up.

"Did she say how she was making money?" I asked.

"No, and I didn't ask her. I didn't think it was any of my business."

"When was the last time you saw Brooklyn?"

"Right before I left. She just stopped by one day. She said she needed to do some editing work."

"Editing work? As in photo editing?"

"Yeah. She didn't do any video."

"Did she want to use your system or something?"

"No. She brought her own laptop. It's still in the back."

"She left her laptop here?"

"She said she was going out for a bite to eat, but then she didn't come back. I must have called her a dozen times, especially since I knew I was about to go out of town."

"Did you tell the police about her laptop?"

"Not yet. I just got back a couple of days ago, and it's been a bit crazy. I haven't had a chance."

"Have any police officers called you or left any messages?"

"No. Not one."

"If you like, I can take the computer. My wife's a detective. I can give it to her."

148

"Naw, man. I'd prefer to give it to the cops myself."

"I get it. I'll call her, though, and ask her to swing by. One more question. Was Brooklyn dating anyone recently?"

"She was seeing this one guy, but I never met him. She was pretty tight-lipped about him."

"Why was that?"

"I don't know. She didn't like talking about him."

"Were they not getting along?"

"I don't think that was it. She just seemed to want to keep it private."

"She didn't say his name, did she?" I asked.

"I think his name was Jay. I never got his last name."

"Okay. I appreciate your time. Good luck with your business."

"Yeah, man, let me know if you know someone who needs a video."

"I will. Thanks."

I left the store and texted Alana as I made my way back to the car. I asked her to call me as soon as she could.

It seemed pretty obvious why Brooklyn left her laptop at a colleague's store. She knew something was about to turn bad. We needed to get our hands on that laptop, and we needed to do it today.

Chapter 20
Digital Footprints

Perspective: Alana

One of the most interesting things about law enforcement is just how much technology has changed the game. Don't get me wrong. Detectives still need to get out there on the streets, talk to people, and try to connect the dots; but traffic cameras, bank and phone records, surveillance video, and computer searches play a much more critical role. Everyone leaves a digital footprint, and it's almost impossible to truly erase it.

I left my desk after texting Poe about going back to work and headed straight for our IT department. Doug is our resident computer nerd. I hate to use that term, but it's actually one he seems to take delight in calling himself. I found him sitting behind his desk. He had a cup of coffee dangerously close to the keyboard. I never understood why he of all people seemed to always do that.

"Hey, Doug, can I ask you a question?"

Doug looked up at me, and I could see the look of surprise in his eyes.

"Alana, you're back."

"Just started again today."

"What happened with....?"

"My husband? You didn't hear?"

"I heard they let him go, but I still don't know what all went down."

"I'll have to fill you in later. Maybe we can do lunch sometime."

"Lunch? Really?"

Yeah. I know. It was shameless manipulation on my part. He had a thing for me, but the guy was harmless.

"I need to see if someone ran a specific search on a suspect. More than that, I need to see when they ran it."

"Who are you checking on?"

"Suspect's name is Genesis Riley."

"No. I mean what co-worker are you wondering about?" he asked.

"Don't know yet. I don't even know if I'm on the right path."

Doug pulled up a program I didn't recognize and typed Genesis Riley into the search bar.

"Looks like someone did access her DMV records."

"Who?"

"Shaw. It's his access code, and he also conducted the search from his computer."

"When was the search made?"

"A month ago."

"A month ago? Really?"

"No question. It was done at eight-thirty-three at night."

Doug turned to me.

"What's the significance of this?" he asked.

"Like I said. I'll have to fill you in later. Can you search another name?"

"Sure."

"Try Brooklyn Van Kirk."

Doug typed her name into the program.

"Austin Shaw again. He did the search on Van Kirk several months ago. March nineteenth to be exact. Also from his computer."

"That was eight months before she was killed," I said.

"Isn't she the same person your husband was accused of murdering?"

"Yeah. She's the one."

"Why would Shaw conduct a search on her before she was killed?"

"I don't know."

"Do me a favor. Don't let anyone know I gave you this information," Doug said.

"What information?" I asked.

I smiled and patted Doug on the back.

Doug attempted a smile in return, but it kind of came out as this half-grin and half-pained expression. I knew Shaw intimidated a lot of people in the office. I guessed Doug was one of them.

"Am I going to get into trouble for this?" he asked.

"Not at all."

I thanked Doug and walked back toward my desk. I looked at the time on my cell phone. It was approaching lunch. I pulled up the contacts list on my phone and dialed Allison Jenkins, who was there at the search of my house when Poe was arrested.

"Hello, this is Jenkins."

"Allison, this is Alana. I was hoping you'd be able to see me sometime today. What's your schedule like?"

Allison informed me she was on her way to lunch, and I did that annoying co-worker thing where I invited myself to join her. She hesitated but eventually agreed to meet.

I left the station and drove ten minutes to a sandwich shop in a small shopping strip. Her police cruiser was parked directly in front of the shop. I walked through the door and saw the place was packed. It didn't surprise me. The food was great and also reasonably priced. It was a favorite place for cops and other city workers, although Allison was the only uniformed officer there now. She'd managed to grab a table near the back. I walked up to the table.

I saw her look at the badge on my waist as I sat across from her.

"You're back?" she asked.

"This morning. Price and I came to an understanding."

"Glad to hear it. I was hoping you would."

"I'm assuming there was an office pool over whether I'd beg for my job back."

"There was, and I'm pretty sure I just won."

"What made you so sure?"

"I didn't think your husband was guilty."

"Why's that?" I asked.

"I don't know. Just a gut instinct. He looked completely shocked that we were even there. I've been on a lot of arrests. You can always tell when they know why we're at their door. They may try to act surprised, but the eyes always give it away."

"Thank you again for looking out for my niece."

"It was no problem. We weren't expecting anyone else to be there."

A waitress came to the table, and Allison asked for a club sandwich and a Coke. I declined to order. The waitress left, and I turned back to Allison.

"My husband has been cleared, and Captain Price has authorized me to look into the case, especially as it pertains to the murder of Molly Randolph."

"You got the Randolph case? Not Shaw?"

"That's right."

"And you think they're connected?" she asked.

"Yes. I do."

"How so?"

"It's a bit of a long story."

I hated saying that, especially since I knew it wasn't fair for me to give her the third degree but not answer her questions in return.

"Tell me how the morning went down. When did you find out it was my husband you were arresting?"

"About an hour before we left for your house. None of us knew a thing before then."

"What did Shaw tell you?" I asked.

"Not much. He said your husband was going to be arrested for murder. He made some vague reference about an affair. That was it."

"Did he say anything about me?"

Allison hesitated.

"Don't worry. This conversation stays between the two of us."

"He warned us all not to contact you. He said there would be serious ramifications if we did."

"I'm sure."

"Davis and I went to your front door with Shaw. Shaw was the one who made the actual arrest. Davis took your husband out to the car. I watched over your niece. I stayed outside and notified the department there was a child present. I asked them to contact you."

"Then forensics came in?"

Allison nodded.

"They were already there. They went into the house right about the time I contacted the department."

"How many people total?" I asked.

Allison paused a moment while she tried to recall the scene.

"There were at least four forensics techs there. Four cops, too: Shaw, Davis, me, and Wilkins."

"Do you know who found the cell phone?" I asked.

"He didn't tell you?"

"No."

"It was Shaw. It wasn't like he was trying to keep it a secret, either. He seemed to want everyone to know that he'd found it. I assumed he'd have told you, like he wanted to rub it in your face."

"And the victim's hair in the master bathroom? Who found that?"

"I don't know. I think one of the forensics techs did. Shaw was outside with me when it was reported."

"He came outside after he found the phone?"

"Yes, and it came over the radio that you were on your way. Shaw came outside to warn me not to let you in the house."

"Of course he did. Do you remember how long it was from the time the search started and when Shaw found the phone?"

"I don't. I don't think it was that long, but I'm just not sure."

"Not long, though? Like maybe ten minutes or twenty minutes?"

"Don't know. Maybe twenty minutes, but that's just a guess."

"Was there anything that jumped out at you about the search?"

"What do you mean?" she asked.

"Anything out of the ordinary? Anything strange?"

"You mean other than the fact it was your house?"

"Yeah. I'm sorry you had to go through that."

"Why are you sorry?"

"Because I know it wasn't your call. It couldn't have been easy for you."

"It sure as hell wasn't easy for you, either. I can't imagine what you both must have been going through. I'm just glad it worked out."

It hadn't worked out, not really, but I didn't see what good it would be to debate the point. Two young women were dead, and we still had no idea who'd killed them. We also didn't know who'd framed Poe, but I was getting closer and closer to feeling comfortable with naming the suspect.

The waitress came back to deliver Allison's sandwich and drink. I thanked Allison for her time and her willingness to even talk to me.

I left the restaurant and phoned Poe after I climbed into my car.

"So you decided to go back to work. Did you at least make Price get on his hands and knees and beg you to come back?" he asked.

"Trust me. I wanted to, but no, I didn't ask him."

"Is there any way you can come to Lahaina now? I have a surprise for you."

"What is it?"

"I found Brooklyn's laptop."

"Please don't tell me you broke into her apartment."

"Would I do something reckless like that?"

"Do I need to even answer that question?"

"I suppose not, but that's not how I found it."

Poe then told me about his encounter with the video producer and how he was only willing to give the laptop to a police officer.

"Well, it's a good thing I've got the badge back, isn't it?"

"I'll text you his business address, and get this: She left the laptop at his place two weeks before she was killed."

"He didn't think that was weird?"

"Of course, he did, and he tried calling her multiple times to give it back. There has to be something on that laptop. There's got to be a good reason she left it there."

"So you gave me some interesting information. Let me return the favor."

I told Poe about the computer search that revealed Shaw had searched for Genesis Riley's information before he'd even had a reason to talk to her. I also informed him that Shaw had been the one to find the burner phone in Poe's home office.

"That is interesting. Sounds like you've had a productive morning."

"You, too."

"But I haven't even told you all of it. You still need to watch that video of some guy delivering the money to Molly's front porch."

"What are you talking about?" I asked.

Poe told me about the video camera Molly had installed to secretly capture footage of the person who'd been delivering her payouts.

"Shame it didn't capture his face, but that would have been too easy, wouldn't it?"

"Don't worry. We're getting close," he said.

"Okay. I'm on my way back now. I'll meet you at that video shop."

I ended the call, and the address for the store appeared on my screen a few seconds later.

Poe was right. We were getting close, but things have a way of twisting and turning just when you think you've figured it all out.

Chapter 21
The Laptop

Perspective: Poe

I met Alana outside the Beautiful Memories video shop. We went inside, and I introduced her to Ted Anders. She showed him her police badge, and he handed over Brooklyn's laptop.

Something interesting happened after that. He told Alana the password to the computer. Apparently, Brooklyn had mentioned once in the shop that she wondered why she'd created such a long password. Ted had asked her what it was before he'd realized that she probably wouldn't tell him. She did, though, and it was a long one: maui is really expensive. All lower case letters.

I can't speak for Alana, but I found it pretty odd that she'd have let Ted know her password. He told me he never used her computer, so there really wasn't a good reason to tell him. Actually, there was one reason that I could think of: She wanted him to be able to access it if something were to happen to her. I knew I was firmly planting both of my feet into conspiracy theory territory, but I couldn't come up with another explanation.

I followed Alana back to our house. I grabbed a beer and joined her at the kitchen table. She powered the laptop on, and the security log-on box appeared in the middle of a photograph of a Maui sunset. I actually recognized the photo as one Brooklyn's former boss had taken. Of course, I could have just assumed he'd taken it. Maybe Brooklyn actually had, and her boss just took credit for it.

"Time for the moment of truth. Does the password work?" she asked.

She typed "maui is really expensive" and the sunset image was replaced with the desktop display a moment later.

"You're in," I said.

I leaned toward her, and we looked at the computer. The screen was almost completely filled with folders.

"Anderson. Hawthorne. Black. Kelly. They're all labeled with people's last names," she said.

"Open one of them. They're probably all wedding photos."

Alana clicked a few of the folders open, and we saw a variety of photographs that ranged from families at scenic Maui locations to weddings at a variety of resorts and beaches. I did a quick look at all of the names of the folders. There must have been at least twenty last names and combinations of last names. That's when one jumped out at me. It was in the bottom right-hand corner of the screen.

"'Asshole.' I'm not sure I want to know what's in that folder," I said.

Alana double-clicked on the folder, and we saw dozens of images of someone we both immediately recognized: me.

"I guess you're the asshole," she said.

"Thanks. I was hoping you were going to let that one pass."

I found the description of me a bit ironic. If you've read any of my other books, you'll know the word "asshole" seems to be a favorite description of my personality, especially by women. I'd kind of gotten used to it by now, but I did wish someone would get creative and use another insult.

"These look like surveillance photos. Everything's been taken at a distance," she said.

Alana was right. All of the images had a compressed look typical of a lens zoomed all the way to its maximum focal length. The shots were of me at various places across the island. I saw several of me entering and exiting Harry's. There were also shots of me in our driveway, as well as me walking the dog. It was more than a bit creepy. I also realized something unfortunate. My hair was starting to thin.

"This girl followed you everywhere," Alana continued.

"I can't believe I never spotted her."

"Who assumes someone is taking photos of you from the bushes?"

It was a good point, but I still thought I should have been much more attentive, especially after receiving the death threat the day after our wedding.

"What was she taking these photos for? Was she going to set up a hit on me?"

"She was clearly obsessed with you. They're several shots of you outside Harry's. You can tell they were taken at different times since your clothing changes. It wasn't a secret you owned the place. I think I remember you telling her," Alana said.

"Let's step back a second. Why did Brooklyn leave her laptop with her business partner? It couldn't be so someone would see these images of me."

"If anything, these photographs paint her in a terrible light. She didn't do anything illegal by taking them, but it clearly indicates she was thinking about it."

"Does that mean there's something else on this laptop that we haven't found yet?"

"Let's check her email."

Alana opened the Internet Explorer application and looked through her browser history. The most recent listing was for Google Mail. She clicked on the link, and the web page changed to the email site. Fortunately, Brooklyn had set the computer to remember the username and password. Alana was able to quickly gain access to her emails. Brooklyn had pinned one of the emails to the top. Alana opened it and saw it was an email Brooklyn had sent herself. There was no subject header, and the only thing in the body of the message was another web link.

Alana clicked on it, and we were rerouted to an old article about a high school football game.

"I wasn't expecting that," I said.

"Me, neither."

"What's the date on that article?"

"Looks like it was published over a decade ago. It was written by the local newspaper."

I read the headline.

"Maui High School wins championship."

Alana turned to me.

"Why in the world would Brooklyn be interested in this?"

I didn't respond since I had no idea what the answer could possibly be. I started to read the story and found out on the third paragraph.

"Bryan Sanders," I said.

I saw the muscles in Alana's neck tighten. She had good reason. Sanders was the guy who'd attacked her more than a year ago.

"Looks like he tossed the winning touchdown in the game," I continued. "Good for him."

"Guy goes from being a football star to a world-class sociopath."

"How well did Brooklyn know him?" she asked.

"Not well, or at least that's the impression I got. She claimed she only knew his first name."

"But you said she was the one who let him into the gallery to kill Gabriel."

"Yeah. Still, she might have been doing that on someone else's orders. That doesn't necessarily mean she was close to Sanders."

"This doesn't make any sense. How can a football championship relate to anything now?" she asked.

"Especially since Bryan Sanders is in prison as we speak. She couldn't have been scared of him after that, so what was the point in searching through his background?"

"There's bound to be much more recent stuff on him. Social media accounts. News stories from his trial. Why would Brooklyn want to go back so far?"

I read through the rest of the story, but no other names appeared with the exception of the football coach. It wasn't a name that sounded even vaguely familiar.

Alana minimized the sports story and looked at the list of emails again.

"She cared enough about his article to pin it to the very top."

"Was she trying to make sure someone found it quickly?" I asked.

"Had to be."

We spent the next hour combing through her emails from the last six months. Most of them were correspondence with clients. I didn't take a running tally, but if I had to guess, I would say she did about eight photography jobs in that time. That totaled to around 1.33 jobs per month. Based on the rates she quoted in the emails, she probably made around fifteen-hundred to two grand per month. That corresponded to Ted's claims that Brooklyn hadn't been doing well with her business.

I didn't know if Brooklyn had any other jobs. If she did, they weren't ever mentioned in the emails. That left me with the inescapable conclusion that she'd been beyond desperate when someone, whoever that might be, approached her and offered her money to help put me behind bars.

Speaking of that subject, there were zero messages about me in her Gmail account. She'd either deleted them a long time ago or she did everything by phone or in person.

"Did you ever get access to Brooklyn's phone records?" I asked.

"Mara did. I know what you're going to ask. There was nothing in there about you, minus those staged emails about the affair."

"Not even something that might have appeared to be written in some kind of code?"

"No. Nothing. That's not unusual, though. She probably used another phone. I would have."

"Try her documents folder," I suggested.

Alana opened it, and we searched through the twenty most recent Word documents she'd written. Most of them were contracts and invoices between Van Kirk Photography and her clients. There were no non-business documents, and there were certainly no files that related to Bryan Sanders or me or even Molly Randolph.

I don't want to imply the laptop was a bust, but it did leave me fairly disappointed. I didn't need to see the surveillance photographs to know the woman had been pretty pissed off at me. I couldn't blame her. I'd forced her into a bad spot, but I didn't have a choice. I needed to find my wife's attacker. I'm sure you would have done the same thing.

The surveillance photographs did bring up an intriguing question. Why even take them? They didn't show me doing anything weird. They certainly didn't show me following her, so I didn't see how they could possibly be used to frame me for doing something to her or even having an affair with her. As far as I could tell, I wasn't anywhere near her Kihei apartment complex in any of those photographs.

They might have been used to show a potential killer the typical places I traveled to on the island. If that was the case and Brooklyn had intended to hire someone to get rid of me, then how did she end up dead and not me? Don't get me wrong, I'm not complaining about still being alive.

Other than the photographs of me and the old news story about Bryan Sanders' football heroics, everything on the laptop appeared to be work-related. It wasn't a complete dead-end, but it was close.

I looked at the time on my watch. It was already mid-afternoon.

"Are you going back to work?" I asked.

"No. I think I want to spend some more time on this laptop. There has to be something we missed."

"Maybe we're over-thinking this. Maybe she just accidentally left her computer at the video shop."

"I doubt it. Why would she do that, especially since her business obviously relied on this computer?"

"Consider this theory: She told Ted she was going out for something to eat and would be right back. What if someone approached her at the restaurant and she didn't have the chance to go back. Maybe they wouldn't let her. Do you even know what she was doing the last few days of her life?"

"I don't know. I don't think I buy that. Her phone records show she was actively using the phone. I think you're implying she might have been kidnapped or something so she couldn't have gone back for the laptop."

"You're right. It's a lousy theory."

"It's not lousy. It's….well, you're right. It was pretty bad."

"Thanks for your honesty," I said, and I laughed.

"No problem."

I looked at my empty beer bottle.

"I think I'm going to get another beer. Want one?"

"No, thanks. I'm good."

I started for the kitchen when the doorbell rang.

"I'll get it," I said.

I headed for the front door. Maui the dog raced past me. He was in full-on attack mode.

"If it's the police, I'm going to tell them I'm not home," I continued.

"Don't even joke about that," Alana yelled from the other room.

I looked through the peephole and saw the one person who would make me prefer another arrest to talking to them. It was Alana's mother.

Chapter 22
The I-Love-Poe Club

Perspective: Poe

The way I saw it, I had two possibilities. I could either open the door and graciously let Ms. Hu inside my home, or I could run back into the living room and hide under the coffee table with the dog. Then a third possibility came to me. I could always dash into the backyard, dive into the swimming pool, and try to hold my breath until she left. I realize mother-in-law's get a bad rap, but mine deserved it. She really did.

I don't know how long I stood at the front door with my hand on the doorknob and the dog barking his head off. It might have been one second. It might have been ten. Hell, it could have been a full minute. My brain seemed to shut down as I anticipated the uncomfortable interaction that was about to come.

"Who is it?" Alana yelled, and her question snapped me out of my trance. I opened the door.

"Hello, Ms. Hu."

"Good evening, Edgar."

I never knew what kind of greeting I'd get with her. Sometimes she called me Edgar. Sometimes Poe. Sometimes I got a "Hey, you." I still hadn't deciphered what they all meant in terms of her attitude toward me when she said it.

I held the door open for her, and she walked into the foyer.

"Is Alana home?"

"Yes, she's in the back."

I led Ms. Hu to the kitchen. Alana was still seated at the table. She looked up from Brooklyn's laptop, and there was no misinterpreting her surprised expression. I wasn't sure how to interpret that. Something had clearly happened between the two of them, and it wasn't good. Alana hadn't mentioned that, nor had she given me a clue that something had even occurred. It didn't take much imagination to know what it was about: me.

"Hello, Alana."

"Have you come to apologize?"

Apologize? That was a shocker. I don't mean to say that Alana had never confronted her mother. She just made it a rule to never do it in front of me. Sure, we were all technically related to each other now, but I wasn't blood. They talked differently around me than they did when I wasn't around. How do I know that? Because most families are like that. Alana had told me, as well, without going into specifics.

"Perhaps I should let you two have some time to yourselves," I said.

Yeah, it was a cowardly move, but do you blame me?

"No. You should stay. This is your house," Alana said.

"I understand that, but it might be easier for you two to talk if I'm not around. I certainly don't want anyone having to carefully choose their words because I'm here."

"Oh, I don't think that will be a problem for my mother. She never carefully chooses her words. She says whatever she damn well pleases."

"Don't curse in front of me, Alana," her mother said.

Alana stood. This was about to get really good or really bad. Where was my popcorn?

"I didn't get around to telling Poe about our last conversation. Maybe I should tell him now," Alana said.

"That's why I wanted to come by. I regret some of the things I said."

"Some?"

Ms. Hu didn't respond.

Alana turned to me.

"My mother came by our house the night you were arrested. I thought she was coming by to give me comfort. Instead, she came by to tell me she was more than willing to be a witness for the prosecution."

"That's ridiculous. I said no such thing."

"You're right. You didn't use those exact words. I think what you said is that you never liked my husband and you knew it was just a matter of time before he left me."

I was pretty sure that was my cue to exit the room, but I couldn't now. My feet stayed glued to the carpet.

Ms. Hu turned to me.

"I was wrong. I'm sorry. I came by to say that. Also to say I'm glad the charges were dropped."

"I don't know what to say, Ms. Hu. I've always tried to get you to like me. Alana and I are in this for the long haul. I absolutely don't want things between you and me to be bad."

"Neither do I."

I know exactly what you're thinking right now. The woman is full of it. Yeah, I realized that, too, but I was in a tough spot. There was no way to win this battle. I knew the woman was lying. She didn't like me, and she never would. Nothing I ever said or did would change that. I'd held out hope that I might be able to swing her to my side at some point. I was never under the illusion that she was going to join the I-Love-Poe club, but I thought she might, just might, come to the understanding that it was better for all of us if she just faked being nice.

"Well, you've said your piece. I think you should go now," Alana said.

"There are still some things I'd like to say to you. In private, if possible."

"I thought you just said you wanted things to be better between you and Poe. Now you're asking him to leave the room?"

"It's okay, Alana. I was actually just getting ready to take the dog on a walk," I said.

I grabbed Maui's leash off the back of one of the stools in the kitchen and called to the dog. He sprinted toward me like I was holding out a piece of meat. Apparently, he didn't want to be around Ms. Hu any longer than I did.

I hooked the leash to his harness and took him outside through the garage.

I had no way of knowing how long their conversation would last, and I didn't feel like taking the dog on a multi-mile walk, especially in the heat of the mid-afternoon.

I turned left at the end of the driveway and headed for Foxx's house. I didn't know if he'd be home, but I had the code to his front door. I didn't think he'd mind if I crashed at his house for the next hour.

Foxx's SUV wasn't in the driveway, but that didn't mean he hadn't parked it inside his garage. I walked up the front porch and entered the code on the lock. I heard the deadbolt turn, and I opened the door.

"Foxx, you in here?"

I didn't get a reply, but I walked inside anyway. I undid Maui's leash, and he took off running. He and I had lived in this house for a couple of years, so he knew his way around.

I walked into the kitchen to grab myself that second beer I wanted before Ms. Hu rang the doorbell. I opened the refrigerator and pulled out a Negra Modelo. I grabbed the bottle opener off the side of the refrigerator and popped the top. The beer was ice cold, and I took a long pull.

The liquid was halfway down my throat when I almost choked on it. Why, you might ask? Well, it had something to do about the woman's scream behind me.

I turned around and saw a completely naked woman in the den. She looked at me a second, then covered her breasts with one hand and her lower region with the other. I averted my eyes, but not before I saw Foxx run out from the master bedroom. I didn't see him well enough to know whether he was also completely naked, but he probably was. I doubted they were there as part of a book club.

"What the hell's going on?" he yelled.

"Sorry, man, I had no idea you had company."

"What are you doing here?"

"Mom-in-law is at my house."

"Say no more."

Then Foxx introduced me to his friend. I still kept my eyes looking away from them.

"Stacy, this is Poe. Poe, this is Stacy."

"Nice to meet you," I said.

Maui the dog barked a couple of times, and I guessed he was trying to get Foxx's attention.

"And that little monster is his dog."

"Hello," the woman said.

Her voice seemed strained, and I didn't blame her. This was awkward as hell.

"Sorry again. I'll just grab the dog, and we'll go back home," I said.

"Don't worry about it. We'll be in the back. Finish your beer. Watch TV. I know how Alana's mother is."

I'm sure Stacy, whoever she might be, wasn't too fond of that suggestion, but I also wasn't in any kind of rush to go home. So I took him up on his offer.

"I'll just go out back by the pool. Nice meeting you, Stacy."

"Nice meeting you."

I took my beer and walked toward the sliding glass door. I heard Maui's feet on the tiled floor behind me. I opened the door, and we both went outside. The weather was still hot, but we could at least cool ourselves in the shade under the patio umbrella.

Maui the dog bypassed the umbrella and ran straight for the far back of the yard. He had this weird obsession with barking at the waves as they crashed into the rock jetty just off the shore of Foxx's property.

I sat under the umbrella for several minutes until I got really hot. I stripped off my t-shirt and sandals and dove into the swimming pool. Foxx's pool was even nicer than mine, and I spent about thirty minutes swimming laps and just lounging in the cool water.

I thought about the investigation as I swam. I felt fairly certain that the same person who killed Brooklyn also killed Molly. It was probably also the same person who'd framed me. I'd discovered that Brooklyn had been following me for weeks, maybe even months, but I still didn't know what her intentions had been.

I couldn't wrap my head around the fact that she'd been murdered. Sure, people are killed for a lot of reasons: greed, power, revenge, love. They're also killed as a form of self-preservation if the murderer thinks the other person means to do them harm. But what kind of harm could Brooklyn have wanted to do to them? If she wanted me hurt, which the surveillance photographs seemed to indicate, I didn't understand how she could have run afoul of whoever wanted to frame me for her murder. It seemed like they would have been on the same team, so what had happened between the two of them?

There was also that weird article about Bryan Sanders as a high school quarterback. What did that have to do with anything? How did Brooklyn even know to look for it and why? Why was it so important that she pinned it to the top of her email account? Speaking of the email, why had she really left her laptop with her business partner? If she was truly worried about something, then why didn't she just flee the island? She certainly had the money after receiving those large payments for the last few months.

Finally, there was the biggest mystery of all. Would I ever have a decent relationship with Alana's mother? Actually, that wasn't much of a mystery. It didn't take Sherlock Holmes to figure that one out. The woman hated me, and it wasn't likely that would ever change. It looked like Alana had finally figured that out as well. Maybe she'd always known but still didn't want to give up, at least not fully.

I climbed out of the pool and looked at my watch. It hadn't yet been a full hour since I'd left home. Was she still there? Probably not, but I decided to give it another ten minutes just to be safe.

Oh, one more thing. I'm sure you male readers are disappointed in me for not describing the body of the woman in Foxx's house. Well, a gentleman never talks about those things, but I will give you one clue: It was spectacular.

Chapter 23
Clouds like Blood

Perspective: Poe

Sometimes I think the universe is secretly monitoring my thoughts and words and deciding to do the exact opposite of what I want just to piss me off. I'd specifically said I didn't want to keep doing these investigations, and I'd mentioned multiple times that I couldn't deal with bad stuff happening to me or my loved ones anymore.

Sure, that's a naïve way to view life. Bad things happen to everyone, and they always seem to come at the worst times. But I figured it was worth a shot. That clearly hadn't happened, though, and I was starting to suspect someone or something of a higher power was trying to see how much I could endure.

One could always quote that old adage: "That which does not kill you only makes you stronger." I used to believe that supposed truth when I was a younger man and hadn't really suffered any physical or emotional injuries with the exception of the occasional bad romantic relationship. Now, after being on the receiving end of a few good butt kickings, I feel safe in thinking that the person who wrote the above saying never actually had anything bad happen to them. That which does not kill you will always leave you bruised, battered, weaker, and sometimes even crying for a little bit of mercy.

After my brief stay at Foxx's house, I grabbed the dog and walked back to my house. Fortunately, Ms. Hu was gone. The thought briefly passed my mind that she'd pulled her vehicle into my garage to trick me and was currently waiting behind some closed door so she could jump out and surprise me. The woman was not one to trifle with, and I still couldn't figure out what the best course of action should be. I'd clearly been her verbal punching bag, and I wasn't sure how much more I was willing to take.

When I got back to the house, I found Alana exactly where I'd last seen her. She was at the kitchen table and going through the laptop. There's not much point in recounting the exact conversation between the two of us here, so I'll just sum it up with a few lines.

Me: You and your mother work everything out?

Alana: No.

Me: Want to talk about it?

Alana: No.

Me: Find anything else interesting on Brooklyn's computer?

Alana: No.

I spent the next few hours sitting in my office upstairs and writing down everything that had happened to me since getting greeted at my door by Detective Shaw and the other officers. I also included extensive notes on what Alana and Foxx had told me.

I knew I'd use these recollections later to write this book, but I was mainly doing it to try to encourage my subconscious to come up with some fantastic revelation on the case of the murders of Brooklyn and Molly and the failed frame job of yours truly. Unfortunately, my subconscious mind was apparently taking a nap and had zero interest in waking up and trying to figure this mystery out.

After finishing my notes, I sent Foxx a text and apologized again for inadvertently interrupting his romantic afternoon. He wrote back and said it wasn't a problem. There isn't much that embarrasses Foxx.

He sent me a follow-up text a few minutes later and asked me to confirm just how hot his new girl was. I didn't think Alana secretly monitored my texts, but I wasn't willing to risk it, so I wrote Foxx back and said I hadn't gotten a good look at the naked girl.

I commented that I was sure she'd been attractive and wished him a successful relationship with her. I concluded by saying that I hoped he could one day find someone as wonderful, gorgeous, and intelligent as Alana. Foxx followed that up with asking if Alana was actually the one who had my phone and was currently texting him. I didn't respond as to leave it a mystery.

I concluded my evening with a long run. I'm sure you're questioning my sanity as to why I would want to run five miles in the dark. Again, I was still trying to work that subconscious thing. You can't think about too much when you're trying to convince your aching legs to keep moving forward across that hard pavement. Many revelations had come to me as I walked my cool down and headed back to the house. Did that happen that night? Nope. I drew a big blank again.

I went out to the pool and sat on the patio while I listened to the waves. I thought back to my house in Virginia. It offered the less-than-spectacular view of my neighbor's house. My neighbor liked to leave the shades up in his bathroom. I often had the unfortunate experience of seeing him standing at his toilet as he relieved himself. I don't know if he ever saw me watching him. It wasn't like I ever looked for more than a split second. No one wants to see a shirtless three-hundred-pound man standing in front of the john. He had to have known people could see him through the window, though, so why did he leave that damn shade up?

Sorry, these are just the strange places my brain drifted to as I tried to figure out the investigation.

The point of all of this was also to say that I was keenly aware of just how lucky I was to be sitting on a patio chair and staring out at the night sky above the Pacific Ocean. I didn't take it for granted, especially after being threatened with never seeing it again.

I thought about Shaw and wondered what he was doing at that moment. Was he still trying to figure out a way to nail me for a crime I didn't commit? Had he even realized or accepted that I didn't kill Brooklyn? If so, was he any closer to finding out who really killed that poor girl?

I had a couple more beers while I sat at the pool. Then I made my way inside and took a long hot shower to wash the sweat off. Alana and I hadn't really talked much since I'd gotten back from Foxx's house. She was still in a bad mode when we went to bed. I did the typical annoying male thing and asked her once more if she wanted to talk about her mother. She said no again.

I don't know why men seem intent on bugging women when they're feeling less than one hundred percent. Ladies, on behalf of all men across the globe, I'd like to personally apologize for that behavior. That doesn't mean I'm going to stop doing it. I just can't seem to control myself, but I am aware at how much it gets on your nerves, or at the very least, Alana's nerves.

I'd hoped to sleep late in the morning since I was pretty exhausted from the trauma of being locked in jail, as well as the busy time I'd had the day before. The long run hadn't helped matters. Maui the dog had other thoughts, though. He woke me up around five-thirty in the morning as he is often prone to do. The little guy doesn't exactly have the largest bladder, and he's considerate enough not to pee on the bedroom carpet. Still, I wished I could find a way to teach him how to use doorknobs.

I swung myself out of bed and slipped my shorts on. Maui and I walked downstairs. I grabbed his leash, a plastic bag, and flashlight so I could actually find his business in order to pick it up. One doesn't want or need angry neighbors who don't appreciate finding Maui's little yard gifts.

I hooked the leash up to his harness and opened the door. It was still fairly dark outside, and the neighborhood was quiet. The dog does this weird thing where he practically leaps through the open doorway but stops suddenly on the front porch so everyone can take notice of his sudden appearance. It's like he views himself as a pro wrestler who's making his entrance into the ring. I don't know if he's really that cocky or if he's simply compensating for his diminutive frame.

I was about halfway down the driveway when I heard a noise that confused me. It sounded like a car moving slowly down the road, but I couldn't see any headlights. There are two large trees by the curb, one in my yard and one in the neighbor's. I looked in the direction of the noise but couldn't see anything beyond the trees. The car appeared a second later. It was one of those moments where every cell in your body says something is very wrong. I assume that's a holdover from early man's need to survive in the wild, but my sleep-deprived brain was too slow to fully grasp what was going on.

The gunshots sounded like cannons exploding in the night. The first round roared past my ear. The second or third one ripped through my left forearm. The fourth one hit my side, and I went down. I think I heard two more shots after that, but I'm not really sure. I thought I heard some weird whooshing sound somewhere behind me. I saw the car speed off out of the corner of my eye.

I was on my back and looking up at the sky. The moon was almost full that night, and I could see several large clouds floating above me. In a weird kind of way, there was something peaceful about it. I thought I heard the dog barking beside me, but his barks sounded somewhat muted, as if he were barking inside a chamber of some kind.

I pressed down on my side and then lifted my hand up to my face. It was covered with dark blood. Some of it dropped down on my face. It felt warm against my skin.

"Poe! Poe!" I heard from the direction of the house.

I heard footsteps on the driveway, and I saw Alana kneel beside me a moment later.

"What happened?"

"Dark car. Maybe black or dark blue."

"Did you see the driver?"

"No."

I felt her lift up my t-shirt.

"We need to put pressure on this."

I heard her tear the bottom of her t-shirt off, or maybe she tore mine. I'm not really sure.

"This is going to hurt," she continued.

She pressed down on my side, and more waves of pain rushed through my body.

"How bad is it?" I asked.

"You'll be okay. I promise."

Something in her voice didn't sound that reassuring. Actually, that something in her voice wasn't a mystery. I knew exactly what it was. It was fear.

"This is Detective Alana Hu. There's been a shooting at…."

She told emergency services our address. I kept looking up at the sky. The clouds had already moved in those few seconds since Alana had been out with me. They'd taken on this pattern that almost looked like liquid. It kind of reminded me of blood as it flowed from the body.

"My husband has received multiple gunshot wounds. One is to the stomach. Get an ambulance here immediately."

She leaned over me again.

"You'll be all right."

"Where's the dog?" I asked.

"You're still holding onto the leash. It's wrapped around your wrist."

I thought back to those photographs I'd seen on Brooklyn's computer. There were several shots of me walking the dog near my house. The obvious reason for her photos had been that someone was planning something that I wasn't going to like. I'd hoped I'd escaped that fate. I was wrong.

I closed my eyes.

"Stay with me, Poe."

"I think this is bad."

"You'll be fine. Don't give up on me. Don't you do it."

I opened my eyes.

"It was a dark car. Maybe black."

"I know. You told me."

"The security cameras. I'm sure they caught it."

"I'll check them in a little while. I'm not leaving you."

"Is the ambulance coming?"

"Yes. It will be here soon."

"I didn't think it would end like this."

"Nothing's ending. You're going to be okay."

"I love you."

"I love you, but you're going to be okay. You're going to be okay."

I closed my eyes.

Chapter 24
The Dark Sedan

Perspective: Alana

I heard the gunshots and sat up in bed. The shots were so loud that they sounded like they'd come from inside the house. I thought Poe had said something earlier about taking the dog out, but I couldn't be sure if I'd actually been dreaming. I looked to his side of the bed and saw it empty. I knew at once he'd been targeted.

I grabbed my phone and gun, which I always kept on the nightstand, and rushed down the stairs. The gun shots had stopped several seconds ago, and I'd heard a car roar away. I ran outside and saw Poe lying on the driveway. There was already a pool of blood forming around him by the time I got there. The wound in his side looked vicious, and my fear was that the bullet had torn through his vital organs.

"Oh my God, Poe."

I called 911 and told them to send an ambulance. I knew how long it would take them to get there. I hoped he could hold on that long.

"Is the ambulance coming?"

"Yes. It will be here soon."

"I didn't think it would end like this."

"Nothing's ending. You're going to be okay."

"I love you."

"I love you, but you're going to be okay. You're going to be okay."

My brain couldn't process the fact that Poe might not make it, but there was so much blood, and it wouldn't stop coming out of his body.

I called Foxx while I waited for the ambulance. I saw him running down the street within ninety seconds of talking to me. Poe was unconscious by the time he got to us.

"Oh my God, is he…."

"No. He's still got a pulse."

Foxx kneeled down beside Poe.

"You're gonna be all right, buddy. You're gonna make it. Don't be afraid."

I looked at Foxx.

"I need you to do something for me."

Foxx didn't respond.

"Foxx! Listen!"

He turned to me.

"I need you to go inside the house. The front room. Go to the security system and pull up the front yard cameras. Rewind to about five minutes ago. I want you to tell me exactly what you see. What kind of car was it? What color? Did the person get out of the car? If so, what did they look like?"

Foxx didn't move. He looked like he was in some kind of trance.

"I need you to do this for me. Now."

Foxx stood and ran toward the house. I turned back to Poe. He was still unconscious. I leaned down to him and whispered in his ear.

"Don't leave me. I love you too much to let you go. Don't you leave me."

Foxx was outside before the ambulance arrived. What the hell was taking them so long?

"We can't wait any longer. We've got to get him to the hospital now. He's bleeding out. Help me get him into my car," I said.

"I'll carry him. You get the keys."

I picked up the dog and ran into the house. When I came outside again, Foxx already had Poe on the backseat.

"Can you come with me?"

"Do you have to ask?" he said.

We both climbed into the car. I hit the sirens and backed out of the driveway.

"Put pressure on that wound as best as you can," I said.

Foxx leaned toward the backseat and pressed down on Poe's side.

"His skin is cold, Alana."

"He's probably gone into shock."

I pushed down even harder on the accelerator. I turned right onto the main road and flew through the red light. I looked up at it as we passed and confirmed the presence of the security camera. It would capture a car either turning right or left of my neighborhood. It was a fortunate break.

"Did you see who shot him on the home security system?" I asked.

"I saw the car. The driver never got out."

"What kind of car was it?"

"It was a sedan, like a Ford Focus or something that size. The color was hard to tell. Maybe black or dark green or blue."

I handed Foxx my phone.

"Find Allison Jenkins for me and call her number. Put it on speaker mode."

Foxx dialed her number and placed the phone on the dashboard in front of me.

Allison answered after several rings.

"This is Jenkins."

"Allison, this is Alana. I need you to check the traffic cameras in Kaanapali. You know where I live. Find the camera near the turn off for my neighborhood. There's only one way in and out, so they had to have gone by it. Check for a dark sedan, maybe a Ford Focus. It should have driven down Honoapiilani Highway within the last twenty minutes. I need the name and address for the person who owns that car, and I want it within the next hour."

"Alana, what's going on?"

"Poe has been shot. Call emergency services and tell them we weren't able to wait for the ambulance. We're headed to the hospital now."

"What's your ETA?"

"I should be there in the next thirty minutes. Tell them to prep for surgery. He has a gunshot wound to the stomach."

I ended the call before she could reply.

"I can barely hear him breathing," Foxx said.

"Hold on, Poe. Hold on."

We passed the ambulance about halfway to the hospital. I looked in the rearview mirror and saw it make a U-turn on the highway and start to follow us back.

Three nurses and the ER doctor were waiting for us as we pulled in front of the emergency room entrance behind the hospital. They pulled Poe out of the backseat and put him onto a stretcher. He was rushed into surgery, and Foxx and I were suddenly left with nothing to do but wait.

My phone rang about thirty minutes after we'd gotten to the hospital. It was Allison.

"What do you have?"

"Five cars passed through that intersection in the time frame you gave. Only one is a dark sedan."

"Did you get the license plate?"

"Yes. The car belongs to Pika Mahoe. He lives in Lahaina. I've already put out an APB."

"I want a patrol sent to his house now. He's probably not there, but we need to check. The suspect should be considered armed and dangerous."

"How's your husband?"

"He's still in surgery."

There was a long pause.

Then Alison said, "I'll contact you again as soon as I hear from the patrol."

"Thanks. I really appreciate you making this happen so quickly."

"Good luck. I'm praying for him to come through."

I ended the call and Foxx walked up to me.

"Did they find the car?"

"No, but we got the owner's name."

"Who is it?"

"Pika Mahoe."

"The guy who was in my bar this week? I never should have let that bastard go."

"How could you predict this?"

Poe was in surgery another hour before the surgeon finally came out. He had an exhausted look on his face, which sent a terror through me.

"Is he okay?" Foxx asked.

"The bullet tore through a small part of his intestines. We had to remove that section. He lost a lot of blood. It was good you didn't wait for the ambulance. He wouldn't have survived otherwise."

"Will he make it?" Foxx asked.

"Yes, but the danger now is infection. We need to keep a close eye on him. I'm sorry, but he's not out of the woods yet."

"When can we see him?" I asked.

"He's still in recovery. Give us about twenty minutes. Then one of you can come back."

"Thanks, Doc," Foxx said, and he hugged him.

Foxx is a tough guy, but he can also be as sensitive as they come when the right people are involved.

My phone rang just as the doctor walked away.

"This is Detective Hu."

"They've found the car," Allison said. "It was abandoned near the corner of Honoapiilani and North Kihei. They found several spent 9mm bullet casings in the front seat."

"Any news from the patrol?"

"Nothing yet."

"Call them. They need to get their asses to his house now."

I ended the call.

"Did they find him?" Foxx asked.

"No, just his car, but they'll get him soon. There aren't many places he can hide."

"Does he blame Poe for Molly's death? Maybe he thinks Poe killed her for helping to frame him."

"He has to. Why else would he do this?"

Foxx didn't really have an answer, and we both sat there in silence.

Then Foxx said, "He's going to be all right, Alana."

I knew what he was really saying, and I appreciated his careful approach.

He was telling me to calm the hell down. He was right, of course. There had been a fury and a fear that had been racing through me since I'd heard those gunshots. I needed to let it go. I couldn't let it consume me and cloud my thoughts for what needed to come next. Poe needed me to be focused.

"This is twice you've helped save one of us. I don't know how to thank you," I said.

"Do me a favor and stop getting yourselves into these life and death situations. You're both going to give me a stroke."

I wanted to laugh, but I was too drained to do much of anything but sit there.

"Would you do me a favor? Call Hani in a little while. Let her know what's happened."

"Of course. What about your mother?" he asked.

"Hani can tell her. I'm not calling."

The nurse eventually walked out, and she escorted me to the back where I found Poe asleep. The only thing that could be heard was the rhythmic beating of his heart on the monitor. It was the greatest sound I'd ever heard.

I suddenly realized today was our wedding anniversary. I think we'd both forgotten about it the night before. Maybe Poe hadn't, but I'd been too stuck on that laptop and trying to push my mother's drama out of my head.

I couldn't stop looking at him as I sat there. He meant more to me than anyone. It was ironic since we really hadn't know each other that long, and now I couldn't picture my life without him. He'd come into my life and shaken everything up. He'd changed how I saw myself and what I wanted out of life. He'd given me a sense of confidence I didn't know I possessed.

I thought of Pika. He'd tried to take all of that from me. He wouldn't get away with it.

Chapter 25
Pika

Perspective: Alana

Poe got transferred to a private room. He woke up within the first few minutes of being in the new room. He looked at me, but I'm not sure he could tell who I was. He was pretty drugged up, and I wasn't sure when the fog would finally lift. Foxx stayed with me for the first hour. Then he went home so he could try to get some sleep.

My phone rang shortly after he left. I thought it might have been Hani since Foxx had said he'd called her and told her about the attack on Poe. It wasn't Hani, though. It was Allison.

"They found him," she said.

"Where?"

"His house."

"Have they taken him into custody? Where is he now?"

"There's no point in doing that."

"Why? What happened?"

"He's dead."

I ended the call and turned to Poe. He was out. I exited the room and asked the nurses to contact me when Poe was awake. I left the hospital and walked out to my car. It was a hot day, and the sun blared down on me. I was about halfway to Pika's house when I realized I was still in a tank top and shorts. I didn't want to go to a crime scene looking like this. A shower and change of clothes would have to wait, though. This was more important.

Pika's home was in Lahaina, not far from Molly's. There were two police cars parked in the front of the tiny beige house. One belonged to the two officers Allison had sent earlier. The other vehicle belonged to Allison. She came out of the house and walked to me as I climbed out of my car.

Her eyes widened as she looked at my outfit. Then it dawned on me it wasn't just the informal clothing. My white top and shorts were covered in Poe's blood.

"How is he doing?" she asked.

"He's going to pull through."

"I have a gym shirt in my bag. It's clean. Would you like it?"

"Yes. Thank you."

I followed her to her car. She popped the trunk and fished a black t-shirt out of a leather bag. I climbed into the passenger seat of her car and quickly changed into it.

I got out of the car and thanked her again for the shirt.

"So, what do we have here?" I asked.

"They did a walk around the property when they didn't get a response at the front door. They found a broken window pane on the side of the house."

"Where is the body?"

"In the kitchen."

I followed Allison inside, and she led me to the back of the house. The place had been thoroughly tossed. Every drawer was pulled out and its contents dumped. Furniture cushions had been pulled away. Area rugs were turned upside down. Even photographs on the wall had been pulled off and were lying on the floor.

The two other officers were standing in the middle of everything. They both turned to me at the same time.

"Detective," one of them said, and he nodded to me.

"Go to the neighbors' houses. Start knocking on doors. See if anyone heard or saw anything. Someone must have made a hell of a racket in here," I said.

"Yes, ma'am," the other officer said.

Allison and I walked into the kitchen, and I saw Pika's body in front of a small, round table. He was about a foot away on one of two matching chairs. His head was slumped forward, but his body hadn't fallen off the chair because his hands were tied behind him and connected to the back support. There was blood all over the front of his torso and on the tops of his legs. There was also blood covering a large section of the tiled floor.

"They slit his throat ear to ear," Allison said.

It was the same manner of death as Molly Randolph. There was something that was different, though. Pika had been tortured. Three of his fingers had been severed and were placed on the table in front of him.

I placed my hand on his bare arm. The skin was cold already.

I looked around the house. In addition to the kitchen, there were two small bedrooms, one bathroom with a shower but no tub, and one medium-sized living room. Every room had been trashed, including the bathroom where all of the contents of the cabinet under the sink had been scattered across the floor. The cover to the toilet tank had been removed and was lying cracked on the floor of the shower. The killer had clearly been searching for something, and I got the distinct impression they hadn't found it.

I turned and saw Allison standing in the bathroom doorway.

"Did Pika call in the theft of his car?" I asked.

"I'll check."

I walked back into the kitchen and took another look at Pika. This time I saw three cuts in the bottom of his shirt. It looked like he'd been stabbed in addition to having his throat slit.

I went outside just as one of the officers returned to the house.

"Lady next door said she saw something last night. Some guy arguing with the victim."

"Okay. Thanks. I'll go talk to her."

I walked to the other house. The woman stood on her porch and stared at Pika's house. She looked like she was in her sixties. She had short gray hair and was tall and heavy. She looked a bit like a retired football player.

"Ma'am, my name's Detective Alana Hu. I understand you saw something last night."

"Is he dead? The other cop wouldn't tell me," she said.

The woman didn't waste time.

"Yes, ma'am, I'm sorry to report that he is."

"He was a nice boy. Didn't deserve it."

"No, he didn't. No one does."

But I could think of a few people who probably did.

"What did you see?" I asked.

"This guy came to talk to Pika last night. He was one of you."

"He was a police officer?"

"He's wasn't wearing a uniform, but I saw the badge on his waist."

"What time was this?" I asked.

"Around eight. I just got home. I was walking to my house when I heard them."

"Were they outside?"

"Yeah, on the front porch."

"Did you hear what they said?"

"The detective was really mad. He kept threatening Pika. Said he would arrest him for not bringing the video in. I don't know what video he was talking about."

"Did you see them ever go inside the house?"

"No. I went inside my house, and I watched them through the window. The guy left pretty soon after that."

"Have you ever had any problems in this neighborhood before? Break-ins? Disturbances?" I asked.

"Sure. My house got robbed a few years ago, but nothing recent, not until today."

"Where did Pika normally park his car?"

"On the street."

"Do you remember seeing it last night?"

"Yeah. It was here."

"When do you get up in the morning?" I asked.

"Around seven."

"You didn't happen to notice if the car was still there, did you?"

"Nope. I never bothered to look. No reason to."

"If you saw the detective again, do you think you would recognize him?"

"Yeah. I got a real good look at him."

I pulled my phone out of my pocket. I opened the photo app and selected a shot of Poe. I walked up to the woman and showed it to her.

"Is this the guy?"

"No. Not him."

I opened the web browser on my phone and logged onto the Maui Police Department website. I found a photograph of Captain Price. I held the phone back to the neighbor.

"What about him?"

"No. That looks nothing like him."

"One more."

I pulled up a shot of Austin Show. I showed her the phone a third time.

"Him?"

"Yeah. That was him. He was the one arguing with Pika."

I turned when I heard a vehicle drive up behind me. It was the forensics team. I turned back to the neighbor.

"Thank you for your time, ma'am."

"What was Pika into?" she asked.

"I'm not sure exactly, but we'll find out."

I walked back to Pika's house and greeted the forensics team. We only had four people in the department, so I was one-hundred percent sure these were the same people who'd gone through my house just over a week ago. I hadn't seen or spoken to any of them since I'd been back.

I approached Hailey Roth, who was one of the younger members of the team. She was a tiny woman, barely standing five feet tall, so I knew she couldn't be the one who'd appeared on the secret video Molly had recorded outside her house.

"Can I speak to you a moment, Hailey?"

Hailey walked over to me, while the rest of the team headed for the house. She didn't say anything, and I could easily read the discomfort in her body language.

"The killer most likely got into the house through a broken window on the side," I said.

"We'll print it first thing."

"After you get done here, I'd like you to get back to the station and go through the car they found this morning off Kihei Road. I'm sure they've impounded it by now. The car was stolen from this property. Please compare the victim's prints with any prints you find in that car."

"Okay."

"One more thing, and I know this is uncomfortable, but who was the tech who found Van Kirk's hairs on the clothing in my house?"

"Can I ask what this have to do with this case, ma'am?"

"It has everything to do with it. Please answer my question."

"I found the hairs."

"Did someone direct you to the hamper?"

"What do you mean?"

"Did you go to the hamper on your own or did someone tell you to search it?"

"We always go through the clothing, but Detective Shaw made a point of telling me to search it."

"He told you to go through the bathroom or did he specifically mention the hamper?"

"He informed me that he'd found a cell phone in your husband's office. He then told me to check the dirty clothes."

"Was there anyone in the master bathroom when you entered?"

"No. I was the only one in there the entire time."

"Who else was on the second floor?"

"It was just Detective Shaw and myself at first."

"Where were the others?" I asked.

"Everyone was on the first floor. I believe a couple of people were assigned to the outside to check the garage and the back of the house."

"You said he told you he'd already found the phone when you got up there."

"That's right."

"So were you the one to put the phone in the evidence bag or did he do that?"

"I didn't do it, ma'am, but I assume one of the other techs did."

"Check for me. I want to know who bagged it."

"Of course."

"You've handled other crime scenes for Detective Shaw. Does he normally direct you where to concentrate your efforts?"

"Sometimes. It just depends."

"Depends on what?"

"Your husband's case was a big one. I got the impression he didn't want anything potentially overlooked."

"Thank you. Please let me know what you find in there, as well as that car."

Hailey started to walk away. Then she stopped and turned back to me.

"Ma'am, I want you to know I did everything by the book. I have nothing against you or your husband."

"I didn't accuse you of that."

"I know you didn't, but people in the office are talking."

"What are they saying?"

"Your husband's attorney said one of us planted that evidence."

"How do you know that's what she said?"

"You know how, ma'am. These things have a way of getting out."

"You assume I believe the same thing his attorney does based on what I've just asked you?"

She didn't respond.

"The next time you hear someone talking about this subject, please tell them this: I proved beyond a doubt my husband couldn't have killed that girl. That phone and those hairs got into my house somehow. Neither my husband nor I put them there. So, yes, someone planted them. I'm not saying it was you or anyone else on that team, but someone put them there."

"Yes, ma'am."

"Thank you."

Hailey left, and I watched her as she entered Pika's house. I knew she was angry with me, but I didn't care. She had a job to do, and she needed to concentrate on it, despite the fact that I doubted they'd find anything in that mess.

Molly's crime scene had rendered no evidence. This one probably wouldn't, either. The killer was careful. He knew what we looked for, but it was only a matter of time before he made a mistake. They always did.

Chapter 26
A Working Theory

Perspective: Poe

I opened my eyes and saw a dark and smooth surface several feet above me. The clouds had gone, and I had no idea where the stars were. I tried to roll over to look for the car. I had to get the license plate. The pain struck me as I tried to twist my body. I instinctively grabbed my side. I felt a think pad across my stomach. Something wasn't right. Where was I?

"Poe, don't move. Just lie still."

"Alana?" I asked into the darkness.

"No. It's Hani. Alana will be here soon."

"Where am I?"

"You're in the hospital."

"Is Alana all right?"

"Of course. She's the one who brought you here."

"What happened?"

"You were shot in your side and your arm. The doctors had to operate, but they fixed you up."

"Why is it so dark in here?"

"Because you were sleeping. Would you like me to turn the lights on?"

"Yes."

I heard Hani stand, and then I saw her a moment later as she walked across the room and turned the lights on. I had to blink several times to get my eyes to adjust.

Hani walked over to the bed and stood beside me.

"You certainly get yourself into a lot of trouble."

"I was walking the dog."

"Foxx says they found the car that belonged to the guy who shot you. I don't think they have him yet."

"Who was it?"

"He said it was some guy you both talked to in the bar this week. I don't know his name."

"His name's Pika Mahoe," a female voice said.

I turned my head and saw Alana enter the room.

"Thank you for staying with him," she told Hani.

"It wasn't a problem."

"How's Ava?" I asked.

"She's good. Foxx has her now. We met out in the parking lot an hour ago. They're probably back to his house by now. I'll bring her by to see you once you have a bit more time to heal," Hani said.

She turned to Alana.

"I'm sure you two want to be alone, so I'll be on my way. Please let me know if you need anything. Happy anniversary, you two. Sorry you're having it here."

"Thanks, again," Alana said.

"Yes, thank you," I said.

Hani nodded and left the room. Alana shut the door behind her. She walked over to the chair Hani had been sitting in and pulled it closer to the bed.

"How much do you remember?" she asked.

"Everything. I think."

"You passed out from the loss of blood. Foxx and I drove you here. You were in surgery for almost three hours. How's the pain? Do you need me to bring the nurse in?"

"It's a seventeen on a scale of one to ten."

"I'll go get her then."

"Not now. I don't want more drugs just yet."

"But if you're hurting."

"I need my head clear, at least somewhat. Pika couldn't have shot me."

"I know, but why do you say that?" she asked.

"There wasn't any hostility when I met him. He actually tried to help."

"I know he did, but then I thought he might have come to think you killed Molly."

"Where is he now?"

"He's dead, Poe."

"How?"

"Someone murdered him in his home."

"When did this happen?"

"The M.E. places his time of death around midnight last night. He'd been dead for several hours when you were attacked."

"Hani said it was his car. So they stole it?"

"Yes, but there were only two sets of prints in it. One belonged to Pika and the other to Molly Randolph. Whoever took the car must have been wearing gloves. There aren't any prints on the shell casings, either. We found one bullet in the back tire of your SUV. Two others were imbedded in the bricks of our house."

"Did you find the gun?" I asked.

"No, and Pika didn't have one registered to him. Of course, that doesn't mean he didn't have one. There are some other things I learned today."

"What?"

Alana told me how she'd discovered Detective Shaw had been the one to find the burner phone in my desk. He'd also apparently told one of the forensics people to check the clothes hamper in the master bathroom.

"That's really weird," I said.

"Why?"

"That he would be so obvious about it. You'd have thought he would have planted the phone and then let someone else find it."

"Maybe not. That could have been even worse. He walks upstairs, stays a couple of minutes, and then comes downstairs? For what reason and how would that have looked? Plus, he couldn't risk going up with anyone else. They could have easily caught him."

It was a valid theory, and I hadn't been able to think of anyone else that fit. The frame job had to have been from a cop. Who better than the lead detective on the case?

"Get this. Shaw was also seen arguing with Pika the night before he was killed. Why was he even talking to him? The Molly Randolph case is mine."

"Who saw him?"

"The next-door neighbor. She overheard them fighting about a video. It had to be a reference to the one Pika gave you."

"Did you tell anyone about that video?" I asked.

"No, but I did enter it into evidence. He obviously went through it."

"Suppose he did. Why would he kill Pika over it? He had to have watched the entire file. There's nothing on that video that implicates Shaw. The person on that video could be any guy wearing a dark sweatshirt."

"That's why he tossed the place. He was looking to see if there was another video that showed more. He was bound to think that Molly might have hidden more cameras. I would have."

"So why would Pika have brought just that one file to me? Why not bring all of them?"

"Maybe he thought Pika might have found more cameras after the fact. Shaw had killed someone. He had to be sure he covered all his tracks."

"What are you going to do now?"

"I already spoke with Price. He's getting a search warrant."

"For what? Shaw's house?"

"We're going early tomorrow morning."

"They're letting you lead it?"

"No. Captain Price says it's a conflict of interest. I had to beg him just to stay on the sidelines. Price himself is supervising the search."

"How many people are going? I wouldn't be surprised if Shaw doesn't already know about it by now."

"Only Captain Price and I know at this point. He's going with a minimal team. He'll call them early this morning and inform them then. Hopefully, if there is a mole, they won't have enough time to alert Shaw."

"You said you're staying in the background on this one?"

"Yes."

"Do me a favor and stay way in the background, maybe behind the largest tree you can find. Shaw's dangerous. He won't go quietly."

"We'll be all right."

"That's what I thought. Who knew walking the dog was so dangerous. By the way, when are they letting me out of here?"

"Doctor said at least a week."

"That long?"

"Poe, you were shot. When did you think you'd get out? Tonight?"

"I've got stuff to do."

"Like what?"

"I don't know. Whatever things people on Maui do."

"You mean like lay around in the sun and drink Blue Hawaiians."

"Yeah. Things like that. I have my tan to think of."

"What tan? You're the only person I know on the island whose skin seems to repel the sun."

"You'll thank me years from now when I have less wrinkles than most people."

"That's exactly right. I need you to stick around. It's our anniversary today. I know you already got me these earrings, but I got you something, too. I stopped by the house to grab it before I came here."

"You didn't have to do that."

Alana reached into her suit jacket and removed a small gift. It was wrapped in blue paper and was thin and rectangular. She handed it to me.

Despite the wrapping paper being thin, it still took most of my remaining strength to tear it open. I couldn't believe how weak I felt.

"It's a Moleskin notebook for you to write down your thoughts on your investigations. I looked up wedding anniversaries, and you're supposed to get paper for year one," she said.

Okay, readers. Time for some brutal honesty. I hadn't really expected her to get me anything for our anniversary. Well, maybe a card. It's not that Alana's not generous. She is, and I know she cares deeply for me. She certainly proved that by rushing me to the hospital that morning. But diamonds versus a Moleskin notebook? Come on. It's not even close.

"You like it, don't you?" she asked.

"Of course, I do. I love it. Thank you."

Chapter 27
I Know What You're Doing

Perspective: Alana

I stayed with Poe for a few more hours until he fell asleep. I looked at the time on my cell phone. It was nearing nine o'clock. I needed to get some sleep myself if I was going to be fresh for the search of Shaw's house in the morning. I knew Price wouldn't let me inside, but I wanted to be on the outskirts for any revelations that I was sure would come.

I left the hospital and walked outside to my car. The night sky was clear, and the air was cool. The drive back toward Kaanapali was uneventful. The traffic was light, and I made relatively good time. I decided to swing into Harry's and thank Foxx personally for everything he'd done that morning. He was a good friend. The older I got, the more I came to realize just how hard that was to find.

The bar was packed, as it usually was. Foxx had done a remarkable job of making a successful business even more prosperous. Poe didn't really need the money, at least that's what he'd told me, but he'd wanted to help a friend. Foxx was in desperate need for something to do, especially after losing his girlfriend Lauren. He'd convinced himself that buying Harry's was that something. Poe hadn't been sure. I knew he dreaded the thought of owning a bar or restaurant. Looking back, he needn't have worried. Everything had gone great with the business, and the earnings had added to Poe's portfolio.

I parked in the rear of the parking lot and walked inside Harry's. Normally, I'd see Foxx behind the bar. He didn't sling drinks, but instead he could always be found talking up the guests. Many tourists told Poe that a big part of their reason for returning to Maui and not one of the other islands was Harry's. It was quickly becoming a legendary watering hole.

I didn't see Foxx at the bar, though. I looked around the crowded bar but didn't find him anywhere. I walked up to the bar and waited a few moments for Kiana to finish serving a couple.

"Hey, is Foxx still here? I thought I saw his SUV in the parking lot."

"I think he's in his office."

"His office? At night?"

"I don't think he's feeling so well."

"Okay. I'm going to poke my head in."

"Sure thing."

I walked to the back of the bar and knocked once on the office door. I didn't get a reply. Maybe I just hadn't been able to hear it over the loud noise of the crowd. I opened the door a crack and saw Foxx sitting behind his desk. He had a drink in front of him. It looked like Jack Daniels or some other dark liquor.

I walked inside and shut the door behind me.

"You okay, Foxx?"

"Yeah. Just tired. It's been a long day."

"Can Kiana close up for you?"

"Sure. She's done it before."

"Why don't you go home?"

"I probably will in another hour. How is Poe by the way?"

"He was asleep when I left him. I came by because I wanted to thank you again for this morning."

"It wasn't a problem. You know I'd do anything for the guy. I'll go to the hospital again in the morning."

"I'm sure he'll appreciate that. Anyway, I better get going. I'm pretty tired myself."

"I'm sure. I'll walk you out."

"No need. Stay here. Enjoy your drink."

I left the office and made my way through the crowd. I exited the bar and was halfway to my car when I heard someone call out to me.

"I know what you're doing. I'm not going to let you get away with it."

I turned around and saw Shaw walking toward me.

"What are you doing here?"

"I should ask you the same thing. I'd have thought you'd be at the hospital."

"And how did you know I was there before? Have you been following me? Is that why you're here now?" I asked.

"It's a bar. I can't stop by for a drink?"

"At the same time I'm here?"

"Coincidence."

"Aren't you going to ask me how Poe's doing?"

"I'm sure he'll be fine."

"I'll let him know you were concerned."

"You seem to be under the illusion I'm out to get your husband, like it was some grand plan. I never had anything against the guy, until he murdered that woman."

"I proved he wasn't there at the time of her murder. Why can't you get that?"

"I don't know, Alana. There's still that little thing about the victim's hair in your bathroom."

"I've thought a lot about your refusal to let this go, and I can only come up with two possibilities. The first is that you tried to frame him."

"And the second?"

"You're too stupid to comprehend what's really happening."

Shaw got closer to me.

"I know exactly what's happening. You're trying to cover for him by setting me up."

"How am I setting you up?"

"You went to the IT department and had them check on my computer searches."

"Who told you that?"

"What difference does it make? Are you denying it or not?"

"I'm not denying anything."

"I don't give a damn what they said. I haven't done anything wrong."

"So you're saying you didn't search Genesis Riley's background weeks before Brooklyn was murdered?" I asked.

"What are you talking about?"

"You looked up her contact information. Why?"

"I didn't do that."

"Yes, you did. It was your access code. Your computer terminal."

"Why would I look her up? I didn't even know she existed until she came forward after Van Kirk's murder."

"That's the same question I kept asking myself. Why would you look her up?"

"You're trying to set me up," he said again.

"Really? I somehow got a hold of your access code and did the search myself, and I did this just in case my husband got falsely arrested for murder? Think about what you're saying. There was only one reason you looked her up. You needed a false witness against Poe."

"Why would I do that to your husband? I don't give a damn about him either way."

"You also looked up Van Kirk before she was murdered. Why?"

"You're crazy. You're seeing all sorts of conspiracy theories."

"Where were you this morning?"

Shaw laughed.

"Is this when you accuse me of shooting your husband? I suppose you think I went to Pika Mahoe's house, slit his throat, stole his car, and then drove it to your house to shoot your husband while he walked your damn dog."

"You seem to know a lot about a case you're not involved in."

"A cop's husband gets shot. The details come out."

"You never answered my question. Where were you this morning?"

"I don't have to answer you. You think you got something on me, take it to Price."

Shaw turned to leave.

"I haven't accused you of any crimes, not yet. I just said you looked up Genesis Riley way before you had any reason to. Maybe you were just stalking her. Maybe you saw her profile on some dating site."

Shaw turned around.

"Go to hell."

"I also think it's ironic that you're the person who found the burner phone. There were eight people in my house, and you're the one who finds it within the first five minutes of searching? Either you're the luckiest cop in the world or you knew exactly where to go. Or maybe I should say you knew where you wanted to pretend to find it. Did you even bother opening the desk drawer, or did you just walk in the room, immediately turn around and say you found it?"

"You come for me, you're going to regret it," he said.

"Is that a threat?"

"Take it however you want."

"It sounded like a threat to me," Foxx said.

Shaw turned around again and saw Foxx walking over to us.

"This doesn't concern you, asshole."

"You're on my property. I'd say that makes it my business."

"It's all right, Foxx. He was just leaving."

"Who is this guy?" Foxx asked.

Shaw walked over to him and held out his badge.

"I'm Detective Austin Shaw. That's who I am. You want to make an issue of this?"

"Is that badge supposed to scare me?"

Foxx pointed to me.

"She's got one of those, too," he continued.

"You've got two seconds to get back inside that bar," Shaw said.

"Or what? I've got this place covered with cameras. How are you going to justify arresting someone for just standing in their own parking lot?"

"Get your ass in there!" Shaw yelled.

"Now you're really starting to upset me. Don't curse in front of the lady."

Shaw poked Foxx in the chest.

200

"You're just too big and dumb to know when to back down."

"Enough!" I yelled.

I got between Foxx and Shaw.

"Both of you. Calm down," I continued.

"You'll gets yours. It's coming for you," Foxx said.

"Is that right? And who's going to bring it? You?" Shaw asked.

"Maybe. Just maybe."

"Get inside, Foxx. I'll be right in," I said.

"No. You were going home. I'll follow you back."

"Oh, so the husband's away. Now we see why you're so quick to defend her."

"She's my best friend's wife, and if you disrespect her like that again, I'll take that badge and…"

"No more, Foxx," I said, cutting him off before he could finish something that I was sure would be quite colorful. "Let's go."

Shaw laughed.

"I'll see you at work tomorrow, Alana. Maybe we can go to IT together. We'll see what they have to say about your computer activity."

Foxx walked me over to my car.

"Your husband's guilty. It's only a matter of time before I nail him again," Shaw yelled.

"Keep walking. He's not going to bait us," I said.

"Too late for that."

"I don't need you in jail."

"I'm fine," Foxx said.

I opened my door and climbed inside my car. I started the engine but didn't back out of the parking lot until I saw Foxx get into his SUV.

Foxx followed me back to my house. I drove my car into the garage and shut the door behind me. My phone pinged, and I saw a text message from Foxx telling me to call if I needed anything. I texted him back: Thanks again for your support today.

His reply: No prob. Shaw is a dick.

I laughed. Leave it up to Foxx to always cut to the chase and provide the perfect wrap-up to a long and stressful day.

I went in the house and opened the sliding glass door to the backyard. Maui dashed outside so he could use the bathroom. Poor dog. He was probably ready to burst.

I thought of my conversation with Shaw while I waited for the dog to go the bathroom. He'd asked me what I was taking about when I told him I knew about the computer search for Genesis Riley. I didn't expect him to admit it, but I'd been watching his eyes closely. He'd looked genuinely surprised. I didn't know if he was surprised I knew or surprised that the search had been done with his access code and from his computer terminal.

I also tried to figure out how he'd even learned about my discussion with the IT department. I doubted that Doug would have told him. He couldn't stand Shaw, but had Doug told anyone else? He had to have talked because I hadn't said anything to anyone except Poe and Captain Price. It's not like Price would have tipped his hand to Shaw, especially after authorizing a search warrant on one of his own people.

I pushed these doubts away as I realized the most likely explanation was that I'd read Shaw's surprise wrong. It had been nothing more than a good performance. His entire meeting with me was simply an intimidation tactic, but it wasn't going to work.

My phone rang a few minutes past midnight. I jolted awake, not sure of where I was. I looked at my phone and saw Captain Price's name on the display.

"Alana Hu."

"Alana, emergency services got a call twenty minutes ago. Disturbing the peace near the Kihei area. The call came from one of Shaw's neighbors."

"Was he involved?"

"We think so, but he wasn't in his house when the patrol got there."

"Is his car gone?"

"Yes. I'm worried he might have gotten word about the search. I'm sending a unit to your house now."

"You think he might be coming for me?"

"I should have called you earlier. I'm sorry, but he confronted me this evening. He said he had proof you were trying to frame him for the murders of Brooklyn Van Kirk, Molly Randolph, and her boyfriend."

I told Price how I'd already had my own confrontation with Shaw in the parking lot of Harry's.

"Did the neighbors see anyone else there?" I asked.

"No. They were asleep when the shouting woke them up. They said they saw Shaw's car leave, but they didn't see anyone else."

"What do you want me to do?"

"Stay where you are. We'll handle this. The patrol should be at your house momentarily."

I got dressed while I waited for the team to arrive. I had no intention of staying at the house, nor did I intend to try to track Shaw down. I didn't think I was his intended target, if he even had one. I thought there was a more likely victim, and I wasn't about to leave his room unguarded.

The patrol had gotten there by the time I made my way down the stairs. I backed the car out of the driveway and told them where I was headed. They tried to argue for all of two seconds, but I think the look on my face told them all they needed to know.

It took me forty-five minutes to get to the hospital. Poe was still asleep by the time I got to his floor. I entered the room, shut the door behind me, and took a seat in the corner of the room. The chair faced the door, so there'd be no way someone could get in here without me noticing.

I didn't hear from anyone else until Price called me just after seven in the morning.

"Are you still at the hospital?" he asked.

"Yes."

"I see you took my request to stay in your house seriously."

I wasn't about to apologize for protecting Poe, so I said nothing.

"We still haven't located Shaw," he continued.

"Did you find anything in his house?"

"Yes. There was a note."

"What did it say?"

"Two words: I'm sorry."

"What did his place look like inside?"

"A table was turned over. A broken window. Someone threw a vase at it. Impossible to tell whether Shaw did this himself or whether it was a fight with another person."

"Have you tried tracking his phone?" I asked.

"No use. He left it in his house beside the note. Traffic cameras have him leaving the Kihei area and heading west. We didn't pick him up in Kahului, so he must have been headed toward Maalaea and Lahaina."

"Do you have any idea how Shaw knew about the IT search?"

"No, but it shouldn't be hard to figure out who told him. How's your husband doing?"

"He's still asleep. I think I'm going to stay here for the day."

"Of course. Let me know if you need anything."

I ended the call and assumed I wouldn't hear anything else for the rest of the day. I was wrong. Price called back in under an hour and asked me to meet him at a beach that wasn't far from where Pika's car was found.

When I arrived, I saw three police cars, an ambulance, and Price's vehicle. They were all parked on the side of the road that bordered the beach. I parked behind Price's car and got out.

I walked onto the beach and saw where everyone was gathered. Shaw's car was parked on the sand, and it was facing the ocean. I saw a couple talking to one of the officers. They were both dressed in shorts and t-shirts.

I turned as Price walked toward me.

"Is Shaw in there?" I asked and nodded toward his car.

"Yeah. It's not pretty."

"What happened?"

"That couple found him. They were walking down the beach for exercise. They said they saw red on the car's window but just thought it was the colors of the sunrise reflecting off the glass. When they came back, they realized what it really was. The wife called 911."

I walked over to the car and saw blood all over the driver's side window. I wasn't sure how they couldn't have realized what it was the first time they passed it, but they were probably talking and not really paying that much attention. Most people didn't these days. Everyone was distracted.

"Where's the gun?" I asked.

"On the floor board, just in front of the brake. Gun's a Sig Sauer P320."

I turned in the direction opposite from Price and saw the answer had come from Allison. She walked up to the car.

"That's not his service weapon," I said.

"It's a 9mm, same caliber that fired at your husband," Price said.

"We'll run a ballistics test as soon as possible," Allison said.

A note that said "I'm sorry." A death that seemed to be a suicide. I looked around the area. It was a peaceful place, but most beaches on Maui were.

I walked over to Price.

"Did you find anything else in his house other than that note?"

"No, but we got the call about his car shortly after you and I spoke. The house needs to be gone over much more thoroughly. Who knows what we'll find."

"Was the note typed or handwritten?"

"Handwritten."

"Are you ruling this a suicide?" I asked.

"Not yet, but it certainly looks that way. The man wasn't just angry when he saw me last night. He was also panicked. I'm guessing he knew what you had on him," Price said.

"It wasn't enough for an arrest. He must have known that."

"Try to look at this through his eyes. He knew what he did, and he knew it was only a matter of time before we found it."

"Does this mean it's over?"

Price looked over at Shaw's body.

"We can't know for sure, but I suspect so."

He turned back to me.

"Go back to your husband. Take care of him. I'll call you again as soon as we get anything new," he continued.

I walked over to Shaw's car and took one last look. Then I headed back to the road. I climbed into my car but didn't immediately start the ignition. The handwritten note did give some credence to the notion that this was a suicide.

I doubted someone would have risked writing in their own hand when they easily could have typed it. On the other hand, I didn't think it would be that hard to mimic someone's writing if you were just writing two words, and short words at that. Still, if it had been someone else, why not kill him in his house? Why put him in a car and drive him several miles to a beach? This wasn't a heavily traveled section of road, but it still got traffic. There were several other places that would be much more remote.

I drove back to the hospital. Poe was awake by the time I got there. I hadn't told him anything about Shaw. I didn't want my first words to him that day to be about a suicide.

"Any chance I can convince you to run up to Harrys and get me a burger? This hospital food will make you sick," he said.

He paused a moment.

Then he asked, "Yeah, I know it was an old joke, but was it really that bad? You look like I just kicked Maui the dog in front of you."

Poe knew me too well. It wasn't like I was going to be able to keep the truth from him for long. I told him about the confrontation with Shaw outside the bar, as well as the disturbing-the-peace call later that night and Shaw's apparent suicide on the beach.

"You really think he killed himself?" Poe asked.

"I don't know. Maybe."

"It all fits. He found the phone in the house. He did those searches of the witnesses before there was anything to actually witness."

"I know. I've gone over that in my head a thousand times on the way over here."

"So what's still bothering you, beside the fact you had to see all that?"

"The guy was furious last night. He didn't strike me as being someone to give up without a fight."

"How well did you really know him? People react to stress in different ways."

"So was Shaw wrapped up in that smuggling ring? Is that why he went after you?"

"Makes perfect sense. He waited for the one-year anniversary of that phone call."

"You think he was the one who called?"

"I've been thinking about that. The voice was different, but I suspect Shaw was working for the guy. He would have needed someone on the inside. A detective makes a pretty good pick."

"You think this person, the one who called you last year, put Shaw up to all of this?"

"I do. He had Shaw frame me. I don't know why he didn't just kill me. Thank God he didn't. But they underestimated someone. They didn't know how good you are."

"Or maybe Shaw just got sloppy."

"I wouldn't say that. He did a damn good job of stacking the evidence against me. We saw those surveillance photographs of me that Brooklyn took. I'm sure she shared them with Shaw. They knew my routine. There was no way to predict I'd go to Baby Beach that morning. I almost always stay at the house in the mornings. It was just freak luck I had to meet Hani that day. It was also lucky that I took that photograph. What could Shaw do at that point? He'd already killed Brooklyn."

Poe was right. It did all fit. It had ended as quickly as it had all begun. Maybe that's what was bothering me. My adrenaline had been pumping so hard, and now everything was done. I needed to sit down, catch my breath, and allow the process to work. They would find more incriminating evidence in his house. I felt confident of that. There was also that gun on the floor of the car. There was still the ballistics test to conduct. It would probably match the bullet pulled out of Poe, as well as the other rounds pulled out of the brickwork on our house and the rear tire of the SUV.

"How are you feeling? I assume better since you made an attempt at humor when I came in the room," I said.

"An attempt? Wow. That really was a terrible joke."

"You've had better."

"Well, I was just shot, so I could always use that as an excuse."

"If you really want that burger, I can call Foxx. He said he's coming to see you this morning. I'm sure he wouldn't mind bringing you something from Harry's."

"Do you think I could ask for a beer with that?"

"No. And especially no more Purple Hazes. We're done with that brand."

Poe laughed and then he grabbed his side.

"Oh, God, that really hurts."

"Take it easy. You don't want to tear the stitches," I said.

"Maybe we should get your mother over here. That will keep me from laughing."

"And it will get your blood pressure up. No way."

"She means well," he said.

"No, she doesn't."

"You're right. She doesn't."

He laughed again.

"Man, why did I just do that?" he asked.

I walked over to the bed and leaned down to him.

"You are the craziest person I know."

I kissed him gently.

Chapter 28
Chance Encounters

Perspective: Poe

I spent the next several months recovering from the gunshot wounds and trying to make some sense of the murders of Brooklyn Van Kirk, Molly Randolph, and Pika Mahoe. Whatever path I went down in my line of thinking, I kept coming back to the same conclusion. They'd all been indirectly caused by me.

I knew it was Shaw's desire to get back at me that caused him to seek out Brooklyn's help for revenge. Molly had gotten dragged into it due to her close physical proximity to me. Pika had been killed on the off chance that Molly had told him something she shouldn't have.

Yeah, I hadn't been the one to murder them, but I couldn't shake the feeling of guilt, and I didn't see myself getting over that for a long time.

Speaking of Shaw, he hadn't been officially accused of carrying out the murders. I wasn't really sure how that actually worked. How can you charge a dead person, after all? The cases, as far as I knew, were still open, but they'd been abandoned for all practical purposes.

Alana had continued her investigation for a few weeks after the discovery of Shaw's body on that beach, but everything kept pointing back to him as the architect of the mayhem. She'd moved on to other assignments now, and neither of us had talked about those cases in weeks. We were both doing our best to put everything behind us, even though that was probably impossible.

The ballistics test confirmed that the gun Shaw had used to kill himself was the same one used to shoot me. I supposed I should have been happy to know the person who tried to kill me wasn't going to be a threat anymore, but that's not how I felt. I was more confused than anything else.

I didn't know why Shaw had designed this elaborate plan to frame me for murder so I'd spend the rest of my life in jail. Why not just kill me instead? Furthermore, why did he try to kill me after he failed at the frame job? Was it just because he was so angry that his plan had fallen apart? The only conclusion I'd come to was that I was probably never going to figure out what his true motivations were.

I'm sure you're wondering what Alana decided to do regarding her law enforcement career. If you recall, she'd put off a permanent decision until she'd wrapped up the murder investigations. Well, she decided to push her decision off again by giving herself a year to think about what she really wanted to do. That may seem like a long time to make up one's mind, but I've found that a year really flies by the older you get.

We didn't see a good reason for her to put a lot of pressure on herself when she didn't have a strong gut instinct either way. I thought she did, but she wasn't willing to admit it to herself. She loved the job, and she couldn't see herself doing anything else, but she was still pretty pissed off by the notion that so many of her co-workers turned their backs on her after I got arrested. We both understood their logic on an intellectual level, but we humans are emotional creatures. We seldom if ever succeed in removing our hearts from the situation.

Speaking of removing emotion for a decision-making process, it was the main reason why Mara Winters had invited me for lunch at our favorite sushi restaurant. I'll get to that bizarre little comparison in a moment. Mara and I were seated at a table near the front door. It was one of the worst tables in the place, but the restaurant was packed so we didn't have much choice.

"I know I've thanked you a million times before, but I really appreciate you helping to bail me out when I got arrested," I said.

"I'm glad I could play a part, even if it was a small one. Alana did most of the work. That's a hell of a wife you have. I've never seen someone so determined."

"She is that."

I didn't see the point in telling Mara that Alana demonstrated elements of that determination in everyday life, including what we would have for dinner, what movie we'd watch, where we'd go on vacation. You get the point. Please don't misunderstand me. I'm not complaining. It had become somewhat of an endearing trait, and I solved any potential conflicts between us by simply answering "Yes, dear." It was an old school solution that still worked wonders.

"How are you feeling these days? It's been a while since we've talked. Is everything healed?"

"I keep waiting to get back to one hundred percent, but I'm not sure that's ever going to happen. My abdomen gets aches and pains when the weather changes, and my arm isn't quite as strong as it was before."

"How is your emotional state?"

"You mean am I in need of therapy or something?"

"Maybe not that, but you went through a lot. Most people wouldn't have been able to handle it."

"I'll be fine. Thanks for asking," I said.

"What about your investigative career? I've intentionally not asked you about that before because I didn't want to put any pressure on you."

Something told me Mara was about to do exactly that. I knew she cared about me, maybe not on the level a close friend or loved one does, but she certainly had my best wishes in mind. That said, she never invited me to one of these lunch dates unless she needed something from me.

"Is there an assignment you have now?"

Mara smiled.

"Is it that obvious?"

"Well, you said you were buying, and you encouraged me to order an extra shrimp tempura roll. I figured some request was coming my way."

"Maybe I'm just trying to thank you for that large legal bill I hit you with."

There was that, and I'd paid it just a few days after getting the invoice in the mail. There had been a noticeable lack of a discount on her hourly rate. I didn't hold a grudge, well, maybe a little one, but people should get paid for their expertise.

"Is this a murder case?" I asked.

"Nothing nearly that serious. It's my niece."

"I didn't even know you had one."

"My brother also lives on the island. He and his wife have one daughter. She just turned twenty-two."

"Is she in some kind of trouble?"

"No. She just got engaged."

"Okay. Now I'm totally confused. Why do you need an...."

I stopped as I suddenly realized what this was all about.

"Mara, you know I have a strict rule about not following cheating spouses."

"Technically, they're not married yet."

"It's still in the spirit of my rule."

"I get your point, but I'm not saying we think he's cheating. My brother and his wife love the young man, but I believe he needs to be vetted."

"Can I ask why?"

"My family comes from money, much like yours."

"Make the kid sign a pre-nup. Problem solved."

"It's not just that. A marriage is more of a business arrangement than anything else. I want to make sure he's a suitable partner for her."

"I'm not sure I agree with your statement."

"Why is that?" she asked.

"There is this little thing called love. In my experience, that counts for a lot."

"At first, sure, but half of all marriages in America end in divorce. That happens because of love."

"How do you figure?"

"People have their blinders on. They can't see beyond their passions, certainly not in the beginning when so many big decisions are being made."

She sounded like she was speaking from experience. If so, it couldn't have been a good one. It occurred to me that I didn't really know Mara's own relationship background. In the years that I'd worked with Mara, she never once mentioned a romantic partner. People always have a way of slipping that into everyday conversation. "My husband did this. My wife said that. My partner thinks whatever." With Mara, there had been none of that. Everything was about the law or a client of hers. I didn't know if she'd intentionally kept that part of her life from me or if that just wasn't a factor for her. It didn't happen often, but some people shunned romantic relationships. Maybe Mara was one of those people. Either way, it was none of my business. I wasn't about to change that now.

"What exactly would you like me to check out?" I asked.

"I've already done some minor looking into him."

"What have you found?"

"Nothing major. I've checked his social media accounts and done a few other online searches."

"You want me to go deeper? Follow him around, stuff like that?"

"Basically. I don't want you to kidnap the guy and torture him into confessing any indiscretions. I just want to make sure he is who he claims to be."

Bottom line: I didn't want to touch this job with a fifty-foot pole, let alone a ten-foot one. I owed her, though, and I wanted to maintain a good relationship with her since I wasn't willing to write off the investigative career just yet. There was another reason, and it was the prevailing one. I was bored silly. I needed to get out of the house and have something to do.

"Send me whatever information you have on him, and I can get started today."

"I appreciate it."

"When is your niece's wedding?" I asked.

"It's in six months. They're getting married at the same resort you did."

"It's a beautiful place. I'm sure they'll love it."

Mara and I changed the subject and started talking about an old law school friend of hers named Mary Anne Portendorfer. The reason we drifted onto that topic is because I'd actually met Ms. Portendorfer at the hotel where Alana and I were married. I don't want to go too deep with the details of that one-day case now, but it involved Mara's friend trying to cover her fling with a timeshare salesman or something like that. The guy had lifted her diamond ring while she slept in her hotel bed. She'd hired me to get it back.

"I have bad news about Mary Anne," Mara said.

"Is she okay?"

"Physically, yes. Emotionally, no. Her husband just filed for divorce."

It didn't take much of an imagination to figure out why.

"Apparently, Mary Anne took a liking to the landscaper they hired to install a Japanese garden in their backyard. Her husband caught them in bed together when he returned home from work early," Mara continued.

Despite my best efforts, I couldn't stop this cheesy country and western song from playing in my head while I pictured Mr. Portendorfer walking in on Ms. Portendorfer and some sweaty gardener.

"The woman seems incapable of staying faithful," Mara said.

"I wonder if Mr. Portendorfer demanded his diamond ring back."

The ring had been given as a symbol of their earlier reconciliation, which was apparently the result of an earlier affair.

"I imagine he'll be content to just leave her."

"How is she taking all of this?" I asked.

"She's devastated. She's begged him to take her back."

It didn't make much sense to me. I couldn't comprehend how someone who loved their spouse so much would habitually cheat on them.

"Maybe she'll get lucky and the thing with the landscape guy will turn into something meaningful. At the very least, she'll have a well-groomed yard," I said.

Mara looked at me like I'd just lost my mind. Apparently, my sarcasm was losing its effectiveness.

"I gave up trying to figure her out a long time ago. I guess that's why we don't talk but every several months or so."

"Did she call you or the other way around?"

"She called me. Get this: She's planning another trip to Maui to try to get over her heartbreak."

"For the love of God, let me know the dates so I can book a flight to another island. I don't think I could handle another encounter with her."

Mara laughed.

I was about to make a comment on what I viewed as Mr. Portendorfer's ultimate good fortune when I saw someone I hadn't seen in a while. I didn't remember her name, but I couldn't forget the face. She was one of the three people who were on my porch when I got arrested for the murder of Brooklyn Van Kirk. She and a male companion - he was dressed in civilian clothing - were walking out of the restaurant. They had to pass by us since we were near the door.

As she got closer to our table, I saw the name "Jenkins" on the nametag of her uniform. We made eye contact, and I gave a small wave. I kind of felt stupid for doing that. She was one of the people responsible for my false imprisonment, but it hadn't been her fault.

She didn't wave back to me. Instead, she nodded and gave me a half-smile. Her male friend didn't look at me. Maybe he hadn't even noticed her and me making eye contact.

Either way, the whole thing seemed like an insignificant encounter. I had no idea just how much that lunch was going to change things.

Chapter 29
The Funeral

Perspective: Poe

I was only about a day into the investigation of the potential wedding partner of Mara's niece. Actually, I was maybe all of an hour into it. I'd learned that he worked at a pretty nice hotel in Kaanapali that was fortunately only ten minutes from my house. He was in their manager training program. I was able to see the guy in person by sitting at the hotel bar as he talked to some other manager about an issue involving laundry. I ordered a Manhattan to help sell my performance as a tourist on vacation. Sure, it was only ten in the morning, but these are the types of sacrifices one must make while working a case.

I said a silent prayer as I savored my drink and thanked God that my parents had done me the incredible favor of leaving me enough money so that I didn't have to deal with laundry as a way of getting a paycheck. Nevertheless, I was the guy following the guy dealing with laundry, so maybe I was being a huge hypocrite for judging the guy.

I finished my drink and was about to call it a day since I didn't know how much I could learn by following him around the hotel when Alana called me. She told me Captain Price's wife had died. I knew she'd been battling breast cancer, and I'd heard she'd been put into hospice care. I couldn't even begin to imagine how Price felt. The guy's pain must have been unbearable.

The sky was overcast the day of Beverly's funeral, and I worried the rain would start at any moment. It didn't, though. The funeral was nice, if one can use that word to describe such an event. The minister seemed like he truly knew Beverly. I didn't know if the Price family had been regular churchgoers, but the minister told specific stories about the type of person Beverly had been. I regretted not getting to know her. It sounded like she'd been a truly remarkable woman.

A depressing notion then occurred to me. That could have easily been me in that wooden box if Shaw's bullet had been an inch or two to the left. That thought, of course, made me feel guilty for thinking about my own mortality at someone else's funeral. We all tend to personalize everything, though, and I had the feeling that just about everyone was thinking about their own lives at that particular moment.

There were a handful of white chairs under the tent that had been placed in front of the coffin. Lucas Price was on the center chair. I noticed something interesting when I looked at the people seated near him. The man I'd seen with Officer Jenkins was directly beside Captain Price. Speaking of Jenkins, she was on the other side of that man. I made a mental note to ask Alana who the guy was, beyond obviously being a Price family member or close friend.

After the funeral, we all drove to a nearby hotel where the family had rented a large multi-purpose room. There were at least a hundred people there, which made it difficult to even move. I looked around the room but didn't spot Jenkins nor the man she'd been seated beside.

I leaned closer to Alana so no one would hear my question.

"Who was that guy sitting beside Captain Price at the funeral?"

"Which one? There were guys on either side of him."

"The younger one. He looked like he could have been his son."

"That was his son. His name's Jaden."

"Have you met him?" I asked.

"Of course. There he is now."

Alana nodded to her left, and we saw Jaden with Officer Jenkins. They were talking to another couple who I didn't recognize. I hadn't seen them before because a group of four people had been standing between us and them.

"I saw him and Jenkins when I met with Mara the other day."

"At the restaurant?" Alana asked.

"Yeah. They were having lunch together. They passed by our table as they were leaving."

"Did you talk to them?"

"No. I just waved."

"I heard rumors that Allison and Jaden were dating. I figured I had confirmation after seeing them together at the funeral."

"That's a pretty big step to be seated with the family. Are they engaged or something?"

"Don't know, but you're right. It must be more serious than I heard."

I thought Jenkins had guts, dating the son of her boss. I didn't know that I'd recommend that career move.

I was about to ask Alana another question about Jaden Price when a couple walked up to us. Alana introduced the woman as Abigail Ford. The man with her was her husband. I think his name was John. The conversation went as one might expect it to. We talked about how sad it was that Beverly had passed and how young she'd been taken. We expressed sympathy for her family, and Abigail commented that the funeral had been "nice," which made me feel better for having thought that word earlier.

At some point in the conversation, John ended up seeing some other guy he recognized, and he drifted off to talk to him. It had been a smooth move on his part. He didn't say goodbye to us or offer any kind of wrap-up comment. He just kind of vanished.

That left me with Alana and Abigail. It took all of ten more seconds before both ladies forgot I was there and started gossiping about just how serious Allison's relationship was with Jaden Price. Before you female readers get offended, I don't mean to imply that woman gossip more than men. Everyone does, and the Allison and Jaden story was a hot topic.

I didn't really care that they were ignoring me, mainly because I didn't know either Allison or Jaden, so I pulled a "John" and drifted away from Alana and Abigail. I walked over to the bar. The line wasn't very long. I didn't know how that was even possible, so I got to the front within a couple of minutes. I ordered a Jack and Coke. It wasn't my usual drink, but I wanted to order something easy for the bartender to make. He handed me the drink, and I blended back into the crowd.

I looked to see if I recognized anyone, but I didn't beyond Captain Price. I knew I needed to eventually say something to him, but he was currently surrounded by several well-wishers.

I was standing in the middle of the room and kind of zoning out when I heard a voice I instantly recognized. It had been more than a year since I'd heard it last, but it might as well have been yesterday. It was so clearly the same guy. He was back on Maui. Maybe he'd always been here.

It took all of my energy to turn around and see who was talking. My body almost seemed paralyzed. I wasn't afraid. Instead, I felt like I was in some kind of trance, like my mind was slowing down because it was experiencing some kind of sensory overload. The voice had shaken me into a raw emotional state that was an odd combination of curiosity, rage, and bewilderment.

I eventually turned and saw the guy from the rear. Even though I couldn't see his face, I knew exactly who it was. I walked away from him and circled around so I could see him from the front. I took a sip of my drink and did my best to casually glance his way. He was still talking, but by now I was too far away to hear his words. It didn't matter. The voice had already been imprinted on my mind. I thought to those last words he'd said to me on the phone: Now I'm going to have to kill you.

It was him. There was no mistaking it. The guy who'd threatened me was Jaden Price.

I downed the rest of my drink and went back to the bar. I ordered another Jack and Coke. I also ordered a white wine for Alana.

I walked over to her. Abigail was gone, but now Alana was busy talking to Allison Jenkins. I handed Alana the wine, and she introduced me to Allison.

"We've met before," I said.

"Yes. I'm sorry about everything that happened," Allison said.

"There's no reason to apologize. I get the position you were in."

"Excuse me, guys. I need to run to the restroom," Alana said. She turned to me and asked, "Can you hold my wine?"

Alana handed me her wine back before I could even answer and disappeared in search of the restroom. I could have strangled her for leaving me alone with one of the cops who'd arrested me, and, yes, I understand how inappropriate that is to say while describing the scene at the funeral reception.

"Didn't I see you at the sushi restaurant the other day?" I asked.

"Yes. Jaden was able to swing by for a quick lunch."

"Does he work nearby?"

"No. He owns a restaurant in Wailea, but he had the rare morning off."

"So he works long hours?"

"Absolutely. It's hard for us to find time to be together."

"That must be tough."

"How are things going for you?" she asked, but she didn't sound the least bit sincere.

Was I offended? Not at all.

"I'm getting better. It's taken a while to recover, much longer than I would have thought. I still haven't gotten back to my full routine."

"How is that little girl? I think she was your niece?"

"Ava. She's fine, although I haven't seen her in over a week. I used to take care of her all the time, but her grandmother has been doing the babysitting duties since I got hurt."

"I'm sure she misses you."

"I doubt it. As long as she has her little stuffed elephant, she's fine."

Allison laughed.

"I remember she was clutching that thing so tightly when I got her. She was so upset when she dropped it into her crib."

"I know what you mean. It takes all of my strength to get it away from her. She carries it with her everywhere."

Alana came back at that moment, and I handed her the wine.

"Thank you," she said.

Allison looked around the room until she spotted Jaden.

"I better go check on Jaden. See how he's doing."

"Of course. We'll come see him a bit later," Alana said.

"How's he holding up?" I asked.

"Better than one can expect. He's trying to be strong for his father."

"I'm sure," I said.

"It was good officially meeting you," Allison said.

"Same here."

Allison left, and I watched as she walked across the room and headed toward Jaden Price.

I turned to Alana.

"We need to stay at least another half an hour, maybe even an hour. I don't want to rush off now. It will look too suspicious."

"Suspicious? What are you talking about?" she asked.

"I just figured out who set me up."

Alana starred at me in disbelief.

"What are you talking about?"

"Shaw didn't kill himself," I continued. "He was murdered."

Chapter 30
He Would Have Remembered

Perspective: Poe

Alana couldn't make it an hour. She couldn't even make it half an hour. She grabbed my arm after about ten minutes and told me we were leaving. We exited to the parking lot, and I'd just shut the car door when she turned to me.

"What in the world are you saying? We're at a funeral reception. How could you possibly figure out who set you up?"

I started the car and drove out of the parking lot before I answered her.

"Who had Ava when you got to the house? Do you even remember that?" I asked.

"Allison had her."

"Where were they?"

"In the driveway. Shaw didn't want me coming into the house, so Allison waited outside. What does this have to do with anything?"

"Allison told me right before you came back from the restroom that Ava got upset when she dropped her elephant in the crib. Where is Ava's crib in our house?"

"Oh my God, she went upstairs?"

"I specifically told them there was a child in the house when they were dragging me out to the car. I'm willing to bet Allison went looking for Ava before she did anything else. That would put her up on the second floor. Maybe she didn't go before Shaw, but I think she probably did. It would have been easy for her to slip into my office and drop that phone in the desk drawer. You know my office and Ava's room are side by side."

"You're forgetting I was told Shaw went straight for your office. He found that phone within a few minutes of starting the search."

"Who told you that? Allison herself?" I asked.

"No. It was Hailey. She's on our forensics team."

"Maybe he just got lucky. Maybe Hailey didn't remember the timeline right. It doesn't matter. Allison was on that floor."

"I'm sorry, Poe, but that doesn't mean she did anything wrong."

"There's one other thing. I recognized his voice. It's the same voice that called me the day after our wedding."

"The one that threatened you?"

"Yes. It was Jaden Price."

"Jaden Price? The son of a police captain? He's the one who said he'd kill you?"

It wasn't hard to interpret the disbelief in her voice. She wasn't exactly being sarcastic, but she was right on the line.

"Fine. You don't have to believe me, but I know what I heard. Jaden Price was the main guy behind that smuggling ring, and he's the one who orchestrated Shaw's murder, the others, too. Maybe he even killed them all himself."

"This is crazy. It's been more than a year, and you said the phone call only lasted a minute."

"It doesn't matter. I know what I heard. It's him. That's why they avoided me at the restaurant. He didn't want me hearing his voice."

"Maybe he and Allison were just running late. Neither of them know you. That's why they didn't come by your table, and Allison was avoiding you because she felt guilty for having played a part in your arrest."

I didn't respond. I knew there wasn't anything more I could say in that car that would change Alana's mind. I didn't blame her. My theory, such as it was now, wouldn't hold up in any kind of court. It was all gut feelings, but that had never let me down.

Neither of us said much on the rest of the drive. I could tell she was aggravated with me, and I understood why. The case had been an emotional one, which was a pretty big understatement, and we'd both done a lot of work trying to put it behind us. Now I'd just ripped the band aid off that wound.

We got back to the house, and I immediately walked up to my office. I'm sure she interpreted that as me pouting. I wasn't. My brain needed time to process what had just happened, and I couldn't have any distractions.

Alana had the entire master bedroom closet to herself, which had been my idea. I kept my relatively small wardrobe in the closet in my office. I grabbed a t-shirt and shorts and changed out of my suit. I slipped on my running shoes and walked back downstairs. I saw Alana sitting on the sofa. She was leaning forward and patting the dog.

"I'm going for a run."

"Are you all right?" she asked.

"I'm good. I won't be long."

I hadn't actually been on a run since I'd gotten shot. I walked about a full mile as a warm-up, and then I slowly transitioned into a jog. I thought again about my reaction to hearing Jaden's voice at the reception. It had been immediate and instinctual. I'd known on some deep level that he was the one who'd threatened me. Now I was in danger of overanalyzing that experience. Had I really heard what I thought I'd heard? Was he really the same guy? Did it make any kind of sense that the son of one of the island's most respected men would be a criminal?

I picked up my pace the farther I ran. I looked at the odometer on my phone and saw I'd already run four miles, but I kept going. I tried to switch gears and concentrate on Brooklyn.

I knew she'd resented me for forcing her into revealing Bryan Sanders' name. I also knew from Ted Akers, her sometimes wedding video partner, that she hadn't gotten much work out of her new photography company. I didn't think it would be hard for Jaden to convince her to go after me, especially if it meant monthly payments and a chance to get revenge, but did Brooklyn ever start to suspect there was something more going on? At what point, if ever, did she wonder if Jaden Price meant to do her harm?

She also must have suspected that Jaden had some kind of relationship with Bryan Sanders, a guy she knew had murdered multiple people. What did that say about Jaden?

Also, there was still the issue of her pregnancy. Who was the father? Was it Jaden? Is that how he'd convinced her to go along with the text messages? Maybe she didn't think the father of her child, if he was the father, could possibly consider murdering her.

If her killer had been the father, that obviously meant they'd been in a very close relationship. Perhaps he'd told her things that he shouldn't have. Maybe that was a motivation for him silencing her. It also meant something else. He might have told her his connection to Bryan Sanders, such as how he knew the guy, where they'd met, what they'd done for each other.

As far as I knew, Sanders had kept the identity of his boss concealed from the cops. I was sure he'd been offered some kind of deal for ratting out the name of the guy that had run the smuggling ring. He hadn't, though. I'd chalked that up to him not knowing the name of the person, but maybe I'd been wrong. Maybe they were so loyal to each other that no deal would ever make him turn. What makes someone that loyal? It's either blood or a relationship that feels like blood.

It was at that point that I thought I knew the answer to a mystery we'd come across months ago. I ran back to the house as fast as I could. I walked in the house and went upstairs again.

Alana had left the cloned drive for Brooklyn's laptop in my office. She'd asked me to copy it before she put the laptop into evidence. That wasn't technically legal, but she hadn't exactly been feeling like following the law to the nth degree after the way her department had treated her.

I had a large high definition monitor in my office for photo editing work. We'd plugged the cloned drive into my computer and used the large monitor to go through Brooklyn's stuff. It made the eye strain a little less during the long hours of combing through her emails and documents.

I powered the computer up and selected the drive. I found the email Brooklyn had sent herself, the one with the old high school article on Bryan Sanders' football heroics. I read the exact date the article was published, which was approximately ten years ago.

I opened the web browser and did a search for Jaden Price. I found numerous articles about his restaurant in Wailea. It looked like he was doing very successful business. I logged onto Facebook and found him there as well. His profile had his birthday written. I know most people tend to just list the month and the day, but he'd actually entered the year of his birth. Jaden was twenty-eight years old, which would be about right.

I did multiple Google searches for the Maui High School football team that had won the championship ten years ago. I found a couple of other articles, one of which showed a photograph of the team. They had blue and white uniforms with the word Maui written over the numbers on their chest. It wasn't the greatest photograph in the world, but it did have decent resolution. I right-clicked on the photograph and saved it onto the desktop. I then opened the picture in Photoshop and blew it up so that I could see close-up views of the various players. There were four rows of players. I found Bryan Sanders in the first row. The other guy I was looking for was in the second.

A question immediately popped into my mind. How had Brooklyn known to look here? The article would have been too hard to find unless she'd known background information on it. Jaden Price must have told her. There couldn't be another answer.

I heard a knock on the door behind me.

"What are you looking at?" Alana asked.

"Come take a look."

She walked across the room and stood behind me.

"The Maui football team? Isn't that what Brooklyn was searching?" she asked.

"Yeah. Take a closer look at the photo. Let me know what you see."

It only took Alana ten seconds to spot him.

"Jaden Smith. They knew each other."

"Not only was he on the same team as Bryan Sanders, but look at his number."

"Eighty-eight. What's the significance of that?"

"Two things. One, it's also the name of his restaurant, which tells me this time in his life was pretty important to him."

"I think I've actually heard of his place. I had no idea he owned it, though. Captain Price never even talked about it. What's the second thing about that number?"

"Eighty-eight is a common number for a wide receiver. We know Bryan Sanders was the quarterback. Not only were these guys teammates, but they would have spent a ton of time practicing closely together. They had a bond going back years."

I waited for Alana to respond, but she didn't.

"One more thing. They won a championship. I have no doubt Jaden's father was one proud papa. Can you tell me he didn't remember the name of the quarterback his son played with? Yet he made no mention of even remotely knowing Bryan Sanders after he was arrested for attacking you. He couldn't have forgotten."

"I'm sorry," she said. "You were right."

Chapter 31
The Football Coach

Perspective: Poe

It took just a few minutes of searching online to determine that Jaden Price's football coach was still employed at Maui High. Before I'd left the house, Alana and I developed a divide and conquer plan. I'd take the interview with the coach. She'd talk to a woman in her department that she hoped could help shed some additional light on the day I was arrested.

It was actually football season, so I sat in the bleachers and watched the last thirty minutes or so of the football practice. I felt completely silly because I was having flashbacks of my time in high school where the football jocks picked on poor skinny Edgar Rutherford. It's amazing how that stuff stays with you.

The coaches were all dressed in that predictable gym teacher outfit: the white polo shirt tucked into the shorts that are probably a bit too tight for comfort. They concluded the practice by having the team run several laps around the field, and then they had some speech around the fifty-yard line. I was way too far away to hear it, but I was absolutely sure it had to be as rousing as something out of Braveheart because the players all let out some loud hoot at the end of it and ran for the locker room.

I thought I could almost see a young Bryan Sanders throwing that game-winning pass to the son of the local police captain. The crowd must have erupted into crazy cheers and applause. I wondered if anyone could have predicted back then who Bryan Sanders would grow up to be. He'd traded his playbook for a criminal rap sheet. Now he was spending the rest of his life in a prison cell.

He wasn't the only one who'd changed since high school. I had as well. I certainly would never have seen myself standing outside his trailer in the middle of the night and having to be stopped by my best friend from killing him. It had been over a year, but I could still feel the rage that had been inside me that night.

I'd crippled the man, and I still didn't regret it, not one bit. I wasn't sure what that made me. As I eluded to in the beginning of this tale, a part of my soul had changed because of these investigations. I'd wanted to get back to the guy I was before I moved to the island. I knew now that couldn't happen. A strange thing had also occurred since someone, presumably Jaden Price, shot me. I no longer wanted to be that naïve guy that stepped off the plane in Kahului.

I'd printed the photograph of the team so I could make sure I identified the right coach. It wasn't hard to spot him. Despite a decade passing, he still pretty much looked the same. He was a Hawaiian, maybe average height, but he had a square body that looked like he could have plowed through a line of defensive backs. It made sense. He'd probably been a high school or college football star himself and had decided to make a career teaching kids to do the same.

I waited several minutes after the players had run off the field and then I walked under the bleachers and found the coach's office. Coach Kalani's office was the larger one of a group of three rooms. I saw who I guessed was an assistant coach in one of the others. The third office was empty.

I knocked on the open door of Kalani's office and entered. He looked up from a notebook filled with pencil sketches of what I guessed were football plays. I'm sure you can tell just how athletically inclined I am. They were just a bunch of squiggly lines to me.

"Hi. I'm looking for Coach Kalani."

"You found him. How can I help you?"

"I was wondering if I could talk to you about one of your past players."

"Are you a college scout?"

"Not at all."

"Who did you want to ask me about?"

"Two people, actually. The first guy's name is Bryan Sanders."

Kalani said nothing, but I noticed the thumb on his right hand twitch.

"He was the quarterback on the team that won the…"

"I know exactly who he was. You don't have to remind me," he said, cutting me off.

I waited for him to elaborate, but he didn't.

"Can I ask you about him?"

"What do you want to know?" he asked.

"Do you mind if I shut the door? This is a sensitive subject."

Kalani hesitated a moment. Then he nodded.

I walked over to the door and pulled it shut. I then walked back to his desk and sat down on the chair in front of it.

"My name's Edgar Rutherford. About a year and a half ago, Bryan Sanders broke into my house and tried to murder my wife."

Kalani didn't respond to that statement, either. I could see the thoughts spinning behind his eyes, though. He knew something. There was no doubt about that.

"I'm trying to get some background information on Sanders," I continued.

"I'm sorry for what happened to your wife, but I heard he got arrested already. What can you do now?"

"You're right. He's in jail, but I'm trying to establish his relationship with another guy. He was also on the same team. Jaden Price. Do you remember him?"

I watched his hand, and sure enough, the thumb twitched a second time. This one was more of a spasm.

"Do you know him?" I asked again.

"Yeah. I know him."

"How close were Sanders and Price back then?"

"They were inseparable. Why are you asking me about Price? Did he have something to do with your wife's attack?"

"I'm sorry to drag you into this, and I must ask you to keep this conversation between the two of us. I believe Jaden Price may have committed some serious crimes."

"Are you a cop?"

"No, but my wife is. I do private investigations."

"She must work with Jaden's father."

"Yes. Captain Price."

"I'm sorry, but I can't help you."

"Can I ask why?"

"You just said your wife's a cop. Anything I tell you will eventually end up on Price's desk. I'm not interested."

"I can assure you it won't."

"Don't bullshit me. I don't need you coming in here and bullshitting me."

His outburst had been sudden, and it wasn't hard to see the rage that was deep inside him.

"My wife has no intention of telling him. Captain Price can't know about any of this."

Kalani didn't respond.

"You said you heard about Sanders' arrest?" I asked.

"Yeah. I heard about it."

"Did it surprise you?"

"As a matter of fact, it did."

"Why is that?"

"Because I would have thought it would have been Jaden Price who got arrested."

"Why?"

"Because he's a sociopath, and I don't use that term lightly."

"What kind of trouble did Jaden get into during high school?"

"What didn't he do? He got away with it all. Nobody could stop that kid."

"Why not?"

"Why do you think? It was his father. The guy always protected Jaden. I tried kicking him off the team, but Austin Price was good friends with the principal. All it took was one call to him, and Jaden was back on. What was I going to do? I needed to keep my job."

"Mr. Kalani, I know you're not this upset because of some juvenile antics and because the principal slapped your hand. What did Jaden really do?"

"It won't help you. Whatever you're trying to nail him for now, it won't matter. It's done, and nothing you can say will make me try to bring it back."

"So, that's it? You can't help me."

"I'm sorry."

I'm not really sure what I was expecting to hear. Maybe I was trying to confirm that Jaden Price was a bad guy and that I wasn't just imagining things. At the very least, I'd gotten that.

I stood.

"Thank you for your time."

Kalani nodded.

I got ready to turn, but then I did something without really thinking about it.

"I want to show you something."

I lifted the bottom of my t-shirt. The injuries had healed, but the scars were still thick and ugly.

"Jaden Price did this to me. I can't let him get away with it."

I turned and walked toward the door.

"He raped my daughter," Kalani said.

I stopped and turned back to him.

"They went out on a date. She was so excited. The star wide receiver. I didn't know what he was really like before then. I should have. He was a cocky kid, but a lot of these guys are at this age. I should have known, though. I should have never allowed her to see him. When she got back that night, my wife and I knew something was wrong. She wouldn't tell us until the next morning. We took her to the hospital. We called the police. We did everything we were supposed to do. None of it mattered. She said it was rape. He said it was consensual. His father covered it up. No one would prosecute, so maybe you can understand my reluctance to get involved."

"Did you ever talk to Captain Price about it?"

"He came to my house the day after we reported the rape."

Kalani gave an ironic laugh.

"I actually thought he was coming to apologize for what his kid had done. What an idiot I was."

"What did he say?"

"He threatened us. He told us that he would make our life a living hell if we didn't drop the charges. Then he implied that my daughter was a whore. My sixteen-year-old daughter. His kid took away her innocence. She was never the same after that. If you think you're going to go up against Jaden Price, you better be prepared to take out the father first. He won't let you get anywhere near his kid. It's not going to happen."

I thanked Kalani again for his time and walked back to my car in the parking lot outside the stadium.

There were only two questions that were running through my head as I made the drive back to my house. The first was "How much did Captain Price know about the murders committed in the last several years?" The second was "How could I prove what Jaden had done?"

Photographs of football teams weren't going to do it. The guy might be a piece of human garbage, but he wasn't dumb. He'd done a damn good job of covering his tracks. We really didn't have anything on him, and I didn't see how that was going to change.

Chapter 32
You Lied

I hadn't been able to sleep much the night after the funeral. Poe's theory had seemed like a pretty far stretch at first, but I couldn't dismiss the connection between Jaden Price and Bryan Sanders. The thought that the Price family was involved had shaken me hard.

It brought up obvious concerns, as well as feelings of deep betrayal, the primary one being the degree to which Captain Price was involved. Had he known I was going to be attacked? If not, how long afterward did he learn it had been Sanders? I wondered if he hadn't known for sure until Poe had proven it beyond doubt.

There was something else. As far as I could tell, Captain Price was the only person other than Foxx and me who knew what Poe had done to Sanders, yet he hadn't arrested Poe. I now wondered if that was to partially atone for his guilt.

I tried to formulate my plan as I drove to work. I had three people I needed to speak with. Doug was the first on my list. I found him at his desk staring at the computer screen and shoving a bagel into his mouth. I pulled up a chair and sat down beside him.

"Good morning, Doug."

"Good morning. How are you?" he asked between chews of his bagel.

He hadn't bothered turning away from his monitor either.

"I'm okay. I need to have a sensitive conversation with you, but I'm not sure the best way to start it."

That got his attention. He put the bagel down and turned to me.

"What's this about?"

"Do you remember a conversation we had some months ago? I asked you to tell me who'd done an internet search on Genesis Riley and Brooklyn Van Kirk."

"I remember. It was Detective Shaw, wasn't it?"

"Yes, and I asked you to keep that between you and I. Here's the thing. Shaw confronted me a few days after that. He said he knew I'd been doing research on the use of his computer. There were only two people that knew about that, so who did you tell?"

"I didn't tell anyone."

"Are you sure? Because I certainly didn't say anything."

"Why would I tell? I didn't want Shaw to know I was checking up on him."

"I'm not saying you told Shaw, but maybe you mentioned it to someone else, and they told him."

"I didn't. I swear."

"People like office politics, Doug. I know that. I'll understand if you told someone. I just need to know who it was."

"Alana, I wouldn't betray your trust. Never."

"Okay. I believe you. I need you to do something else for me, though."

"Just name it."

"I want you to let it slip that I asked you to do another search, this one on Allison Jenkins."

"What do you want me to search for?"

"Nothing. You won't find anything."

"I don't get it. You want me to confess to doing a search I didn't do?" he asked.

"Exactly. Don't pick the biggest office gossip. That would be too obvious, but don't tell someone that can keep a secret."

"You want this to get back to Allison?"

"Of course."

I stood.

"Does this have something to do with Shaw killing those people?" he asked.

"Thank you, Doug. I appreciate you doing this for me."

I left before he could ask another question.

I really did believe Doug when he said he didn't tell anyone about the search of Shaw's computer use, yet Shaw had known. That meant the leak had to have come from me, and it did. I had told someone. I'd told Captain Price.

My second stop of the day was with Doctor Rachel Bennett, who was our chief medical examiner. She and I had started at the department around the same time, and we'd worked together on most of my cases. She was a dependable and loyal person, and I considered her a friend.

"Alana, nice of you to come by. I was actually planning on calling you soon to see if you wanted to get lunch sometime."

"I'd love to, but it might have to wait a couple of weeks. I'm trying to wrap up a case."

"Which one?"

"It's actually the Van Kirk investigation."

"Van Kirk? I thought that was put to bed."

"Not quite. Regarding the autopsy you performed, I'm guessing you were the one who told Detective Shaw that the victim was pregnant."

"I did. It was heartbreaking."

"Did Shaw ask you to take a DNA sample from the child? I know he tried to blame the murder on the person he assumed to have been the father."

"He did ask me. I remember he provided me a sample from the suspect."

"You don't need to call him that. We both know who it was."

"Sorry. It's just…"

"I know. Did you get a chance to run the test?"

"Yes. Your husband wasn't the father."

"And you told Shaw that?"

"I did."

"Just curious. What was his reaction?"

"He really didn't have one."

"It didn't seem to bother him?"

"No. He appeared kind of neutral about the whole thing."

"Did you tell anyone else that Poe wasn't the father?" I asked.

"No. Just Shaw, but it's all in my report. Anyone who has access to the report could have learned that fact."

"If I were to provide you with a new DNA sample from someone else, could you run another paternity test?"

"Of course."

"Great. By the way, can I get a copy of that DNA test?"

"Sure. I can do that right now. Do you want a hard copy or would you like me to email it?"

"Email would be great. Thanks, and let's do that lunch soon. My treat."

I didn't ask Rachel to leak that I had spoken with her about the DNA test. She was a discreet person, and I knew she wouldn't tell anyone about our visit. Still, I'd made it a point to say hello to a few different people as I'd entered and exited Rachel's office. I wasn't working a case that would have required me to see her, at least not a current one that was official. If someone decided to keep tabs on me, it would be fairly easy for them to discover that I'd had a meeting with the medical examiner.

I waited until the end of the day before meeting with the third person on my list. I knew this one was going to get rough. The woman had lied to me, and I couldn't let that slide.

Poe had just texted me about his meeting with the Maui High football coach. You already know what he discovered, so I won't repeat it here. Just after reading his messages, I sent my own text to Hailey Roth. I asked her to meet me outside the station.

I left the office several minutes before that so I could get to my car and pull it up to the front. Hailey stepped outside a few seconds after I stopped by the curb. I saw her looking around for me. I did a small tap on the horn, and she spotted me.

She walked to the car as I rolled down the passenger window.

"You wanted to see me, ma'am?"

"Get in the car, please."

Hailey opened the door and climbed inside.

"Is everything okay?" she asked.

"Give me a moment. I don't want to have this conversation here."

I drove us across the street to a coffee shop. I parked in the back of the lot and turned off the car. Hailey went to open her door.

"We're not going inside. I want to talk in the car."

"Ma'am, what's going on?"

"Did you think you were going to get away with it?" I asked.

"Get away with what, ma'am?"

"You lied to me."

"About what?"

"Several months ago, when we were outside Pika Mahoe's house, we had a conversation about the day my husband was arrested. Do you remember that conversation?"

"Of course."

"Why did you lie to me?"

"I don't know what you're talking about. I didn't lie about anything."

"So, now I'm upset. I was willing to chalk the first time up to you being under a lot of stress. I thought maybe you just didn't remember things correctly. There were multiple murders, and you really haven't been on the force that long. I know the pressure we're all under to solve these things. But now that you're sticking to your story, I know that I can't trust you."

I waited for Hailey to respond, but she didn't.

"I specifically asked you who was on the second floor when that burner phone was found in my husband's office. You said it was just you and Detective Shaw, only we both know that's not true. So either you're not a very observant person, in which case you need to be removed from the forensics department immediately, or you lied to me to cover for someone else. Which is it?"

Hailey said nothing.

"I did some asking around today. I find it interesting that you and Officer Jenkins used to be roommates. Do you know why I find that interesting?"

"No, ma'am."

"Do you take me for a fool?"

"No, ma'am."

"No, ma'am. Yes, ma'am. Whatever you say ma'am. You're pretty good at playing this little timid girl act, but I know what you are. When I'm done with you, your ass will be on the street. Just because you work for the department, it doesn't mean you don't have to follow the law. You'll be damn lucky if you don't get arrested. You lied to a detective. You obstructed justice. I know for a fact that Allison Jenkins was on the second floor of my house. I know she went into that bedroom before anyone else. You had to have seen her. I want to know why you concealed that information from me."

"She asked me to."

"Why?"

"She heard the rumors that someone from our team planted that phone."

"That's because someone did plant it."

"She swore it wasn't her. She said it was Detective Shaw. She asked me not to mention that she was up there."

"Why would you agree to that? What in the world would convince you it was okay to do that?"

"She was just looking for the child. She swore that's all she was doing."

"I don't believe you. I think you're a part of this. If she had just been looking for my niece, you both would have said so."

"She's my friend."

"She's your fiend," I repeated, not sure I'd heard her correctly.

Actually, I knew I'd heard it correctly. I just couldn't believe that was her excuse.

"She's always been there for me," she said.

"Let me guess. She passed you the Kleenex box when you had some problems with some guy. Is that it? You're done little girl. You're out."

I started the engine.

"Please, I didn't know."

"What didn't you know?" I asked.

"I thought Detective Shaw committed those crimes. That's what everyone said."

"Everyone? Who specifically told you it was Shaw?"

"It was after we got the ballistics results on the gun Shaw used to kill himself. I matched them to the one that shot your husband. I told Allison that, and she said you'd suspected Shaw all along of framing him."

"She said that?"

"Yes."

"Why aren't you and Jenkins roommates any longer?"

"She moved out. She lives with her boyfriend now."

"You mean Jaden Price."

"She moved in with him a couple of months ago."

"When did she start seeing Jaden?"

"It's been a little more than a year."

"How did she meet him?"

"It was at his restaurant. She said she heard that it was good and wanted to try it out. She invited me to go with her. We met him at the bar. She gave him her number."

"Okay. Let's go back to the day my husband was arrested. Exactly where and when did you see Allison on the second floor?"

"I was walking up the stairs when I saw her coming out of the bedroom."

"Which bedroom? The one with the crib?"

"No. She didn't have the baby then. She said she was looking for the child. I saw her walk into the other bedroom, and she came out with the baby after that."

"When you saw her coming out of the first bedroom, was she in the doorway, or was she fully into the room?"

"She was fully inside and then she walked out."

"You didn't find that a little odd?"

"What do you mean?"

"Why would she need to walk completely into a room to see if there was a crib inside? She could have easily just poked her head through the door."

"What are you saying? Are you accusing her of putting that phone there?"

I ignored her question.

"I need to know where you stand. Are you willing to say on the record that you saw Officer Jenkins leaving that bedroom?" I asked.

She hesitated.

"This is your moment, Roth. You either tell the truth or you stick to your original story, which we both know is garbage."

"I'll testify to what I saw."

"Good. Good."

I put the car in reverse.

"I won't say anything about this," she swore.

"I don't care who you tell. Talk to Allison or don't talk to her. It doesn't matter to me."

We drove back to the parking lot of the police station in silence. I stopped at the same spot I'd picked her up. I didn't look at her. I didn't say anything.

Hailey opened the door and climbed out.

Chapter 33
Payback

Alana phoned me after her meeting with the forensics lady. It's a great feeling, isn't it, when you get confirmation of your theories? Allison had been on the second floor of my home, and now we had someone willing to testify to that. Unfortunately, it still didn't prove she'd planted the phone and the hairs. It also didn't do anything to show that Jaden Price was involved.

"We need to turn Allison," I said. "We need something on her that will convince her to give up Jaden."

"I've already requested a warrant for her phone and bank records. I don't have high hopes, though. She's a smart girl."

"Don't be so sure. Jaden might have easily manipulated her into doing something she wouldn't ordinarily do. Look at Bryan Sanders. He convinced him to murder multiple people, and Jaden's the one walking around free."

"Why do you think Sanders never flipped on Jaden?"

"Loyalty. There is no other explanation."

"And if Allison has the same loyalty?"

"She won't. They haven't been together long enough."

"Are you on your way home?"

"Not yet. There's one more stop I want to make. I'm almost there now."

"Where are you going?" she asked.

"I'm not sure I want to answer that, at least not without my lawyer present."

"You're going to his restaurant, aren't you?"

"Damn. You are perceptive."

"This could be a good move. Make sure he sees you."

"You're not upset?" I asked.

"No. It's time we put them on the defensive. Don't worry. It's not like he's going to shoot you in the middle of his place."

"That's what I assumed, too. The way you put it, though, it sounds a little cold."

"Sorry. I'm not indifferent to the danger, but I'd rather go on the attack then sit back and wait for them to make the next move."

"I understand."

"By the way, I'm guessing Shaw never told you this, but the DNA tests confirmed you weren't the father of Brooklyn's unborn child."

I said nothing. I knew I couldn't be the father, but I wasn't sure how to respond to something like that.

"Are you there?" she asked.

"Yeah. Just thinking about that kid. He or she never had a chance, did they?"

"Unfortunately, no."

"The baby seems to have been overlooked in all of this."

"Not by me. You think the child was Jaden's?"

"Probably. That video guy said Brooklyn was dating a guy named Jay. Jay. Jaden. Seems like it has to be the same guy. What are the chances Allison knew that?"

"Fifty-fifty. Maybe that's one of the reasons Jaden killed Brooklyn. He didn't want Allison to find out about the baby."

Alana and I spoke for a few more minutes. I ended the call as I drove into the parking lot of Jaden's Eighty-Eight restaurant. It was still early in the evening, and it was a Monday, so the lot wasn't very full.

I backed into the parking space on the off-chance that I needed to make a quick exit. I entered the restaurant and told the hostess that I was going to sit at the bar.

The interior of the place was gorgeous. It had a modern design with lots of shiny metal and glass. The back wall was essentially a giant window with tremendous views of the ocean. The sun was low in the sky, and shafts of red and orange light reflected off the metal beams.

The stark design wasn't something you saw on Maui very often. Most places seemed to have dark wood or very laid back designs that made it seem as if the owners had put little money into the establishments. There was something refreshing about that to me, but I could see how someone would easily be blown away by this place.

It pissed me off to admit this, but Jaden Price had great taste, or maybe he just let his designer do his or her thing. Let's go with that choice.

There were only a couple of other guys at the bar. They were sitting down on one end and seemed completely engrossed in some football game on the bar's television.

I sat on the opposite end, and the sole bartender approached me. She had short black hair and dark eyes. She looked like she might be twenty-five at best.

"Good evening. What can I get you?"

"A Manhattan."

"I haven't made one of those in a while."

"Really? I thought it was a classic."

"We're on Maui. People tend to want something a bit more tropical."

She started mixing my drink.

"How long are you in town for?" she asked.

"I actually live on the island. I'm in Kaanapali."

"Is that right?"

"I came out here a few years ago. Fell in love with a local cop. Decided to stay."

"Congratulations. I'm Meg by the way."

"Poe."

"Nice to meet you, Poe."

"What about you? How long have you lived here?" I asked.

"Most of my life. My parents are artists. They moved here back in the eighties."

"Artists. There are quite a few of those on Maui."

"They're everywhere, but maybe that's my favorite thing about this island."

"I know a few myself. What about you? Are you an artist?" I asked.

"I'm trying to be. Not sure if this art degree is going to get me anything but debt, though."

"What kind of artist are you?"

"A painter."

"Have you heard of an artist named Lauren Rogers?"

She handed me my drink.

"Are you serious? Of course, I have. She was probably the best known artist on Maui."

"My best friend was engaged to her."

That wasn't technically true, but every indication pointed to them moving in that direction.

"When my wife and I got married, he gave me one of her originals. It's in our bedroom," I continued.

"I knew she was killed, but I never heard the full story of what exactly happened to her."

"It was a jealous rival," I said.

"Your friend told you that?"

"Basically. He still misses her. His home is covered with her artwork."

"God, I'd love to see that sometime."

"He and I own a bar in Lahaina called Harry's. You should swing by some time. I'm sure he'd be willing to show you her work. You just need to coordinate a time."

"I've heard of Harry's. Little dive bar a couple of blocks off Front Street."

"Yeah, that's it."

"What brings you over to this part of the island?" she asked.

"Someone told me about this place. I've been looking for a restaurant to take my wife for our anniversary."

"You can't go wrong here. Everything on the menu is delicious."

"What's your favorite entrée?"

"Probably the ribeye, but really, everything is good."

"Did Jaden Price open this place or did he buy it from someone else?"

"I don't remember what it was called when he bought it, but it was definitely a tourist trap. He gutted the building and completely redid the theme. How do you know Jaden?"

"My wife's a cop. She works with his father."

"That's right. His father's the chief of police or something like that?"

"Yeah, something like that."

I took a sip of my drink.

"You make a good Manhattan," I continued.

"Thanks. Would you like to order anything to eat?"

"Maybe in a little while. Hey, is Jaden working tonight?"

"Not on Mondays. It's the only night he takes off."

"Makes sense. I used to work at a restaurant when I was in college. Mondays are dead."

"Tell me about it. I try to do everything I can to not get this shift."

"So what happened tonight? Someone call in sick?"

"You got it. I won't make anything tonight."

I took another sip of my drink. I hadn't been lying. It was an excellent Manhattan.

I put the drink down on the bar and slipped my phone out of my pocket. I opened the photos app and found a shot I'd taken of one of Brooklyn's website photos. It was a picture of her with her Canon camera.

"I was wondering if you'd seen someone around here. Do you mind if I show you a photograph?"

"Sure. Who is it?"

I showed her the photograph of Brooklyn.

"Do you recognize this woman?"

The bartender's smile instantly vanished.

"Why are you asking about her?"

"I'm guessing you know her."

"Yeah, but you didn't answer my question," Meg said.

"My wife's a detective. I'm helping her with something."

I reached into my wallet and removed one of Alana's business cards.

"Here's her card. You can call and verify if you like."

I slid the card across the bar. She looked at it without picking it up.

"Anyone can make a card that says anything."

"You're right. They can."

I reached back into my wallet and removed a fifty-dollar bill. I placed it on the bar and then put my drink on top of it.

"Mondays do suck, don't they? It sure would be nice if you could have a good shift tonight," I continued.

Meg hesitated.

Then she said, "Her name was Brooklyn. I don't remember what her last name was."

"Was? So you know she died?"

"Hard not to know, especially if you work here."

"Why's that?" I asked.

"Because she was here all the time. It was a real shock when we heard she got murdered."

"Am I safe to assume Brooklyn was here to see the owner of this restaurant?"

"That's right."

"Who told you she was killed?"

"Jaden did."

"How did he take it?"

"He's not an emotional guy, but I'm sure he was torn up about it."

"He likes to hide his feelings?"

"Yeah."

"Was there anything odd or different about their relationship? Something that might have made it stand out?"

"Your drink looks empty. Can I get you another one?" Meg asked.

"Of course."

She took the glass and the fifty-dollar bill under it.

"I wouldn't say there was anything odd, but she was here a lot," she said.

"A lot? As in too much?"

"I got that impression. Jaden made a couple of remarks around me."

"What did he say?" I asked.

"I don't remember the exact words, but they were something to the effect that he was beginning to view her as a stalker."

The bartender put the second Manhattan down. I took a sip. It was as good as the first.

"Have you met his new girlfriend?"

"You mean Allison? Yeah, she's real nice," Meg said.

"How long have they been dating?"

"Tough to say."

I was tempted to sigh, but I didn't so I wouldn't offend her. I got the message, though. I opened my wallet and removed another fifty. I put it under the new glass. I didn't need to ask my question about Allison and Jaden a second time.

"They've been dating for over a year."

"Did his time with Allison overlap his dating of Brooklyn?"

"Maybe. I think that's one of the reasons he was so frustrated about her coming around."

"When I worked at that restaurant during college, the managers would work the longest hours. I don't think they ever went a week without working at least sixty to seventy hours."

"It's the same here."

"I remember they would always eat at the restaurant, too. Lunch and dinner. There was this one manager who always ordered the same thing. It was a burger, cooked medium, with Monterey Jack cheese, onions, lettuce, and tomato. Fries, of course. I don't know how he stayed so thin. He had that same meal at least twice a day for six days a week. Kind of disgusting when you think about it. I bet Jaden eats lunch or dinner here."

Meg nodded.

"The managers where I worked would always ask the bartenders to ring up their personal orders. Does Jaden do that with you?" I asked.

"Sometimes."

"Is there a particular drink he likes with his meal?"

"That depends. Are you talking lunch or dinner?"

"Which shifts do you work?"

"I always work the dinner shift. I go to school during the day."

"Then which drink does he prefer at dinner?"

"He always has a scotch."

"What's his brand?"

"It's actually a Japanese scotch."

"Yamasaki?" I asked.

"You've heard of it? That's surprising. Most haven't."

Unfortunately, and to my great dismay since I didn't want to have anything in common with Jaden, it was also my preferred brand of scotch. Foxx had introduced me to it.

"Will you be working tomorrow night?" I asked.

"Yes."

"How many years do you have left in college?"

"Three more. I got a late start."

"Tell me. Have your parents been successful artists?"

"How is that any of your business?"

"It's not really, but it applies to what I'm about to ask you. A deal I want to make."

"No. They're not successful. My mother is unemployed. My father works at an art gallery selling other people's work."

"Did you pay your first year's tuition, or did you have to take out student loans?"

"I paid some of it, but not all."

"How much in loans did you have to take?"

"Again, how is this your business?" she asked.

"The deal. It's coming. Don't worry. So how much is your loan?"

"About ten grand," she said.

"Okay. Here's my deal. Tomorrow night, you'll make sure you're the bartender who takes Jaden's order. When he's done with his Yamasaki, I want you to take the glass. Grab it by the bottom so you don't disturb the rim of the glass. Bring the glass to me at the end of your shift."

"Why would I do that?"

"In return, I'll pay off your student loan."

Meg laughed.

"You had me going for a while. I really thought this was going to be something good."

"You thought it would be better than paying off your loans? What were you expecting? Pay off your parents' mortgage?"

"I was expecting a serious offer."

"I may not look like much with my t-shirt, shorts, and sandals, but my offer was more than serious. Bring me the glass, bring me his fork, too, and I'll pay you ten grand."

"How would you know they're even his? I could give you anyone's glass. Hell, I could give you your own back?"

"Because I already know how the test will turn out, so if it doesn't, then I'll know you conned me. Let's alter the deal. I'll pay you half when you deliver those items to me. You'll get the second half when I get the test results."

"Why do you need it if you already know what the results will be?"

"Because my gut is not the same as concrete proof."

"How do I know you'll pay me the second half?" she asked.

"You don't, but five grand is better than you'll make here. I'm good for it, though. I'm also guessing you've learned to spot a bullshitter from a mile away after doing this job. Do I impress you as being one?"

"You mentioned tests. What kind of tests?"

"Don't worry about that."

"What do you and Jaden have going on?"

"We're playing a bit of a game. He paid one of my bartenders to take something from me. I'm returning the favor. So, would you like to make a deal?"

"Okay. Let's do it."

I handed her my business card and took Alana's off the bar.

"Call me when you get off work tomorrow night, and we'll figure out a place to meet."

"You better have that money," she said.

"Don't worry. I'll have it."

I stood.

"About those two Manhattans," I continued, and I opened my wallet to pay her for the drinks.

"They're on the house," she said.

"That's not what I was going to ask, but thank you."

"What were you going to ask?"

"I was going to say that they were delicious. Have a good night, Meg. I'll see you tomorrow."

Chapter 34
Allison Jenkins

Perspective: Alana

It had been several days since I'd spoken to Captain Price. On the one hand, that wasn't surprising. He'd taken two weeks of bereavement leave. That said, I also felt confident that he'd heard about my investigation into Allison Jenkins. There was a part of me that expected him to order me off the case, or at the very least, demand that I justify my reasoning and then reject it on the grounds that I didn't have the evidence. He hadn't, though. He'd been completely silent.

I scheduled the interview with Allison and informed her that she needed to have her attorney or union representative present. She didn't ask me the purpose of the meeting. She didn't really say much of anything, which in itself spoke volumes.

I also requested the presence of Piper Lane, the prosecutor who'd gone after Poe. She and I had patched things up, as much as one can expect to given the circumstances. I told her everything we'd discovered, and she agreed that we had a case.

I was the last person to enter the interview room that afternoon. I sat down and placed the folder I had on the table in front of me. Piper Lane was on my side. Allison and the union rep, John Chase, were on the other.

"I assume you know why we're here," I said.

"Not really. I've heard you're looking into the murders committed by Detective Shaw again, but I'm not sure why you apparently think I'm involved," Allison said.

"Let's get to it then. Let's go back to the day you were at my house, the day you arrested Edgar Rutherford."

"I didn't arrest your husband. Detective Shaw did."

"Very well, the day Detective Shaw arrested my husband. Talk me through what happened after he was removed from the house."

"Your husband had informed us there was an infant in the house. I believe she's your niece. Detective Shaw instructed me to locate her and watch over her until a family member could come get her."

"What did you do after Shaw gave you those instructions?"

"Your husband had told us she was on the second floor. I went up there, got the child, and came back downstairs."

"That's interesting. You went directly upstairs, went right to the bedroom where her crib is located, and got her."

"No. I didn't go directly there. I'd never been to your house before. I had to look inside one or two of the other bedrooms before I found her."

"So you did go into the other rooms?"

"I didn't go inside, per se. I just looked from the doorways."

"You didn't go inside my husband's office?"

"I'm really not sure which room was his office, but the only one I walked into was where the child was located."

"When I spoke with Hailey Roth, your former roommate, she indicated to me that you instructed her not to tell me or anyone else that you'd even been on the second floor."

"I never asked her to say that. Why would I do that?"

"Because by then there was ample evidence that the burner phone and the victim's hairs were planted."

"Really? I'm still not aware of any evidence that shows that beyond a reasonable doubt. You proved your husband couldn't have committed the murder. That's all."

"He didn't commit the murder, but are you still saying that was his phone?"

"No. I'm saying that he may have been mistaken when he said the phone hadn't been there that morning. He could have simply not seen it. It might have been planted days before we carried out our search."

"Let's go back to Ms. Roth. You're saying she lied to me when she said you asked her not to reveal the fact that she saw you coming out of the home office?"

"Yes. That's exactly what I'm saying."

"Why would she lie?" Piper asked.

"I'm not really sure, but I have my suspicions."

"Which are?" Piper asked.

"Jealousy."

"What would she have to be jealous about?" I asked.

"You were right when you said Hailey and I had been roommates. We lived together for three years. We split all the costs. I chose not to renew the lease with her when I moved in with my boyfriend. It put her in a tough financial position. I knew that, but I didn't see any reason to hold back my relationship just to help her pay the rent."

"Let me get this straight. Hailey Roth is lying about you because she's having trouble paying the rent?" Piper asked.

"People do all sorts of uncharacteristic things when they're under stress, especially financial stress."

"The boyfriend you just referred to, that's Jaden Price?" I asked.

"Yes."

"When did you meet Mr. Price?"

"About a year ago. We met at his restaurant."

"I've heard his business does very well."

"I believe so. You'd need to ask him."

"You live with Jaden and you don't know if his restaurant does well or not?" Piper asked.

"He doesn't share the books with me, but he seems happy about how things are going."

"I know you're aware of who Brooklyn Van Kirk was. Did you know that Mr. Price and Ms. Van Kirk were dating when you met him?" I asked.

"He said they'd gone out a few times. I don't think he considered them as dating."

"Really? We spoke with a member of the wait staff at his restaurant. They said she was there all the time."

"I think Brooklyn wanted the relationship to be something it wasn't."

"So she was harassing him?" I asked.

"I guess you could say that. He confided in me that he wished she would stay away."

"That's interesting. He told you that a woman, a very attractive woman at that, was constantly coming by his restaurant and bothering him?"

"Yes."

"That didn't set off alarm bells?" I asked.

"No. I trusted him."

"I'm impressed. If my boyfriend told me a woman was following him, I'd think there might be a pretty good reason she was doing that."

"What does this have to do with anything, Detective Hu?" John Chase asked.

"I'm getting to it. This is a fact-finding discussion. Officer Jenkins hasn't been charged with anything."

"A fact-finding interview about her love life? Either get to the point quickly, or we're ending this meeting," Chase said.

"Your husband was accused of having an affair with Van Kirk. Did you believe him?" Allison asked.

"I did."

"So why is it strange that I would believe Jaden?"

"Because you really haven't known him very long, and I'm married to Poe. You're only dating Mr. Price."

"I'm living with him."

"Detective Hu, enough with the personal questions," Chase said.

"Yes. I think that's about enough of that."

I reached into my folder and removed several pieces of paper, which I placed in front of Allison and her attorney.

"Do you recognize these?" I asked.

Allison looked at the documents but didn't say anything.

"Those are copies of your credit card statements from the last year," Piper said.

"We've highlighted a few of the transactions. Can you tell us what those are?" I asked.

Allison flipped through the pages until she found the statements with yellow highlights on four lines of expenses.

"They appear to be car rental charges," she said.

"They are, four car rentals with four different car rental companies. All of them are located at the airport," I said.

"I rented a car. So what?"

"You rented four cars, not 'a' car."

"Why did you go to four different rental companies?" Piper asked.

"I wanted to try out different companies, see which ones had the best service."

"Well, don't leave us hanging. Which one was the best?" I asked.

"There's no reason to treat Officer Jenkins with disrespect," Chase said.

"My apologies."

"We contacted each of those companies. You rented two sedans, one SUV, and one minivan," Piper said.

"If you say so."

"If I say so? You don't remember what you rented?" Piper asked.

"I rented whatever they had available."

"Why did you even need to rent a vehicle? You have your own car, don't you?" I asked.

"Yes, but it's been in the shop."

"That often?"

"Yes."

"I thought you might say that. We did notice a few charges to a car repair shop. We checked with them and got copies of your records. You've only had oil changes and a state inspection in the last year. Your car seems to be running fine."

Allison said nothing.

"Did you get your car fixed at another shop?" Piper asked.

"I must have."

"What was the name of the shop? Where is it located?" Piper asked.

"I'm not sure."

"How did you pay for those repairs? It seems like you use your credit card for everything. You even charge two dollar drinks at the local coffee shop," I said.

"I remember now. I rented the van and the SUV because I needed to transport something large."

"What did you need to transport?" Piper asked.

"Jaden bought a large screen television. He asked me to rent something that would be large enough to move it."

"Which vehicle did you use to move the TV?" I asked.

"I think the van."

"So what did you move with the SUV?" Piper asked.

"I don't remember. It was months ago."

"Okay. I won't bother asking about the sedans. Let's just get to point of these rentals so we don't try Mr. Chase's patience anymore," I said.

I removed a series of color photographs and placed them in front of Allison.

"These are images from various traffic cameras around the island. You'll notice they show four different vehicles: two sedans, a minivan, and a SUV," I said.

"The license plates correspond with the vehicles you rented. The dates these images were recorded also perfectly match the dates you rented the vehicles. Therefore, it's our conclusion that's you driving those vehicles in the photographs," Piper said.

"Do you know what those dates also match?" I asked.

Allison didn't respond.

I held up the photograph of the first sedan.

"You rented this car the day before Brooklyn Van Kirk was murdered. You returned it late the morning she was killed."

I held up the photograph of the SUV.

"This was rented the day Molly Randolph had her throat slit. It was returned the same day."

I pointed to the third and fourth photographs.

"The sedan was rented the day Pika Mahoe was murdered. The minivan was the same day Detective Shaw was killed," I continued.

"Those traffic cameras put you in the exact same locations on the island where the murders occurred. Can you explain that?" Piper asked.

Chase whispered something in her ear before she could respond.

She nodded.

"Officer Jenkins has no comment," Chase said.

"I'm sure she doesn't," Piper added.

"The two sedans and the SUV only had one person in the front seat. Unfortunately, we can't make out the driver. They're two people in the van, though. Here's what I think happened. You drove Jaden Price to Detective Shaw's house. You both rendered him captive and you or Jaden then drove Shaw's car to the beach while the other followed in the van. You shot Shaw in the head and staged it to look like suicide. Then you and Jaden drove away together in the van," I said.

"We tracked the van all over the island with those traffic cameras. You went from the airport directly to Shaw's, then to the beach, then back to Jaden Price's condo. The van was returned that afternoon. We know for a fact that you were at work, so we assume Jaden was the one who returned it to the airport."

"This is all just hypothetical nonsense. I didn't kill anyone."

"What forensics evidence do you have that places Officer Jenkins at any of the crime scenes? Do you have fingerprints, hair samples, clothing samples? You can't place her at the scene," Chase said.

"I don't need it. I have those car rental charges on her credit card and those traffic cameras. Four people dead, including a decorated detective. The jury will want someone to pay. I hate that it's a dirty cop. I really do, but I can win with this evidence all day long," Piper said.

"Did you know Brooklyn was pregnant?" I asked.

Her reaction didn't let me down. Her eyes widened, and she visibly flinched.

"I thought you might not. Shaw didn't go around announcing it. He wanted to wait until the DNA tests proved Poe was the father. When they came back negative, he kept everything quiet. It didn't look good for his case," I continued.

Piper reached into the folder and slid the DNA test results to Allison.

"That's the test right there. Mr. Rutherford is not the father," Piper said.

I turned to Piper.

"Sounds a bit like a bad talk show, doesn't it?" I asked.

"I don't see the humor in this," Chase said.

"No, it's not funny. None of it is," Piper said.

"Was it your idea or Jaden's idea to get the beer bottles from my husband's bar? We know Molly Randolph was paid to swipe them," I said.

"I didn't frame your husband."

"Do you know what Poe did this week? He went to Eighty-Eight. I'm sure you know that's the name of Jaden's restaurant. He did to Jaden exactly what was done to him. He paid a member of the staff to take a glass from the bar. Do you know whose glass it was? It was Jaden's. He drinks Yamasaki scotch. We used his DNA on that glass to run another test."

I turned to Piper.

"Ms. Lane, who is the father?"

Piper didn't say anything. She just slid the DNA test results to Allison. She didn't even look at them, but John Chase did.

"Brooklyn Van Kirk was strangled. Molly Randolph and Pika Mahoe had their throats slit. I couldn't understand why Brooklyn wasn't killed with a knife. At first I thought you or Jaden assumed it would be too strange to have Brooklyn's hairs in my bathroom but not her blood on the clothes. Now I realize it was something entirely different. You knew that child belonged to Jaden. He was two-timing you with Brooklyn. He told you he was just using her to set up Poe. He was doing that, all right, but it was so much more than that. He got her pregnant, and that's one of the reasons she had to go. Only you were the one who did it. You strangled her because she tried to take someone who belonged to you. It was your rental car. The traffic cameras show you went there. You're going down for this Allison."

John Chase whispered into her ear again. Before either of them could respond, I spoke again.

"I'm assuming you contacted Captain Price about all of this. I'm also assuming his advice to you was to say nothing. He's not going to bail you out of this. You're not his son. He's the only one walking away from all of this."

"It doesn't have to be that way," Piper said.

"You have a deal to present to Officer Jenkins?" Chase asked.

"I do, and the deal is good for sixty seconds. Then it's off the table. Give us Jaden Price."

"And in exchange?" Chase asked.

"Immunity from prosecution. She'll also need to resign from the police force, effective immediately."

"Can I have a moment with Officer Jenkins?" Chase asked.

"You can have sixty seconds," Piper said.

"I think we may need a few more minutes, if you don't mind."

"I do mind. I'm not happy with this deal, but my boss has ordered me to offer it. Personally, I hope she rejects it because she belongs in jail," Piper said.

This time it was Allison's turn to whisper into Chase's ear. He nodded and turned back to Piper.

"We'll need the offer in writing," Chase said.

"Of course. I've already prepared it. I assumed she'd take the deal."

Piper took the last piece of paper in the folder and handed it to Chase.

"Start talking, Allison. Give us Jaden Price," I said.

She did.

Chapter 35
Captain Price

Perspective: Alana

Jaden Price was gone. He wasn't at his house or at his restaurant or anywhere near any of his friends' and associates' homes. He hadn't left the island on a commercial flight. We'd also checked the private airports. No one by the name of Jaden Price or anyone resembling Jaden Price had chartered a flight. We went to the various marinas and asked about boats that were large enough to make the journey off the island. No one had seen or heard from Jaden Price.

This didn't mean he hadn't left the island. Money can easily buy people's silence, but I thought it was more likely that he was still on Maui. It's not the largest island, but it also isn't the smallest. There were plenty of places he could hide. He wouldn't be able to forever, though.

Captain Price was predictably of no help. He claimed to have not spoken with his son since the funeral. I found that hard to believe, but Allison said she'd been unaware of any meetings or phone calls between the two men for months, with the sole exception being the funeral. It was possible that Price had seen the writing on the wall and had done everything he could to avoid his son, but I didn't think that had been the situation. I believe Allison was helping to cover for Captain Price in exchange for potential help from him in the future.

There was also a comment Allison had made to me. She'd said that Captain Price had bragged about his son's restaurant to her. She'd gone there to check it out. That's when she'd met Jaden. Why would the captain brag about his son, though, if they weren't speaking with each other? It didn't make any sense, so I felt pretty comfortable in my assessment that the captain had been lying.

I could almost guarantee that Allison would have told Jaden about her scheduled meeting with me. Jaden had to have known what it was going to be about. He probably also knew there was a good chance she'd flip on him. That would leave him plenty of time to prepare for what would come next and make his escape.

Poe's theory on all of this was a different one. He thought we should just sit back and wait for Jaden to find us. That said, he wasn't willing to make either of us an easy target. We had police protection for the house for the first twenty-four hours. After that, Poe hired a private security firm. There were two men positioned in the front of the house and another two in the back. If he'd had his way, Poe would have asked them to follow me around at work.

A few days went by after the interrogation with Allison, and we still didn't have any leads on Jaden's whereabouts. Poe was going stir crazy, so we decided to make a trip to Harry's. That wasn't the only reason we'd gone there, though.

Half of the security detail followed us while the other half remained at the house. One guy made regular walks around the parking lot and the rear of the bar. The other stayed inside within a short distance from us.

Poe and I sat at our favorite booth in the back. Kiana brought Poe a Manhattan while I stuck with water. I wanted to stay sharp for the meeting we were about to have. It would have made more sense to have this conversation in his office, but Captain Price had requested Poe's presence. There was no way he was going anywhere near the station, and he didn't want the captain inside our house. We compromised and chose Harry's.

"May I have a seat?" Price asked.

It was somewhat of an odd question. After all, we'd come here at this time to meet him. Maybe he'd just read the obvious discomfort on my husband's face.

I glanced over at Poe, and he seemed intent on not saying anything. I turned back to the captain and indicated to the empty side of the booth. He sat down and placed his hands on the table between us.

"I'm not really sure how to start this conversation," he said. "I'm sorry for what's happened."

"When did you know?" Poe asked.

"I'm sure you won't believe this. I wouldn't if I were in your position, but I didn't know what Jaden was doing. My son and I had drifted apart. My wife's funeral was the first time I'd seen him in over a year."

"I'm sorry about Beverly. I know we didn't get a chance to speak at the funeral. I really cared for her," I said.

"I know you did, and she thought the world of you. You were one of her favorite people," he said.

"Your wife's death was a tragedy, and I'm sorry as well for her loss. But this conversation is about your son. Do you know where he is?" Poe asked.

"If I did, he'd be in custody right now."

"You've been protecting him for years. Now we're supposed to believe you're willing to turn your back on him? I'm not sure I buy that," Poe said.

Captain Price turned to Poe.

"Jaden was always getting himself into trouble, but it was never anywhere near the level it is now. I had no knowledge of that smuggling operation. As far as I knew, we'd arrested the people responsible for that more than a year ago. Your wife thought the same thing. It seems like you were the only one who knew there was someone else out there. Maybe you should have said something before."

"Is this your absurd attempt to push some of the blame my way? Is that what you're really going to try to do?" Poe asked.

"No. The only person to blame in all of this is my son. Allison Jenkins, too. If I had my way, they never would have offered her immunity. She belongs in jail."

"And you? How do you escape all of this?" Poe asked.

"Not that this is any of your business, but I plan to take an early retirement once my son's been apprehended, and he will. He can't escape this island without us finding him first. We've got every route cut off."

I knew that wasn't true. Captain Price did, too. I wasn't sure why he'd even said it. He may not like my husband, but I didn't think he believed Poe was stupid. Everyone at this booth knew that money had a way of opening doors closed to ordinary citizens. Yes, we'd frozen Jaden's accounts, but there was no way of knowing how much cash he had on hand.

"So your son's a maniac and you get to keep your nice government pension? Is that how this game is played?" Poe asked.

"I'm sorry for what he did to you. There is no excuse, and I thank God that you weren't killed. But I don't need to listen to that smart mouth of yours," Price said.

"Get out of my bar," Poe said.

"That's enough. Both of you," I said.

Captain Price turned to me.

"I'd like just a couple of more minutes of your time, if you'd allow it."

I turned to Poe.

"Can you give us a moment? I'll be fine," I said.

Poe pointed at Captain Price.

"Two minutes. Then you're out of here."

Poe stood and walked over to the bar.

"I'm sorry, Alana. I know he has every right to be furious at me."

"Was your son the one who ordered the hit on me last year?" I asked.

"I don't know. I really don't. I never would have imagined he was the one behind all of this, not in a million years. I know what he is now, but there's still a part of me that sees him as that little kid playing in the sandbox in our backyard. It's so hard to comprehend what he's done. First my wife is taken from me, and now this. I have nothing left."

"You said you hadn't spoken with your son in over a year. Why was that?"

"It was something as stupid as money. He asked my wife and me to invest in that restaurant of his. I didn't want to do it, but she did. We gave him the money, and he refused to pay us back. It really put a strain on us. I knew I should have let it go, but I couldn't swallow the fact that he'd taken from us. Then Beverly got sick, and I think I was looking for someone to be angry with. I took a lot out on Jaden. He refused to talk to me after that. He'd only visit his mother if I wasn't at the house."

"Where do you think he is? You probably still know him better than most. Where is he hiding? Who's sheltering him? There has to be someone on the island helping," I said.

"We've checked with everyone I know who has any kind of relationship with Jaden. Allison gave us a list of names, too. No one claims to have seen or heard from him. I have no idea where he went."

Captain Price looked over to the bar. I followed his gaze and saw Poe staring back at us. The captain turned back to me.

"I better go. I'm sorry for upsetting Poe. I'm sorry for everything."

I didn't know what I could say in response to his apology, so all I did was nod.

Captain Price slid out of the booth and exited the bar.

Poe walked back over to me.

"Did you believe him?" he asked.

"Not one bit."

"How did I do?"

"You played the part of the furious spouse perfectly. Anything else and he would have been suspicious. And my performance?"

"He might have bought it. You seemed pretty much on the fence about the whole thing. He knows you guys have a long history, but he also knows you're paid not to automatically buy what people are telling you, even if it's your supervisor."

"Do you think he knows where Jaden is?" I asked.

"Of course. I watched them pretty closely at the funeral, especially after I saw your former co-worker sitting beside them. There wasn't any bit of discomfort between father and son. Either they're the world's greatest actors or Price was lying to us. Besides, they could have easily asked Allison to sit between the two of them if they really hated each other."

"Why meet with us tonight? What was he hoping to gain?"

"He had to meet with us. You guys have a close relationship. Sure, you've talked about the case after Allison's interrogation, but you told me yourself that he's had to recuse himself for the obvious conflicts of interest. How would it look if he didn't personally apologize to your husband after what Jaden did to me?"

I knew Poe was right, but I still thought there was more to it than that. Poe did, too. I could tell by the look on his face.

"Price irritates the living hell out of me. He helps cover up a rape in high school and then he has the audacity to come here and claim he didn't know his son was into anything that bad? We're supposed to buy that crap?"

"What did you expect him to say? That he knew everything that was going on?"

"You're right, but it still pisses me off. Where's Foxx? Why isn't he out here yet?" Poe asked.

We turned toward the bar just as Foxx was walking out of the back office. He made his way over to our booth and sat down beside me.

"Did you see anything interesting on those cameras?" Poe asked.

"Oh yeah. Very interesting. You're going to love it."

Chapter 36
Sunset Dead

Alana and I spent the next day hanging out at the house. I did my morning routine of swimming laps in the pool and then drying off in the sun. We watched a couple of movies afterward. One of was a World War II film starring Mr. Pitt. If you've read these books before, you know Alana has a fascination with that war. I'm sure she also has a thing for Brad, but who doesn't? The other film we watched was a comedy-drama about this guy from Pakistan who falls in love with an American woman, only his family won't accept her. It was a surprisingly strong film and a welcome relief from the gore and brutality of the first movie.

Toward the end of the day, I suggested that we drive to the beach to watch the sunset. There's a spot near Kihei where I like to take photographs. It has a string of attractive palm trees that make for great foreground objects with the ball of the setting sun in the back.

I walked outside to the security team and told them we were taking a drive. I informed them they could have the night off. They looked at me like I was crazy. I probably was, but they accepted my request and drove off just as Alana and I were backing out of our driveway. We had the top down on the convertible, and it was a pleasant drive to the beach. The air was cool, and the low sun brought out those deep blue colors in the ocean that I spoke of earlier.

The sun was just starting to go down as I pulled off the road and parked at the edge of the sand under the aforementioned palms. I pulled a couple of beach towels out of the trunk, and we walked onto the sand. We spread the towels out, and Alana sat on one of them. I stripped off my t-shirt and made my way into the water. The water was warm, as it usually was on this part of the island, and I waded deeper until the gentle waves came up to my chest.

I spent the next several minutes watching the sun get lower and lower in the sky. Today it was a mixture of pinks and oranges and less reds. There were just a few clouds, and the bottoms of them reflected the pink, so it looked like they were giant balls of cotton candy.

This beach wasn't that far from where Shaw's body had been found in his car. The thought of Shaw reminded me of something he'd said during his interrogation of me. He'd said that I liked to spend my days running around the island playing cops and robbers. I knew it had been an intentional cheap shot designed to get me angry and make me lose my composure. It was an obvious tactic, but you'd be surprised how often it still works. Most people can't control their emotions. Once they get upset, it's pretty hard for them to back off and lower their heart rate. I was certainly no exception to that, but I hadn't been baited by him during that interview.

His comment had stuck with me, though, and I'd thought of it often since that day. Had I been this arrogant jerk who liked to play detective when the mood suited him? Maybe. It's hard to be totally self-aware, and sometimes I have the unfortunate tendency to be overly so. I had been responsible for putting several guilty people behind bars. That had to count for something. Still, I questioned whether my actions had ultimately done more harm than good. People had gotten hurt, even killed. Sure, it hadn't been directly my fault, but I couldn't shake the feeling that I'd played a role.

I glanced back at the beach, and I saw Alana looking toward me. Maybe she was actually looking past me at the sunset. She was the most important person to me. I know you've heard me say that a million times, but that's what was going through my mind at that moment as I watched her. She needed to be safe, and she wasn't right now.

I thought back to another comment I'd heard during my time in jail. Mara had mentioned while we were in the courthouse that she'd realized at some point that I was playing a game of chess. I knew she'd meant it as a compliment, but I hadn't been able to fully take it that way. The word "game" had thrown me off. Both Mara and Shaw had used that particular word. Was that all this was to me, a game? It couldn't be.

I don't remember if it was me or Mara who'd said this, but Alana was compared to the queen in the game of chess. We'd said that the queen was the most important piece on the board. That was true, but I thought there was a better word to use to describe that piece. That word was "dangerous."

I leaned back in the water and ducked my head under. The water felt refreshing on my face. I broke the surface of the ocean and looked at the sky again. The sun was even lower by now, and there was a long band of red stretching across the horizon. It looked like the top of the water was on fire. It was breathtaking, and I wondered if it would be the last time I ever saw such a thing.

I ducked in the water one more time and stayed under for about a minute. I tried to control my heartrate as I felt the warm water around my body. In some way, the water was where I felt most at home. I was surrounded by it at all times, and there was tremendous comfort in that. I came to the surface again and turned back to Alana.

For good or for bad, I had to admit to myself that I had been playing a game. My grandfather had been a master at chess. My mother had told me that. I thought she'd been a master herself, but she'd said more than once that she'd never been able to beat him. I hadn't been able to beat her, even though I thought I was fairly good at the game. Was I good enough to beat Jaden Price, though? I didn't know.

I was almost back to Alana when he walked past the line of palm trees. He was dressed in faded jeans with a hole in one knee. He also had on a navy blue t-shirt and a black baseball cap. He looked like a thousand other guys on this island. He would have easily blended in with the crowd. The only thing that stood out was the pistol in his right hand.

"Did you think I'd left the island? Did you think I'd let you get away with it all?" he asked.

There are many things that go through your mind when you have a gun pointed at you. I should know. It's unfortunately happened to me more than once.

The first thing that pops into your head is whether or not you're actually seeing what you think you're seeing. Your brain tries to process why someone would want to hurt you. What is their motivation? Is there some way this could all be a mistake?

This stage takes less than a second to answer, and the next part is panic. It's completely predictable, and it does absolutely no good. It clouds your thoughts, and the adrenaline racing through you can make you unstable.

The third stage is desperation. You try to figure out what you can do to possibly get yourself out of this mess. Can you reason with them? Can you buy them off? Is there any way you can possibly escape? Can you actually take the fight to them and have some chance, no matter how miniscule, of winning?

None of these stages happened to me on this day. I was more concerned with Alana. She stood just as I reached her. She was between Jaden and myself. I extended my arm and placed my hand on hers. I slowly pulled her back and stepped in front of her. He wasn't going to get a clean shot at her.

Jaden laughed.

"Isn't that noble? Do you think that's going to make any kind of difference? Neither one of you is walking off this beach," he said.

I didn't bother asking him any questions. I didn't care what his reasoning was or whether or not he'd felt any kind of remorse for his actions. I assumed he didn't, and it didn't really matter if he did. The dead were staying dead. No one was coming back. No one could repair the damage he'd done.

This had all started two years ago with a friend of Alana's. She'd figured out what Jaden was doing, and she'd gotten killed for it. Several others had died since then. All of that had brought us to this moment. We were on the beach. The sand was hot under my feet. The sun was setting behind us. There was a gun pointed in our direction, and Jaden Price had no intention of letting either of us go.

"You should have accepted my offer," he said.

"To work for you? Why would I do that? I already have everything I've ever wanted."

"And I'm going to take it all from you."

"Goodbye, Jaden," I said.

Three things happened next, and it took just a couple of seconds for them all to occur.

The first was the loud wail of a horn that echoed across the beach. It didn't sound like a car horn or the blare of an emergency vehicle. Instead, it had come from air horn, something you'd hear at a football game or other sporting event. It was completely unexpected and out of place. It had its desired effect. Jaden couldn't help himself, and he committed the second action. He turned his head to his left to see where the noise had come from.

The third thing happened a split-second later. A gunshot rang out. The bullet raced past my side, and I felt the hot air burn my flesh. The bullet struck Jaden in the upper chest. I saw the look of confusion on his face. He dropped his gun, and I watched it as it fell to the sand. He tried to take a step toward us, but he stumbled and dropped to his knees.

I walked over to him and picked up the gun while Alana kept her Glock trained on him. It's an unbelievable weapon. Accurate and deadly with the ability to fire even after being fully submerged in the water.

I'd hidden the weapon under my exercise shorts. The elastic material had kept the gun firmly placed against my body, and the baggy swimsuit overtop had kept the bump concealed. It had also been the main reason I'd walked into the water. I'd assumed he'd been watching us the entire time. There would have been no way for him to see the gun.

Both Alana and I stood over Jaden. I recognized the stages race across his face. I saw him try to process what had just happened. Then panic appeared, followed quickly by desperation. I knew what would come after that, but there was no way he was getting out of this. He was done.

"No, Jaden, I didn't think you'd left the island. I knew you'd come for us."

"Jaden Price, you're under arrest for the murders of Brooklyn Van Kirk, Molly Randolph, Pika Mahoe, and Detective Austin Shaw," Alana said.

The queen, the most dangerous piece in the game.

I turned as I saw Foxx drive up to the beach. He jumped out of his SUV and ran toward us.

"Your timing was perfect," I said.

"I see the air horn worked."

"Perfectly," Alana said.

I knew Foxx had been listening to our conversation the entire time. Alana had placed her cell phone on the beach towel beside her. It was in speaker mode. She'd called Foxx's phone just before we'd climbed out of my convertible.

Alana grabbed her phone and called emergency services. She gave them our location and ordered the ambulance for Jaden.

I walked over to my car and kneeled down near the passenger side rear tire. I reached under the back quarter panel and pulled off the tracker Captain Price had placed on my car in the parking lot of Harry's. It had already been photographed and printed by Alana in our garage the night before.

I opened the trunk and tossed the tracker inside. I'd assumed Price had told Jaden exactly where he'd placed it and had instructed him to remove it after killing Alana and me. It had been a good plan, almost full proof.

I turned around and saw Jaden lying on his side. Blood ran out of his chest and turned the white sand crimson.

I looked past Alana and Foxx and saw the sun had vanished into the ocean. The sky was still shades of orange and pink.

It was beautiful.

Chapter 37
Venezia

It didn't take them very long to find Captain Price. He was at his home watching television, or at least that's what Abigail Ford told Alana he'd been doing when she'd arrested him. I would have loved to have seen the look on his face. On the other hand, I was kind of glad I hadn't been there. I was disgusted with the Price family and if I had my way, I'd never see either of them ever again.

I was pretty sure Price had known what his son had been up to from the very beginning. You don't cover up your son's high school rape and then assume the guy's gone down the straight and narrow. He knew his son was dirty, and he'd chosen to look the other way. Actually, he did far more than that. He'd abused his power and his position to make it all okay. I didn't know if he'd personally profited from his son's illegal business dealings. It didn't really matter. Price had been complicit in all of it. The guy was garage in my book.

I did owe him for something, though, and I hated to admit it. Nevertheless, I'm always honest with you. I'm not about to change that now. Alana and I debated what made Jaden Price want to frame me versus kill me, at least at first. I think it was his father's doing.

Price loved Alana. One can argue what the nature of that love was, but I think he told his son not to kill me. He knew what it would do to Alana if he did. Jaden couldn't resist just dropping it, though. That's why he called me and threatened me the day after my wedding. He wanted to put the fear of God in me. He wanted to punish me somehow.

Time passed, and my meddling in Jaden's affairs probably started to drive him more and more crazy. Still, there were his father's potential wishes to obey. Don't kill Poe. The next best thing was to put me behind bars. I'd suffer, and he wouldn't have crossed his father. When that plan failed, he couldn't stop himself anymore, and that's how I ended up lying on my back in my own driveway under the night sky.

So many people died, all for his greed and thirst for revenge. He'd survived Alana's gunshot on that beach, but he'd spend the rest of his life in jail. Was that justice? I didn't know.

It was finally over now, and I hoped Alana and I would be able to put it all behind us. It wouldn't be easy, but maybe time would heal the wounds, as people like to say.

I wonder how you readers, especially the ones who have read my previous stories, enjoyed hearing directly from Alana. I know I enjoyed reading what she'd done to save me. My big takeaway was the realization that there were two versions of Alana. There was the one I knew, unguarded, funny, smart, and loving. She was a truly unique and special person. There was also a completely different Alana, though. That person was the detective. She was a woman in a profession dominated by men, and she had to fight every day for respect. In a way, I thought Alana was a linebacker trapped in the small frame of a woman. Cross her or threaten her family, and she'll level you.

I'd never seen that version of Alana, at least not until this case. I thought I had during the Aloha Means Goodbye case, but I hadn't, not really. Even though most of our interactions during those early stages of the investigation had been me speaking with the detective, Alana hadn't put up that wall that she does with everyone else. I don't know why that was. Maybe she doesn't, either. I'd have to remember to ask her about that someday. I'd like to think that she'd been interested in me from the first moment, which is why she'd shown me her softer side, but we all know that's only my ego talking.

Well, I guess we've reached that point where it's time to wrap up a few of the loose ends. I'm sure there's another investigation you're wondering about.

That's the one I was asked to conduct by Mara. It turned out her gut instinct was correct after all. I guess mine was too for the case turned into me catching an unfaithful spouse-to-be. You may recall I overheard him discussing the hotel laundry with his supervisor. Apparently, the young man must have really had a thing for it because I caught him having a fling with one of the housekeepers. I won't go into all the details because it's not quite as exciting or salacious as it may seem. I will say that the housekeeper was a gorgeous young woman of Japanese descent. She actually reminded me a lot of Alana, at least in terms of her physical attributes, not that it justifies the man's indiscretions.

Mara's niece called off the wedding, as one might expect her to do. However, she also did another thing that was somewhat unexpected. She told Mara that she would never speak to her again. Mara had ruined her wedding and her future, at least that's what the niece had said in a heated exchange. It was your classic case of killing the messenger. Mara was hurt, which had been completely understandable. Still, she was glad that she'd stopped her niece from making a big mistake. She was also hopeful that the young woman would one day forgive her.

What were the reactions of Mara's brother and sister-in-law? They were basically the same as their daughter. Mara was now the black sheep of the family. Here's another clichéd saying for you: No good deed goes unpunished.

Speaking of relatives, Alana hadn't spoken to her mother in weeks. I had no idea how long that would last. She claimed it didn't bother her, but I know Alana well enough to realize she wasn't being truthful with herself. She cared for her mother, despite the fact that she can be a downright nasty woman.

Was I still resentful that she'd turned on me? Of course. The lady had used my incarceration as a time to pounce. It was a low move, but I didn't really expect better of her. Maybe things would improve in the years to come, but I wasn't holding my breath.

Here's another thing to discuss. I'm sure you're still in a state of denial regarding how much money I paid the bartender at Eighty-Eight to swipe Jaden's glass. Yeah, it had been an impulsive move on my part, but I didn't regret making it. The DNA results had proven that Jaden had gotten

Brooklyn pregnant. I truly believe that was the fact that pushed Allison over the edge. In my book, that ten grand was money well spent.

That said, I convinced Foxx to have Harry's reimburse me for the money. We just threw it under labor costs so we could write off the expense. Do me the favor and don't tell the IRS. They already get enough of my money, and I'm not sure they'd agree that a bribe was a legitimate labor expense.

Speaking of the bartender, Foxx and I offered Meg a job at Harry's after Jaden's restaurant closed. We'd never replaced Molly, mainly because it felt kind of cold to immediately look for someone else after she'd been killed. Nevertheless, we needed the help, and Meg had proved that she could make one hell of a Manhattan.

Meg also inspired Foxx and me to give back to the island community. Maui is known for its artists, and that's usually a tough living. We decided to sell one of the Lauren Rogers original paintings that Foxx had hanging in his house. We took the million-plus bucks and invested it. We're now using that money to fund a scholarship program for local artists. The entire thing had been Foxx's idea. I think it was a way for him to still feel close to Lauren. She was still the woman he'd loved the most. Granted, there was another lady in his life who now meant even more, but his love for little Ava was certainly a very different kind of love.

As I write about Ava, it makes me think about the beginning of this story. It started with Ava and me searching for a wedding anniversary gift. I find it ironic that it ended in much the same way. My second anniversary was approaching. I told Alana that I wanted to exchange gifts early. She asked me why, and I said that my reasoning would be apparent once she opened my gift.

We made the decision to open our cards and gifts about one month before the actual anniversary. For those of you who don't know, cotton is the gift you give for your second anniversary. Alana gave me five polo shirts, all in different colors. I tend to wear black or dark blue most of the time, and she said she wanted to see me in softer colors. I'm not exactly sure what the specific names of these colors were, but I think sea foam, lavender haze, peach, and robin's egg blue were among them. They weren't my thing. They were nowhere near close to my thing, but I certainly wasn't going to admit that to Alana. I just smiled and thanked her for the thoughtful gifts. My acting must have worked for she smiled back at me.

So, what did I give Alana? I once again completely ignored what was recommended and chose not to give her a gift of cotton. Instead, I bought us a trip to Italy, and I presented the itinerary for the vacation in a card. We would fly to Florence, spend five nights there, then take a train to Venice where we would have another five nights to explore one of the world's most romantic cities. This had been the reason I'd wanted her to open the gift early since my plan was for us to have our actual wedding anniversary in Florence. I knew she needed to give her job advance notice that she was taking time off.

There was another reason I'd wanted to go to Venice. Kiana had told me that the original owner of my bar had named it and patterned it after an establishment in Venice. I thought it would be interesting to see where Harry's had been born.

Alana thanked me profusely and commented that she felt guilty her gift had not been up to the level that mine had. Well, it hadn't, but who is keeping score? I certainly am not. All that I knew was that I loved her, and we were about to have some of the best pasta in our lives.

"Amore mio, we're off to Italy in just a few short weeks."

"I can't wait," she said.

She looked down at Maui.

"Don't tell the dog. He's going to get upset."

"He'll get over it," I said.

"Should we take a gondola ride, or is that something only tourists do?" she asked.

"I'm sure it is, but we will be tourists. I don't see how you go to Venice and not ride a gondola."

"I've heard Venice is a shopper's paradise. Maybe we should bring an empty suitcase so we can have somewhere to put all the stuff we buy. On second thought, maybe we should take two empty suitcases."

Two empty suitcases? What had I gotten myself into?

Did you like this book?
You can make a difference.

Reviews are the most powerful tools an author can have. As an independent author, I don't have the same financial resources as New York publishers.

Honest reviews of my books help bring them to the attention of other readers, though.

If you've enjoyed this book, I would be grateful if you could write a review.

Thank you.

Acknowledgements

Thanks to Lyna Tucker for editing this book and to Mike Merritt for the cover design. Thanks to Polgarus Studio for formatting this book.

Thanks to you readers for investing your time in reading my story. I hope you enjoyed it.

Poe, Alana, Foxx, and Maui the dog will return.

About the Author

Robert W Stephens is the author of the **Murder on Maui** series, the **Alex Penfield** novels, and the standalone thrillers **The Drayton Diaries** and **Nature of Evil**.

You can find more about the author at www.robertwstephens.com.

Visit him on Facebook at www.facebook.com/robertwaynestephens

Also by Robert W. Stephens

Murder on Maui Mysteries

Aloha Means Goodbye (Poe Book 1)

It's Poe's first visit to Maui after numerous invitations from his best friend, Doug Foxx. The vacation quickly becomes a disaster, though, as Foxx is arrested for murdering his girlfriend, a wealthy and world-renowned artist. Can Poe prove his friend's innocence, and can he win the heart of the beautiful detective who arrested Foxx?

Wedding Day Dead (Poe Book 2)

Poe's life couldn't be better. He's just relocated to Maui, and he's dating the sexy detective, Alana Hu. Things take a turn for the worse, however, when Alana's ex-lover returns to the island. Soon, Poe's relationship with Alana falls apart, and he's dragged into another murder investigation where he's also one of the prime suspects.

Blood like the Setting Sun (Poe Book 3)

Poe now works as an unlicensed private investigator. His first client is the eighty-year-old owner of the Chambers Hotel. She's convinced someone is trying to kill her. Her main suspects? Her adult children. Poe thinks she's a bit senile, but then the lady shows up dead. Poe is thrust deep into the Chamber's family history, and it's much darker than he could have possibly imagined.

Hot Sun Cold Killer (Poe Book 4)

Poe is hired by Zoe James to discover the truth about her mother's death a decade ago. The police ruled it a suicide, but was it murder? As Poe conducts this cold case investigation, the bodies soon pile up until the killer has his sights trained on Poe. Can Poe uncover the truth before he ends up dead?

Choice to Kill (Poe Book 5)

Poe helps Alana with a case that is deeply personal to her: the murder of a childhood friend. At first, the case seems fairly straightforward. Soon, though, Poe realizes that things are not always as they seem. He's up against his most ruthless adversary to date, and he'll have to face his worst fear.

Sunset Dead (Poe Book 6)

A murdered mistress. A wrongful arrest. Can Poe and Alana take down a killer from both sides of the law? Poe can't stand to take another case after his last one nearly killed his wife. When he's accused of murdering his supposed mistress, he's forced back into a familiar role to prove his innocence. But can he do it from behind bars?

Alex Penfield Novels

Ruckman Road (Penfield Book 1)

A jogger has spotted a body on the shores of the Chesapeake Bay at Fort Monroe, but the body has vanished by the time the police arrive. The jogger tells Detective Alex Penfield that she recognized the man as Joseph Talbot, a neighbor who lived inside the stone walls of the old Army fort. Penfield goes to Talbot's house, only to discover he's placed video cameras in every room. Penfield learns the cameras were placed to capture strange occurrences in the house that Penfield eventually sees, too. Are there logical reasons for these mysterious events and the disappearance of Joseph Talbot, or is Penfield losing his mind from the trauma of a recent shooting and other dark events in his past?

Dead Rise (Penfield Book 2)

Detective Alex Penfield has to solve a murder case before it happens. His own. Retirement never suited Penfield, but there's nothing like a death omen to get you back in the saddle. A psychic colleague warns the detective that his own murder is coming. When a local death bears an eerie resemblance to the psychic's vision, he can't help but get involved. As the body count rises, the case only gets more unfathomable. Witnesses report ghastly encounters with a man sporting half a face. And the only living survivor from a deadly boat ride claims he knows who's to blame. There's only one problem: the suspect's been dead for 20 years.

Standalone Dark Thrillers

Nature of Evil

Rome, 1948. Italy reels in the aftermath of World War II. Twenty women are brutally murdered, their throats slit and their faces removed with surgical precision. Then the murders stop as abruptly as they started, and the horrifying crimes and their victims are lost to history. Now over sixty years later, the killings have begun again. This time in America. It's up to homicide detectives Marcus Carter and Angela Darden to stop the crimes, but how can they catch a serial killer who leaves no traces of evidence and no apparent motive other than the unquenchable thirst for murder?

The Drayton Diaries

He can heal people with the touch of his hand, so why does a mysterious group want Jon Drayton dead? A voice from the past sends Drayton on a desperate journey to the ruins of King's Shadow, a 17th century plantation house in Virginia that was once the home of Henry King, the wealthiest and most powerful man in North America and who has now been lost to time. There, Drayton meets the beautiful archaeologist Laura Girard, who has discovered a 400-year-old manuscript in the ruins. For Drayton, this partial journal written by a slave may somehow hold the answers to his life's mysteries.

86493270R00162

Made in the USA
San Bernardino, CA
28 August 2018